"I've been sent to investigate the case, Gab."

She closed her eyes for a moment, then opened them. "You?"

"That's right. The Marshals Service has jurisdiction."

"You?" she asked again, her voice rising.

"They sent me because I'm from Flagstaff, Gab," he said quietly.

"Oh my God," she whispered. "Do I need a lawyer? Am I being charged with anything?"

"No, of course not. This is only a statement. Is there a problem?"

She gave a short laugh. "Problem? The Whittakers are dead, we're being hounded by the press, our switchboard is ringing off the hook and my husband—" She stopped abruptly.

"What about him?" Jed asked.

"He isn't here."

"Yes, that's what you said," Jed replied. He hesitated. "I don't want to make this any harder for you than it already is, Gab."

She gave him a searching look. "Is that what you say to all the suspects?"

ABOUT THE AUTHOR

The town of Apache Springs, Arizona, is fictitious, but the Spanish gold is very real. "Every time my husband and I drive to see our daughter, Erika, at school in Arizona, we explore a new part of the state," says Carla Peltonen, half of the Lynn Erickson writing team. "Molly (Swanton—the other half) and her husband vacation there all the time. There is real gold hidden somewhere in the hills. Everybody knows it, but no one can find it. We've wanted to write about it for years, and suddenly we saw how to do it." The result is *Apache Springs*, an adventure that will capture your imagination as well as your heart.

Carla and Molly and their families live in Aspen, Colorado, the inspiration for an upcoming book under the Mira imprint, entitled *Aspen*. Look for it in bookstores this August.

Books by Lynn Erickson

HARLEQUIN SUPERROMANCE
347—SHADOW ON THE SUN
370—IN FROM THE COLD
404—WEST OF THE SUN
439—THE NORTHERN LIGHT
482—SILVER LADY
520—A WING AND A PRAYER
549—PARADOX
564—WILDFIRE
578—THE LAST BUCCANEER
596—DANCING IN THE DARK
626—OUT OF THE DARKNESS

Don't miss any of our special offers. Write to us at the following address for information on our newest releases.

Harlequin Reader Service
U.S.: 3010 Walden Ave., P.O. Box 1325, Buffalo, NY 14269
Canadian: P.O. Box 609, Fort Erie, Ont. L2A 5X3

Lynn Erickson
Apache Springs

Harlequin Books

TORONTO • NEW YORK • LONDON
AMSTERDAM • PARIS • SYDNEY • HAMBURG
STOCKHOLM • ATHENS • TOKYO • MILAN
MADRID • WARSAW • BUDAPEST • AUCKLAND

ISBN 0-373-70656-1

APACHE SPRINGS

Apache Springs

PROLOGUE

IN THE SPRING OF 1589, the small troop of conquistadores left Pueblo de los Corazones on the Sonora River in New Spain and marched north into uncharted territory. They were in search of the fabled Province of Cibola, in which lay the fabulous and wealthy Seven Cities of Cibola, where Indian children played with diamonds, pearls and emeralds.

Hernan Cortez had secured New Spain seven decades earlier, but had not pursued the stories of Cibola. Melchior Diaz, Esteban the Moor and Fray Marcos had searched nearly fifty years before, but had failed miserably, finding only poor Indians who lived in strange, mud-brick towns four and five stories high, an endlessly deep chasm whose river was said to reach the Pacific, and plains full of huge, humped cattle.

Captain Henrique Estancio had new information, though, from a Pueblo Indian slave who spoke Spanish. The man, whose outlandish name was Kokopelli, was old and humpbacked, though he had all his teeth and appeared sinewy and healthy. His face was round and brown, and he wore his gray-streaked hair twisted into a knot on top of his head and adorned with bright parrot feathers. At his waist, on a girdle of yucca fiber hung a cunningly carved wooden flute, which he played with commendable talent.

This slave told the captain that he knew where Cibola was, had been there himself. He drew maps on the dusty ground with a stick. "It is there," he said with convincing surety, and Captain Estancio felt excitement kindle in him. Kokopelli agreed to lead the captain there in exchange for his own freedom.

It was a bargain well struck.

Estancio formed only a small expedition because his funds were limited, and the government of New Spain was less than enthusiastic about yet another fruitless quest for Cibola. He had six men on horses, two cows, some sheep, six extra horses, a dozen pack mules carrying supplies, and Kokopelli, barefoot and bareheaded, with only his flute. And, of course, Fray Benedicto, whose love of God was equaled only by his ineptitude in the wilderness. However, every expedition must have a priest to save the souls of the poor heathens.

They traveled for many days north to the San Pedro River and were finally beyond the borders of New Spain. It was hot and dry, the sun merciless. They crossed the Gila River and the Salt River. The land was barren but for lizards and hawks and scorpions, *despoblado*.

Two horses became footsore and had to be left; the sheep were frightened off by a coyote and scattered. The cows were slaughtered because they were too slow. They reached Zuni, the pueblo, one evening, but its citizens pulled up their ladders and refused to come out, despite the prayers of Fray Benedicto. Too many had been killed by Spanish soldiers in the past, and their memories were long.

They rested there for a day, but two of the pack mules died and the Zuni stole another. They could see the celebration fires atop the pueblo and smell the roasting meat. The drums kept them awake all night, along with the wailing of Kokopelli's flute.

The troop carried with them an assortment of weapons—guns, swords, lances, bows and arrows, javelins, slings, clubs—so they were well armed, but they stayed alert for signs of the nomadic, warlike Querechos, also known as the Apaches, although their lands were farther east, as far as was known.

The terrain rose, and the going was hard over prickly cactus and thick brush and tumbled rock. Water was scarce but ironically, as the animals dropped one by one, they needed less of it.

Still, Kokopelli said he knew the land and they were approaching Cibola, the real Cibola, not the sorry pueblos that yielded nothing save maize and beans, scrawny turkeys and a lexicon of alien spirits.

Full summer was soon upon them, but they were climbing higher now, and although the way was rough, it was cooler. The men still complained, threw away their stifling armor and helmets until Captain Estancio had to quell a near mutiny with threats of death. The men were weak with hunger and thirst, but strangely the priest grew stronger—more gaunt but tireless and uncomplaining. His faith never wavered, and he looked on this endless journey as a challenge, though not one heathen would kiss his gold crucifix or pray with him. He especially wanted to save the soul of the Pueblo slave Kokopelli, who was very intelligent, but the slave only smiled enigmatically at the priest and played haunting trills on his flute.

They were following, roughly, the Little Colorado River to the northwest now, deep into country that Coronado had explored years before. The men muttered that they were being led astray; there was nothing here but more wilderness and snakes. Kokopelli insisted they would find Cibola soon, a large city full of rich people who wore fine cotton clothes and gold and jewels. They would all be rich.

They came upon a place one day where bubbling hot springs spewed from deep within the earth, forming pools, smelling of fire and brimstone. They rested there, bathing in the pools, refreshing themselves. A sadly depleted company they were, with only a few mules left and four horses. Each man had weapons, though, except the priest and the Indian, and some even had pieces of armor left. They refilled their water skins, trapped some squirrels and rabbits and had a feast. Their spirits rose like the smoke from the cook fires.

They set out again, encouraged, but after a three-day trek, they were attacked by Querechos, a war party that surprised them at the mouth of a canyon. They fought a running skirmish with the canny devils for hours. Diego Castillo was killed, and three others were wounded by arrows. The captain rallied his men, and they retreated in order up the narrow steep-sided canyon, where the near-naked savages could only attack one man at a time. The Spaniards were terrified and exhausted, weakened from loss of blood and lack of water. All except the priest, whose faith grew stronger, and Kokopelli, who despite his age and humpback did not tire, nor did the smile leave his lips.

By twilight the Spaniards had fortuitously found a cave, a large, cool, dry cave in the side of a mountain, where they were safe for the moment, although they had to leave their remaining horses and mules for the devils to take. The priest knelt and prayed in their midst, prayed for deliverance from the heathens and from thirst and hunger and fear. The captain asked him to pray also for the success of their mission, but the priest only shook his head and replied, "God does not listen to worldly requests."

It was then that one of the men noticed that Kokopelli was not among them. When had he vanished? Where had he gone? No one had seen him, nor did any of them ever see him again, even though Juan Alvarado swore he heard his flute playing mockingly that night.

The cave was a godsend, so the remaining Spaniards thought, but when day dawned they realized their predicament. The fiendishly clever Querechos merely stayed there, blocking the party from leaving their sanctuary. On the second day Pedro Dorantes died of his wounds and the captain gathered his remaining men, making a desperate sortie from the cave. Carlos Herrera was killed in the fight, and the rest retreated to the cave, licking their wounds.

On the next sortie, Fray Benedicto joined them, wielding a weapon surprisingly well, but they were again pressed back, and that night another man died, shriven by the priest.

The water was gone, the food supply nearly depleted. Captain Estancio's remaining men died, from wounds or from thirst, or from loss of hope. Then only the priest and the captain were left, haggard and gaunt and bearded, their eyes sunken, their tongues swollen.

The priest perished sometime in the night, and Henrique Estancio was left alone in the cave in the midst of corpses and armor and useless weapons and the leather bag of golden pieces of eight he'd carried this long way in the event of trading opportunities. Outside the entrance, he could hear distant thunder, and soon it began to rain, as if the heavens wept for him.

The Querechos cared no more for the rain than for anything else, though, and above the thunder and wind, in the flashing zigzags of lightning, they danced and howled and yelped, celebrating the spirits of the mountains and their own victory over the white eyes, which would soon be complete. Accompanying their revelry was a humpbacked old man who played a flute, his music urging them on to greater and greater exertions for the glory of the spirits. Once the last Spaniard was dead they would leave this place behind, and the spirits would place a taboo on it, so that no one would ever again dare to invade Apache land. As for the dead and their strange weapons, let them lie there forever in warning.

The captain lay on the hard floor of the cave and commended his soul to God, asking for redemption. It was not the fear of death that tortured him, but the horror of dying so far from his own kind. That and the knowledge that he'd led men to the same fate. From between cracked lips he whispered up a fervent prayer that no man should ever follow in his footsteps because of greed, and for four hundred years no one did.

CHAPTER ONE

THEY ARRIVED AT FIRST light: two four-wheel-drive pickup trucks and a sheriff's department Cherokee from Flagstaff. They came grinding ominously up the steep drive that led to the Apache Springs Hotel and broke the silence of the mother-of-pearl Arizona dawn.

Gabriela Zimmerman shivered despite the warmth in the hotel's kitchen, but she kept her hands busy, trying not to think, stuffing sandwiches, fruit and chips into plastic bags. The recovery of the bodies was going to take the better part of the day; the emergency team was going to need food.

"Don't forget to fill the water bottles," she told the cook. "Maybe put ice in them, too. It's going to be really hot out there."

And then her husband, Brian, stuck his head through the swinging doors. "You got the food ready?" he asked, distracted, rushed. "They're here."

Before she could answer he was gone, and the cook exchanged a sympathetic look with her, as if to let Gabriela know that no one blamed them for yesterday's accident.

The lobby seemed to come alive then, some men spreading out topographical maps on the polished Victorian tables, others talking loudly outside on the stone veranda, checking equipment: ropes, radios, knives, rucksacks. There'd be no helicopter used on this rescue operation; the canyon was far too rugged for a safe landing.

Gabriela stacked the lunches on a sheet pan and carried them out to the lobby, her heart catching when she saw all the men, all the gear, all the policemen.

"You'll need this," she said, handing the tray to Ray, a local man from Apache Springs, one of the volunteer Mountain Rescue team members. "And there's plenty of water."

"Thanks," Ray said, giving Gabriela's arm a reassuring squeeze. "Take it easy. This is no big deal. We do this at least once a summer, Mrs. Zimmerman."

"Sure," Gabriela said, "I know. I know."

Brian brushed by her at one point. "Don't look so goddamned worried. It isn't as if it was our fault," he said.

Well, she couldn't help being upset, she thought as she went back to the kitchen. She couldn't take it lightly. She'd been right there when it happened; she'd known those people.

The whole process of collecting and sorting the gear and forming a plan of action took only twenty minutes, and then the rescue team was off in the four-wheel-drive trucks, heading into the broken, mountainous country of northeastern Arizona, the August sun beating down, the dust rising from under wheels and hanging on the air.

Gabriela watched them leave. A tall woman, dressed neatly in a pair of khaki slacks and a red blouse, her wildly curly black hair pulled back into a ponytail, she stood on the veranda and waved goodbye to her husband. Then she folded her arms and took a deep breath and wished the whole ordeal was over. She

couldn't help feeling as if the accident was somehow
their fault. Maybe there was something they could
have done to prevent it, to have saved those lives.
Something. But every time she'd voiced that thought
to Brian he'd either brushed it aside or gone on a ti-
rade. Once he'd even yelled, "Why does everything
happen to me!" She just didn't understand his thinking anymore. And when he flew off the handle like
that it scared her.

She turned and reentered the hotel. It wasn't even
seven in the morning, and the phone at the front desk
was already beginning to ring. Guests awakened by the
commotion wanted to know if everything was all right;
they'd just seen police cars out front. And then the
news media. Papers. Television. Radio stations. From
clear across the country. Call after call.

A producer from a New York City network wanted
to know if he could send his anchorman out and get a
business discount on a room at the hotel.

"We don't do business discounts," Gabriela said
with a sigh. "We're a resort."

"Okay, so let me book a room...."

"We're full."

He swore. "Well, where's the nearest motel?"

"The nearest motel with available rooms might be
up in Flagstaff."

"And where's that?"

"Thirty-seven miles."

"God. Where is this Apache Springs, anyway?"

"Look on a map," Gabriela snapped, and hung up.

By eight she managed to turn the front desk over to
the young college girl who'd worked there for the past
two summers. She hated to dump the whole mess on
Margaret's shoulders, but enough was enough. And

besides, Brian's parents, Otto and Ellie Zimmerman, were waiting upstairs in their fourth-floor apartment for an update. And Ellie was so sick.

Gabriela moved around the kitchen and dining room, reassuring people, having to tell the whole story over and over and over. "Yes," she said a dozen times to the guests, "it was Evan Whittaker and his wife.... Yes, the same Whittaker who's been in the news."

At nine-fifteen she went out to the steaming sulfur pools behind the hotel and checked on the gardener and pool keepers, bringing them all together, hoping to relate the story only once. "Yes, the Whittakers were on the treasure hunt with Brian and me.... No, it was the canyon to the north of that.... Yes, the one near the Apache Reservation...."

And then she was back inside, hurrying, her brain spinning, still trying to get a minute to visit the Zimmermans, when a news team arrived from Phoenix. They had parked their satellite van right in front of the hotel's stone steps. "Can you please move that thing out of the drive," she said, sweat breaking out on her upper lip.

But they ignored her. A crisply dressed woman poked a mike at her, asking, "Mrs. Zimmerman—you are Gabriela Zimmerman, aren't you?"

"Yes, I am, but I..."

The newswoman turned to her cameraman, who switched on a bright light and nodded his readiness. "Mrs. Zimmerman, would you confirm for our viewers the identities of last night's victims? We're told it was District Judge Evan Whittaker and his wife, Clare...."

"Y-yes," Gabriela stammered, confused, blinded, wanting to run.

"The same man who's the president's top choice for the Supreme Court seat?"

"Well, yes, I..."

"And both the judge and his wife are confirmed dead?"

Gabriela stammered her answers, aware of more newsmen arriving. Out of the corner of her eye she saw someone snapping pictures of the old daguerreotypes that graced the lobby's walls: old, yellowed photographs of the famous and not-so-famous who'd once stayed at the hotel. This particular reporter took three photos of Doc Holliday's picture, the one that showed him lazing in a sulfur pool in an old-fashioned bathing costume.

"And it was just the four of you who were hiking?" the newswoman was asking.

"Yes, just the four of us."

When it was over, Gabriela couldn't remember a word she'd uttered, but before she could catch her breath and escape there was yet another newsman shoving a mike at her. When she refused to do the interview, the well-dressed anchorwoman flashed her rival a grin. But Gabriela wasn't going to give in. They'd told the Coconino County sheriff everything there was to tell last night. From now on, his office up in Flagstaff could give the interviews. Oh, God, she thought, finally escaping and pushing the elevator button, why hadn't Brian stayed here today? The rescuers could have located the...bodies without him.

For the first time in more than three hours Gabriela was suddenly encased in silence, the old elevator rising slowly to the fourth floor. She leaned against the back wall, put her hands on her thighs, bent over and groaned. She was losing it. She'd had no sleep all night. By the time she and Brian had hiked out and gotten back to the hotel it had been after dark. They'd called the sheriff and Mountain Rescue, but nothing could be done at night. It wasn't as if the victims were hurt and waiting for help—no, they were dead, and there was no sense endangering anyone in a foolish attempt to recover the bodies in the dark.

Gabriela truly hadn't slept a wink, nor had Brian. They were both too upset, too shaken. And now she felt almost sick, as if a heavy weight was pressing on her. If the accident had happened to anyone else, anyone but the federal district judge whose face had been on the cover of *Time* magazine just two weeks ago, none of this would be happening.

Oh, the Mountain Rescue team would have come to recover the bodies this morning, and there would have been the police reports, but save for a paper or two from Flagstaff, maybe a call from Phoenix, there would have been only the mildest of media interest. After all, this was the rugged mountain terrain of Arizona, and accidents during the busy summer tourist season were common. People got injured in the steep canyon country. People got bitten by snakes, hit by lightning; they broke bones climbing rock faces, drank impure water. During the autumn deer and elk seasons they shot one another. In June there'd been a cougar attack on a hiker. Motorcycles skidded off roads. Three-wheelers overturned on mountain trails and bicyclists took bad spills. In the mountains people died. It was just that it was rare that someone so famous died.

And that famous someone and his wife had been their responsibility. "Great," Gabriela muttered as the doors slid open on four. "Just great."

The fourth floor was strictly off limits to guests. The vast majority of it was storage space—an immense attic with twelve-foot ceilings filled with old furniture and boxes, almost a hundred years of Zimmerman relics. God forbid anyone should throw anything out. The tradition of keeping things had begun with Brian's great-grandfather—the founder of the hotel—Franz Zimmerman. It was the aristocratic Franz who'd immigrated to America in 1898 from Austria, seeking adventure and fortune in the fabled West, and it was Franz who had first realized the potential value of the Apache hot springs where the hotel now sat.

Of course, he'd had to await the arrival of the railroad in nearby Flagstaff. But when it had steamed into the mountains in 1901, Franz was ready for the flocks of tourists who came from Boston and New York and Atlanta—adventure seekers, hunters, historians. There were U.S. presidents and famous writers and even European nobility. After all, the Grand Canyon lay just to the west of Flagstaff, so a week's visit to the famed hot springs fit many an itinerary. The Apache Indians had been coming to the bubbling sulfur pools for centuries, partaking of the curative waters, so why shouldn't the Easterners?

And they did. Franz built a spectacular red-stone, turreted castle in the middle of the wilderness. Thirty guest suites were all done in rich Victorian appointments: dark, ornately carved woods; plush velvet upholsteries; flowered wallpaper; pink Italian marble fireplaces in every room; indoor baths. The lobby itself, with its eighteen-foot ceilings and inviting sitting areas, was as splendid as any west of Denver. The dining room was elegant, the bar dark and private, the outdoor bath houses built against an eighty-foot wall of red rock, the steam from the three vapor pools rising and swirling into the clear, fresh mountain air.

For sixty years tourists had come to fish and hunt and climb mountains, to cure what ailed them in the hundred-plus-degree waters that reeked of sulfur. But with the advent of air-conditioning, tourists had discovered the desert, Phoenix and Tucson, the warm winter sun and year-round tennis and golf. And when the snows of winter whitened the mountains to the east and north of these new sunbelt meccas, the visitors from Boston and Detroit and Chicago—the snowbirds—began to spend their money in the spas on the floor of the desert, basking in the sun. The shift had been inevitable.

Tourists still came to Apache Springs, but mostly in the summer and autumn, and certainly not in the numbers they once did. Otto Zimmerman, Brian's father, often joked that what they needed in Apache Springs was a golf course and an international airport, but in a town whose population was about four hundred, those were highly unlikely prospects.

Gabriela glanced down the dark, cluttered corridor and knocked on the apartment door. She was not looking forward to this visit. She could almost hear Otto now: "How many times have I told Brian to stop those ridiculous treasure-hunt tours? The hotel does fine on its own, we don't need that kind of tourist gimmick."

And Brian's mother, Ellie: "Oh, Otto, you should be glad Brian takes the initiative. He's doing his best to keep the place going. For Lord's sake, can't you get off the boy's back?"

Brian, of course, was hardly a boy at thirty-seven. And as for how well he was keeping the hotel on its feet, that was another story altogether.

"Otto? Ellie?" Gabriela swung the door open softly. The last thing she wanted to do was disturb Ellie, who was in the middle of radiation treatment for breast cancer. And Otto was not so well, himself. He'd suffered two heart attacks several years back, and now both of them were living more reclusively, leaving Brian and Gabriela totally responsible for the management of the hotel.

"Otto?" Gabriela called quietly.

"In here. The kitchen," came his reply. "Fixing some breakfast."

Gabriela crossed the old-fashioned living room that always smelled musty and went into the kitchen. "Yuck," she said, sniffing the air. "What on earth are you concocting now, Otto?"

He turned from the stove, an apron tied around his slim waist, a spatula in hand. "Chinese herbal pancakes."

"Otto says they're a sure cure," Ellie said from her seat at the table. "I say he can eat them himself."

"Boy," Gabriela said, sitting, "I'll second that."

"Coffee?" Otto asked, ignoring the women. "Of course, I've got all kinds of herbal teas...."

"Coffee," Gabriela said, smiling, dreading the soon-to-come questions. She was not kept waiting.

"Brian went with the rescue team, didn't he?" Otto began as he spooned more batter into the iron skillet.

Gabriela nodded. "Right after dawn. But I bet they won't get back until this afternoon. I guess an ambulance is going to meet them out front."

"Little late for that," Otto said, and Gabriela spooned sugar into her coffee, stirring, stirring.

Ellie's brow furrowed. "How did it happen?" she whispered, her once-pretty face now lined and drawn. So thin. Her fair, graying hair was thinning, too.

"They told us last night how the hell it happened," Otto chimed in. "Our son took those poor people on one of his treasure hunts and got them killed is how it happened."

"Please," Ellie said, putting up a hand, "don't start, Otto. Just don't start right now." She looked at Gabriela questioningly.

"We got going late," Gabriela said. "And then Clare got a headache. The altitude, I guess. Anyway, Clare and I decided to let them go on. You know how the judge loves... loved to search the mountains for the treasure. Well, anyhow, he and Brian said they'd only be another hour or so, and Clare and I just kind of wandered around a hillside. She wanted to see the wildflowers...." It was all coming back so clearly, too clearly. Gabriela felt tears prick behind her eyelids. She tried to clear her throat. "Anyway, Clare, well, she didn't seem to mind that they took so long, and I even suggested we go on back to Brian's truck, but her headache was better, and, well, she had this big bouquet of wildflowers and..."

Ellie reached across the table and squeezed her hand. "You don't have to tell us right now, honey."

"No," Gabriela said, "it's okay. I'm fine." She picked up a paper napkin and blew her nose. "It's just that they were such nice people. Regular people. God, they'd been coming here for six, seven years. We really got to know them."

"I know, I know," Ellie said gently.

"Anyway," Gabriela went on, taking a breath, "Brian and Evan were really late meeting up with us. They were both kind of out of breath, excited. Clare even told the judge he was acting like a two-year-old."

"Ha!" Otto said, snorting. "I suppose they found the treasure."

"Be quiet, Otto," Ellie said.

"I don't know why they were excited," Gabriela went on. "I assumed they'd stumbled across some old Indian arrowheads or something.... They were on the reservation, anyway. The point is, it was getting late. We were kind of hurrying. I guess I went on ahead on the steep part of the trail...heights, you know. I remember just wanting to get off the stupid narrow trail. The next thing I knew I heard this horrible scream and...and I..."

What had she done?

"Go on," Otto pressed, his cooking forgotten.

But Gabriela was shaking her head. "I don't know," she whispered. "I honestly can't remember exactly what happened. I got back to them and...and the judge wasn't there and Clare was...God, she was... The rocks were tumbling.... The trail had given way. I was so...paralyzed. And Brian was yelling and..." She couldn't go on. There was nothing to tell. The narrow canyon trail had given way and two people had fallen to their deaths. The only reasons Brian had not been killed were his age and his agility. He'd clung to the wall behind him. He'd hung on and he'd lived. "It was so awful." Gabriela wept.

The silence in the kitchen pulsed for a long minute, Gabriela and Ellie clutching hands, Otto looking grim and troubled. It was Ellie who spoke first. "It's over, it's done," she whispered. "We'll all go on from here. Life goes on, Gabriela."

"I know." Gabriela tried to regain her composure.

"What won't go on," Otto said heavily, "are those goddamned treasure hunts. Brian is done with that crazy obsession. Done. If he wants to go out by himself, that's fine. But no guests. Never again."

Gabriela nodded slowly. It was true. The whole notion of hidden Spanish treasure was crazy. No one believed it. Not really. It was all just a cute old Apache legend. A myth. Brian was clever. He'd think up some other tourist draw, something a whole lot safer than taking city folks on treks through this rough country.

"Spanish gold," Otto said sneering. "Conquistadores. Caves. It's all bull..."

"Otto," Ellie said firmly.

"It was all baloney hundreds of years ago, and it still is."

"Brian knows that," Gabriela said. "He really does. When we got up this morning, not that we slept a wink... Anyway, he said that was it. He was ending the tours."

"A little late," Otto muttered, but then caught himself. "Sorry. It wasn't anyone's fault, I know that." He walked over and pulled Gabriela's head against him and patted the mass of her dark hair. "That son of mine doesn't know what he's got," he said with kindness. "Best darn gal in the county. I knew it the minute you came up from Tucson that spring. Told Brian all about you that very night. Didn't I, Ellie?"

His wife smiled and nodded.

"I sure did," he went on. "I told Brian that he better snag you before you headed back to the university."

"Right," Gabriela said, turning her eyes up to his. "What a bunch of BS, Otto."

"Well, maybe a little. But you've been the best thing to happen to that boy in his whole life."

"Well, thank you." She suppressed a twinge of guilt.

"My pleasure," Otto said and went back to the stove. "You two just hold yourselves together through this television stuff—" he pointed toward the window and the drive below "—and we'll all come through this."

"That's right," Ellie said. "We'll get through everything." And when she said that so emphatically, Gabriela recalled that in two days Ellie was due for another treatment at the clinic in Flagstaff.

"We will get through," she said and managed a smile.

By noon, the stress of the last twenty-some hours was taking its toll. Gabriela did her best to avoid the reporters who'd gathered in the lobby, filled the dining room and jammed the curving drive with their vans. It was unbelievable. There must have been thirty or more of the bloodsuckers. Margaret, however, was holding down the fort just fine with the help of the bartender, Sam, and the young bellboy, Clyde, and Gabriela thought that if she could get just a few minutes' rest, she'd be all right. There was still the ordeal of the rescuers' return to get through....

She sneaked off to her cabin just before one, taking the trail behind the hotel that led along the red rock face and then down into the piñon forest for some three hundred yards. The cabin was nearly as old as the hotel, a real log structure built by Franz Zimmerman in the early 1920s. It had three rooms: kitchen, living room with a big hearth and a single bedroom. It was cozy in the winter and cool in the summer, a great retreat. For nine years now she'd lived there with her husband. Nine years...

She did get a half-hour's rest, stretching out on the couch, a forearm over her brow while she took slow, deep breaths and tried not to think. The trouble was, the more she tried to empty her mind, the more thoughts crowded into it. The Whittakers, arriving three days ago. Evan had been so happy to be away from all the media attention over his nomination for the Supreme Court that he'd been downright jovial. And Clare. Ever the attentive wife, his Rock of Gibraltar...the wildflowers in her hand, the late-afternoon sun catching the silver of her hair...

Gabriela pushed the images away, and then Brian instantly filled the void in her head. She'd never seen him this upset. And her husband had plenty to be upset about lately. For one thing, the hotel was buried in bills. There was the loan from last year's renovation, and the payments were two months behind. Gabriela knew Brian had delayed sending in June and July's sales taxes to the state, too. The bills were due for the new patio furniture out by the vapor pools, and the plumber who'd raced right over and fixed the leaking tub in 103-degree heat had not been paid. That had been back in May. Then there was Brian's own pickup truck, the fancy one with the king cab—the payments were three months behind.

And all because of his gambling.

Gabriela tried hard not to think about that right now, not with the tragedy of the Whittakers' deaths looming so large. Still, she couldn't stop thinking about her husband, his faults, the pain in her marriage. If only he'd talk to her, let her help. That was what marriage was all about, the give and the take, listening, understanding, supporting. But Brian wasn't letting her in anymore. He hadn't for years.

She'd given up on her marriage, and had already discussed divorce with Brian, then this had happened. Well, she couldn't abandon him when he needed her most.

Later, in a few weeks or months, she'd bring it up again.

She rose from the couch when she knew it was indecent to lie there another moment. Worrying about Brian and his troubles—their troubles—wasn't going to help a thing. They'd just have to get through this nightmare and pick up the pieces. Together. She and her husband would do it together.

Back at the hotel things had quieted down. Margaret told her, "Hey, when they all figured the rescue team wouldn't be back for hours, they got bored. Some of them went into town, some are sacked out in their vans."

"Good," Gabriela said. "But I bet it's not going to last."

She was right. The lull was soon over. The rescue team must have radioed ahead for the ambulance from Flagstaff to meet them at the hotel, because it arrived there shortly, stirring up a commotion all over again.

Then the Coconino County sheriff pulled in. He'd been there last night, of course, taken their statements, spoken with the head of Mountain Rescue.

Now here he was again. But this time he left Gabriela in peace. Heck, every reporter there wanted an interview with Sheriff Eric Ulrich, and next year was an election year, after all.

The vehicles of the rescue team drove up soon afterward. Gabriela, along with everyone else, stood outside and watched. At first there was a lot of chatter and vying for positions—cameras, lights, powder on the noses of the TV personalities—but then the atmosphere seemed to grow very still, the air suddenly hot and gravid as the last of the vehicles drove up and its engine was turned off. Gabriela swore to herself that she could hear its motor still ticking in the abrupt silence.

Then the rescue team unloaded two gray body bags.

She felt her pulse quicken, felt sudden sweat start to the surface of her skin as she stared, watching the remains of Evan and Clare Whittaker being loaded into the ambulance.

The whole time cameras were rolling and reporters were whispering ardently, reverently, into mikes—as if they really cared about anything other than their ratings. When the doors of the ambulance were finally closed, Gabriela began to search for Brian in the throng and realized that she'd needed him there beside her all along. No wonder she felt so queasy, so shaken. Why couldn't he have at least stopped to give her hand a squeeze?

She saw him a moment later, over near the sheriff's white Jeep Cherokee. His fair head was bowed, and he was nodding, and from his body language she knew he was extremely uptight. Well, after last night and today, he had a right to be.

With the departure of the ambulance, the hotel seemed to be miraculously empty. The story was over for now. Gabriela breathed an enormous sigh and went back inside, pushing away the memory of the body bags, remembering that the Whittakers were childless—thank God she hadn't had to talk to any children, deal with their grief. Not today. Maybe that was a selfish thought, but there it was.

She stopped for a minute to check on Otto and Ellie again and half expected to find Brian there. But he wasn't; he hadn't been up to see them since late last night. She made an excuse for him.

"I think he's talking to the sheriff," she lied to Ellie. The sheriff had already gone.

It was Otto who said, "You don't have to do that for us. We know our son."

On the way back down in the elevator, Gabriela thought about that. Why did she always feel as if she had to protect Brian, her handsome, charming husband with his boundless energy?

When they'd met he'd been carefree and lighthearted, a great outdoorsman. He could hike and climb and fish and hunt. Not a day went by that Brian hadn't come up with a new adventure to share. His unpredictability had been catchy and fun. Then.

He'd had lots of buddies from his schooldays, and they'd all gather at the hotel and regale Gabriela with stories about Brian's younger days. He'd been a card, a cutup, they'd told her. And he was a western gentleman through and through, slow-talking and droll, with that terribly competent masculine manner western men cultivated.

It had been such a welcome change from her ex-fiancé's single-minded intensity, from their constant fighting. Brian had treated her as a precious object, and she'd basked in his appreciation. She'd adored his parents from the first moment, and she'd adored, too, the lovely red-stone hotel, with its elegant exterior, graceful circular drive, stone porch, the tall windows and gracious lobby. It was an ornate Victorian gem in a Wild West setting, and from the first moment, Gabriela had itched to get her hands on the slightly seedy, run-down place, to repair and refurbish and polish and bring it back to its original splendor. Oh, yes, she'd settled into the secure cocoon of Apache Springs as if she'd been born there.

The years had shown some cracks in Brian's facade, though. He'd become possessive, and where Gabriela had been an equal to her college boyfriend she was, she knew, a mere female to Brian. He didn't get along with his sister or his father, and he'd started gambling.

Now, instead of sharing his life with Gabriela, he shut her out. In an implacable way, he'd put more and more distance between them, until she often felt he was an utter stranger. And that spontaneity that had been so much fun? Now, well, now he frightened her sometimes. Calm and in control one minute, angry and irrational the next. Their marriage had become a precarious tightrope walk as Gabriela fought every step of the way to keep her equilibrium.

She finally found him out by the pools. He was sitting at a glass-topped table, staring up through the vapor toward the red rocks. He had a beer in front of him, but he hadn't touched it.

She sat down across from him and pushed her hair behind her shoulders, stretching out her long legs. "Some day, huh?" she began.

"Yeah, a whole lot of fun," he said, not looking at her.

"Want to talk about it?" she tried.

"No," Brian said flatly.

"Well, I just thought that maybe if we could..."

"I said no."

She narrowed her eyes. "Look, Brian, we can't go on like..."

"Hell," he said, standing abruptly, "will you get off my back?"

"I didn't..."

"You know what that sheriff just told me? He said the coroner's office is going to perform autopsies on the Whittakers' bodies! Can you believe this crap!"

Gabriela thought for a moment. "Well," she finally said, "that's probably just routine, don't you...?" But before she could finish he snorted in disgust and stalked away.

CHAPTER TWO

DEPUTY U.S. MARSHAL Jed Mallory was jogging, his usual three-mile circuit around the suburban neighborhood of Arlington, Virginia. It was early, not even seven in the morning, but he'd already stripped off his gray Redskins T-shirt and stuck it into the damp waistband of his running shorts. It was hot—seventy-five, at least—and oppressively humid. The sun was peering over the horizon, a jaundiced eye in the hazy sky, as if it was thinking twice about ascending any farther.

Damn climate, Jed thought, a routine curse. If it wasn't as sultry as the tropics, it was as cold and raw as the arctic. He'd never really gotten used to it. Ah, forget it, he told himself.

As he ran he tried not to think, but sometimes that was impossible, especially after the case he'd just been on, hunting down a federal fugitive.

It had all begun six years ago when the Iowa State police had arrested a mean SOB who'd been wanted in three other states for murder. He'd been arrested for the murders of seven women in all. He'd finally gone to trial in federal court in Michigan, but escaped with a cunning ploy—he'd faked a heart attack by using some powerful drugs.

Jed had been assigned to the task of hunting him down because, among other duties, the U.S. Marshals Service was charged with upholding federal law. So, along with two other deputies, Jed had been on the chase for the last six months.

They'd gotten the creep, though, eventually, and now it was over, a brief respite until the next assignment. Well, Jed thought, maybe this time he'd be sent to Alaska or Maine, somewhere cool.

He chugged along thinking about the upcoming autumn, the sweat now covering his lean torso like oil as he passed the familiar houses, the neat green lawns, the newspapers thrown carelessly on front stoops. The trees overhead met in places, a verdant canopy, a stifling ceiling that made him feel claustrophobic. It was so thick and wet and alive here, you could almost see the plants reach and stretch and writhe. So unlike where he was from—Arizona, the West, the dry, spare, sparkling place that he visited once a year to see his mother in Tucson.

His hometown, though, was Flagstaff, up in the mountains in the north of Arizona. Seven thousand feet high, Flagstaff was cool in summer, downright cold in winter. It snowed starting in October sometimes, and kept it up well into May. A town named for the tall pine trees surrounding it, and for the one tree to which the pioneers had attached a flag on the Fourth of July. A logging town, then a railroad town, now a surprisingly cosmopolitan small city in a spectacular setting only eighty miles from the Grand Canyon. Clear, pine-scented air, a blue sky, absolute clarity and clean, distinct colors, not the shades of crowding green that he ran past now.

He puffed along, breathing hard but evenly, waved to a retired air force general who was out early, too, every morning. He could just abide Arlington at this hour, empty, lukewarm instead of stifling, without the noise and traffic, the East Coast bustle he'd come to loathe over the past ten years. He should have stayed in the west where there was room to turn around, where there was air to breathe. He knew that now and had finally, last year, applied for a transfer. He was still waiting. He'd been offered Indianapolis but declined. It had to be farther west.

Jed had graduated from the University of Arizona with a degree in law enforcement and there had been several Arizona towns and counties that had tried to recruit him for their local forces. He'd even gotten a call from a personnel guy with the Phoenix police, where his father, Max, was chief. But he'd turned them all down. Jed had to do it his way, with no help from Pop or anyone else. He'd ignored everyone's advice, his favorite professor's, his mother's, his fiancée's. Ignored their begging and reasoning and pleading. And, still trying to get Pop to notice him, he'd shot for the stars, applying to the FBI and the other federal police force, the U.S. Marshals Service, an arm of the Justice Department. Been accepted, too, and decided on the Marshals Service because the FBI seemed to be wallowing in its own glamour.

Jed was absolutely committed to law enforcement and had always wanted to be on the front lines, with the army that kept anarchy from prevailing. It was an important task, fulfilling a basic and vital need of society. He still thought so, but his early idealism had dimmed over the years.

He'd been stuck here on the East Coast for too long, putting up with scheming, political intrigue, infighting between the Service and the FBI, budget constraints, the usual incompetent contingent of workers.

Sometimes he felt he was wasting his time with bickering and endless reports.

A car pulled up alongside him, a gray sedan with darkly tinted windows. He didn't stop, merely glanced out of the corner of his eye, kept going. The passenger-side window rolled down, and a man stuck his head out. "Mallory?"

Jed kept jogging, not answering as the car rolled along next to him.

"Hey, Mallory!" the man yelled again.

He stopped finally, at his own driveway, and leaned forward, hands on his knees, breathing hard, droplets of perspiration spattering onto the pavement. "Yeah?" he said, not looking up.

"You must be nuts, running in this heat," the man said.

"Probably," Jed replied mildly, then added, "What's up, Hawthorne?"

"The boss sent us to look for you. Said you'd be out jogging." Hawthorne shook his head in disbelief.

"What does he want?" Jed asked, straightening.

"He just said for you to report to headquarters ASAP. He's in a rotten mood, I'll vouch for that. He's been up all night on something."

"What?"

"He hasn't told anyone. It's big, though. He's been saber rattling with the Bureau."

"Okay, I'll be there as soon as I shower."

The driver of the car leaned across Hawthorne and said, "What, you're not gonna run all the way to headquarters, Mallory?"

"Now, why didn't I think of that?" Jed asked coolly.

When he got to headquarters at seven-forty-five, his
light blue shirt was already damp under the arms despite his car's air-conditioning. He carried his sport
coat over one finger; his tie was loosened. No uni-
form was necessary at headquarters or on most of the
jobs he was given, only those where U.S. marshals
were doing jobs such as courtroom guard duty or ex-
ecuting a federal order. But the coat-and-tie costume
was bad enough, especially in the heat.

He showed his pass to the guard, made his way
through the building to his own desk to check for
messages, then shrugged into his coat, pulled his tie
straight and headed for the boss's office.

Arthur Gish was a whippet-thin man, fiftyish, with
a gaunt face and a gray crewcut. He was a good administrator, but Jed thought he wasn't cool enough
under pressure. He tended to blow his top. Of course,
Jed was comparing him to that paragon Police Chief
Max Mallory and remembering his father's absolute
equanimity under stress. Pop only threw a fit when it
was effective, and no one mistook one of his rages for
anxiety. Arthur Gish was always anxious, although
maybe that was because he owed his job to his wife's
father, a lawyer in the Justice Department.

Jed knocked and went in. Gish sat behind his desk,
rearranging papers, a scowl on his face, the phone
tucked between his shoulder and jaw. He waved Jed in
and gestured for him to sit down in one of the leather
chairs in front of his desk. Jed sat; the chair felt tacky
in the muggy air.

"No, I said I won't do it that way," Gish was say-
ing. "It's clearly our job. Yes, I'll go to the Attorney
General if I have to, and I don't care if he is fishing in
Alaska. Sure, I'll talk to him myself. No deals." He

put the phone down and rotated his neck as if it were stiff.

"Damn fibbies. Greedy prima donnas," Gish muttered, referring to the FBI.

"Yes, sir."

"Okay, Mallory, we've got a big one. I've been here all night fighting like hell for it. It's ours now."

"That's great, sir."

Gish grimaced. "You recall Evan Whittaker?"

Jed thought for a second. "The federal judge, the one up for the Supreme Court? That Whittaker?"

"That's the one."

Jed waited.

"It seems he's dead, him and his wife both, in some godforsaken place out in the middle of nowhere. An accident." Gish folded his hands on his desk and leaned forward. "Happened the night before last. Their bodies were recovered yesterday afternoon, and I got the news last night."

"May I ask what kind of accident, sir?"

"They were hiking and fell off some cliff." He shook his head. "Crazy."

"Uh, an accident . . ." Jed raised his eyebrows. "So why are we involved?"

Gish frowned again. "I was notified because the initial examination of the bodies indicates injuries inconsistent with the nature of their falls." Gish tapped a stack of papers on his desk. "I've got the medical examiner's report here, the sheriff's report, statements. I want you to do some snooping on this, Mallory. Just you for starters, so no one gets spooked. This is big, Mallory. Whittaker was a personal friend of the president, and he wants this investigated thoroughly."

"Yes, sir."

Gish rubbed his eyes. "Had a helluva time convincing them, but they had to give in. This is a deceased federal judge, and it's our jurisdiction. No doubt about it."

"Excuse me, sir, but Taylor has seniority. Shouldn't he get this case?"

"Normally he would. But this happened in Arizona, Mallory, your home turf."

Jed's head snapped up. "Arizona?"

"Yeah, some cockamamy place, can't remember the name." He pointed to the papers. "It's all there. Near Flagstaff, wherever that is."

"Flagstaff," Jed repeated. He wanted to smile, to laugh, but he kept his expression neutral.

"I figured you'd know the area, not get the locals so riled up. You know how those county sheriffs hate federal agencies butting in. You're a natural, a local boy."

"And the authorities have been notified I'm coming?"

"Absolutely. I called myself. Coconino County sheriff." Gish glanced down, ruffled through some papers. "Um, here it is, Eric Ulrich."

"Uh-huh, good." Flagstaff.

"He promised full cooperation, but he's sure it was an accident. Said they don't have very many homicides in his county. He implied we were paranoid—you know, the usual."

"Right," Jed agreed, but inside he was elated. They were sending him home!

"You'll leave today." Gish pushed a manila envelope and a file folder across his desk. "It's all in there, everything we have so far. I can only repeat, Mallory, you're going to have to get to the bottom of this."

"Yes, sir." Jed flipped open the case file, scanned it. There was the initial medical examiner's report, faxed in yesterday evening, local police and sheriff's reports, statements from various individuals.

He turned another page. Gish was talking, something about keeping in close contact, and Jed was nodding, listening with half an ear. He saw it then, on the next page—the name of the place where the Whittakers had been staying.

Apache Springs Hotel.

Jed's heart gave a strange hop, a kind of stutter. His spine tingled. Gish was droning on, but he couldn't concentrate on anything but the thin slippery fax paper and the names of the two people who were with the Whittakers at the time of the accident: Brian and Gabriela Zimmerman.

He looked up at his boss and realized he was being asked a question, but he had no idea what it was. His stomach was clenched like a fist.

Brian and Gabriela Zimmerman.

"You with me, Mallory?" Gish said.

"Yes, sir, but I'd better tell you something here."

"Go on."

"I know the Zimmermans. Well, I knew them."

Gish looked at him. "Is this going to be a problem?"

"No, sir, but I thought you should know."

"Okay, duly noted. If there's a chance of your compromising the case, tell me now. I'll send Taylor."

Jed thought of Taylor facing Gab, questioning her. "No, I can do it. I haven't seen either of them in ten years. Shouldn't be a problem."

"All right, Deputy, you've got your orders. Remember, this is a possible homicide you're investigating. The president wants results."

"Of course, sir," Jed said, rising. *Gabriela*, he thought.

IT WAS TWO HOURS EARLIER in Arizona, which was on mountain time. That made it close to three o'clock in the afternoon when the landing gear thumped down on the hot tarmac of Sky Harbor International Airport. There was a guy from the Phoenix office waiting for Jed, and he barely had time to take in a hot, dry breath of air before he was on a police helicopter heading north to Flagstaff.

He'd read all the reports in the file, read them three times. He knew every word by heart. Jed wasn't surprised by many things in his job anymore, but he was surprised by some details of this case. The first was Gabriela's presence. What kind of insane, remarkable fate had put her square in the middle of this mess? The second was the lack of motive. No one, absolutely no one in Arizona, much less Apache Springs, had a reason to kill Judge Whittaker.

And third, a nice surprise for once, was the medical examiner in Flagstaff who'd done the autopsies on the Whittakers and written the report Jed held in his hand: Jackson Many Goats. Jackson was an old friend, an Apache Indian who'd grown up in Flagstaff and gone to school with Jed until Max had moved his family to Phoenix. Jed had met Jackson again at the university, and he'd kept in touch over the years. He'd known his friend worked in the ME's office, but now it looked as if Jackson was the head honcho. Good for him.

The helicopter sped on, due north over the bleached-out land of the Sonoran Desert that surrounded Phoenix. A heat haze lay over everything and off to the west thunderheads were amassing, the usual August monsoon that brought afternoon showers to the Southwest.

Jed was assailed by two distinct feelings that were at odds with each other. He was glad to be home, unutterably glad, and at the same time he was as uncomfortable as hell over the inevitable meeting with Gabriela.

Should he have told Gish just how well he knew her? Could his knowing her create a conflict of interest? Damn. He searched his mind, feeling the tender spots the way a person would probe a sore tooth with his tongue. What if this really was a homicide—he had to consider the possibility—and Gab was involved? What if she was guilty? Ridiculous, of course, but could he view her involvement with detachment?

He thought hard, imagining all sorts of scenarios. Yes, he could handle it. He'd always kept business separate from his personal life. He kept things scrupulously in their places. He could do it.

Brian and Gabriela Zimmerman. They'd been married for how long now? Nine years. Yes, nine years. He recalled Brian with utter clarity, although he'd met him only once. A blond, good-looking fellow, strongly built, medium height, barely taller than Gab, who was a good five-nine or ten herself. A smiling, slow-talking sort of guy, the kind who hung out in the local bar and knew everybody in town and whom everybody liked. Good old Brian.

Well, Jed would be careful handling the Zimmermans. He would be completely professional. He'd do his job and let nothing show, not one damn iota of what he was feeling, of what he knew he'd feel when he saw Gab again, of what he'd once felt for her. . . .

HE WAS A SENIOR at the University of Arizona, she was a sophomore. He met her in a geography class, one they were both taking to fulfill a science requirement. She was a tall girl, almost skinny, with a head of wildly curly black hair, clear glass-green eyes and fair skin sprinkled with pale golden freckles. She had a serious look about her that he liked, and a total lack of self-consciousness.

He was attracted to her instantly, overpoweringly, although a serious relationship was the last thing on his mind. And she was crazy about him, too, possessive and a little jealous, which he thought was cute. He called her Gab right off the bat, and he laughed at her objections to the pet name.

"Would you prefer Gabby?" he asked once, and she threw a book at him. Then he tackled her and they rolled around on the floor for a time until he pinned her on her back, and she was beneath him, furious and breathing hard, and he kissed her. That was the end of that argument.

She jogged with him, and he loved her long legs flashing beside him. He would lick the salt off her skin when they were done, and they'd shower together, their bodies all slippery and cool.

They were happy. Truly in love, inseparable. They had quarrels, because she had a temper, and some lasted days, because she was real stubborn, and they sometimes drove each other crazy.

He loved her, though, and could not imagine spending the rest of his life with anyone else. If there was a hitch at all in their relationship it was his father. Gabriela always said his dad was a jerk for the way he treated Jed, as though he had more important things on his mind. But Jed and Gab got over her trouble with Max by promising never to talk about that relationship.

Somehow, they made it work.

Gabriela was from Los Angeles. He drove there with her over spring break, and they told her parents they were going to get married. They were persuaded to wait, at least until Gab was out of school. Jed didn't mind. She was his, and what difference did it make if they waited?

It was on the way back to Tucson after that visit to L.A. that the trouble started.

"I've got the applications," he'd told her, wanting to share everything with her, needing to share, to be as close as he could.

"The ones to law school?" she asked. "Are you going to apply to UCLA like my father suggested?"

"I told you, Gab, I really don't want to go to law school. I was just being nice to your father."

"You don't?" Gab frowned.

"I want to be in law enforcement. You know that."

"I didn't think you were serious. Jed, I mean, really, you're so smart. Your grades are good, better than mine...."

"So? Does a federal agent need to be dumb?"

"Federal agent..."

"I'm applying to the FBI and the U.S. Marshals Service. I'm not sure which I'll choose. Well, that's assuming I'm accepted."

"You know what you're doing?" Gab had said then. "You're trying to impress the great Max Mallory, chief of police. Only you're actually trying to do him one better.... A federal policeman. How could you be so blind?"

After that their relationship took a turn for the worse. The closeness began to disappear, although years later Jed realized it was both their faults. He was wounded, his fierce pride full of holes, and he began to question their relationship, began the arguments, always feeling as if he had to defend himself, defend his father.

They might have made it, even then, because Gab was convinced it was only a stage they were passing through and that they'd meet the challenge.

"I love you," she had insisted. "I'd follow you to the ends of the earth."

And he had loved her. God, how he loved Gabriela.

But then the accident happened.

Gabriela's sister was married that spring to a sociologist with the Los Angeles County schools. The guy counseled teenage kids, the real troublemakers, the ones who were routinely beaten by their folks and then beat the hell out of their peers. Julie's husband—of only ten weeks—went out one afternoon with a local cop when it was reported that one of his cases at school was in a bad situation at home. Bad turned to worse. The cop was wounded in the chest, and Julie's husband took a bullet in the head. He died instantly.

Gab flew out to the funeral. She was gone two weeks, and when she got back to Tucson Jed knew it was over. "He wasn't even a policeman, Jed. He was just with one! Don't you see! Someday the phone's going to ring and it'll be you they're calling about. I can't... I just can't..."

That same summer Gab took a job at the resort hotel in Apache Springs. She needed time to think, she said. And Jed had been accepted by both the FBI and the Service and made his choice despite it all. Young and idealistic and stubborn.

In the end Gab couldn't bring herself to go with him when he left that fall. She went back to finish her junior year. When he flew into Tucson after boot camp, just for a visit, she was busy with her courses, still a student, while Jed was a U.S. marshal.

She cried and said she loved him, and they made love one last, lingering, bittersweet time, but she wouldn't go with him.

They wrote, he called her a few times, but something was broken and couldn't be patched together. It hurt, but he was so busy, discovering a new life, discovering ambition and the Washington Redskins, trips to New York, to the beach, women who looked at him with liquid eyes when they heard he was a U.S. marshal—"like Wyatt Earp."

The next fall he went home to his sister Hannah's wedding, and when he asked her about Gab, just casually, Hannah said to him, "Oh, didn't you know? Gab got married last month. To Brian Zimmerman, you know, from that hotel where she worked."

He was stunned, reacting in a way that surprised him. He went through denial and shock, then anger. How could she have done it? He drove up to Apache

Springs the next day, not sure what he was going to do, but needing to do something. She was working behind the front desk, and she was breathtakingly, agonizingly beautiful. Before he could say much of anything, Brian appeared, and she introduced them, blushing, embarrassed, awkward but terribly proud.

Brian had been real good about the whole thing, a nice guy. He even made the usual joke: "So you're a modern-day Wyatt Earp, huh?" It made Jed grind his teeth in fury. The last thing he saw when he drove away from that damned hotel was the two of them standing at the top of the porch steps of that crazy old stone monstrosity like some characters out of *Rebecca,* Brian's arm around Gab possessively, the lord of the manor himself. And the scene appeared in Jed's dreams for months afterward.

Now HE WAS RETURNING, full circle, it seemed. How ironic. And Gabriela and good-old-boy Brian were the only eyewitnesses to the terrible accident he'd come to investigate. Life sure threw you some curves, he thought, and then he wondered again if he should have excused himself from this job. Of course, he never would have, not even if he'd been given the choice over and over again.

The helicopter had flown over the foothills above the desert, over winding rivers in pale green valleys, and it was now over the deep, dark green of ponderosa pine forests on the higher slopes of the San Francisco mountains. Humphreys Peak, at 12,643 feet, stood sentinel just ahead, and Jed knew Flagstaff curled around its southern base. He leaned forward to see more clearly. He hadn't been back to Flagstaff in years. How many now?

Since before Pop died, eight years ago, because the funeral had been in Phoenix, with all the pomp and circumstance of a policeman's burial. His mother had gotten a card from Gab then and cried over it. But Jed hadn't.

He looked out the plastic bubble of the shuddering chopper and saw the forest stretching away to the north and west, all the way to the Grand Canyon. To the east was the Fort Apache Indian Reservation in Mogollon Plateau country. Nearby was the site of Zane Grey's cabin, whose westerns every Arizona school kid read. Right below were the Anasazi ruins known as Montezuma's Castle, although the Aztec emperor Montezuma had never been this far north. The sun glinted off a lake far ahead, and Jed wondered if it was the one he and Gab had hiked to that time they'd camped out near here.

Lakes and tumbling mountain streams, winding foot trails, canyons and campgrounds, snowcapped peaks and the cobalt-blue afternoon thunderstorms sailing in from the west. Deer and elk, coyotes and jackrabbits. Wilderness and cool, green shadows under the pines. They all brought back a rush of memories.

The helicopter tilted and descended, and now Jed Mallory could see the city spread out before him. Home.

CHAPTER THREE

GABRIELA WAS WRONG. When the ambulance pulled out of the drive yesterday afternoon, she'd honestly believed the worst was over. At the very least, she was positive the media's attention would shift, perhaps to Washington, D.C., to the president and his scramble to find a new politically acceptable nomination to the Supreme Court of the land.

But the phone seemed to be ringing twice as much today with question after question about the accident. It was bizarre. And, evidently, all because Sheriff Ulrich had ordered autopsies performed on the Whittakers, a perfectly routine procedure, really, especially given the judge's prominence.

And the questions the reporters were asking! "Hard Copy" wanted to know if there had been foul play connected to the deaths. And the *National Enquirer* offered Gabriela and Brian twenty thousand dollars for their stories. One yellow-press paper asked if the Apache Indians might have been involved—after all, the accidents had happened near the reservation.

Gabriela talked to some of the media, trying to be polite but firm, others she hung up on. Margaret, still at the desk, was instructed to say nothing at all, only that the Zimmermans were unavailable for comment. And Brian... To begin with, he refused even to answer the telephone, and when he overheard Gabriela speaking to one of the more reputable reporters, he snatched the phone and slammed it down, hollering, "Why can't you keep your mouth shut!"

That was the straw that broke Gabriela's back. "Outside," she said to Brian. "Can I please speak to you for a minute outside?" Her tone was even, but her green eyes were smoldering. On the far side of one of the vapor pools, out of earshot, she put her hands on her hips and said, "Don't you ever talk to me like that in front of our employees. In front of anyone, for that matter. What in God's name has gotten into you, Brian? Can't you see I'm only trying to do my best? To help you?"

Brian studied his wife, his expression finally softening. "I'm sorry," he said. "I guess I lost it in there. I just wish we could turn the phones off. These reporters are driving me nuts."

"We're all under a lot of stress," Gabriela said, relaxing her stance. "Everything will settle down, you'll see."

"I can't believe the questions these jerks are asking," he said. "Just because the sheriff ordered those autopsies. Ulrich is an idiot. He should have known it would stir up a hornet's nest. Any fool could have seen this media hype coming from a mile off. But not him."

She sighed and stepped closer, taking his hands. "He's doing his job, I suppose. Maybe we shouldn't blame him for just . . ."

But her husband stiffened. "Whose side are you on?" he demanded.

"Side?"

He disengaged himself from her. "Yeah, side, Gabriela. Nothing happened out there. Two people fell. That's it. You saw it. Nothing happened!"

"Brian, don't do this," she said. "We're both under pressure right now. Don't make it worse. I know it's hard, but if we stick together through this, we can..."

"Like when you gave your statement to the sheriff?" he interrupted. "That kind of stick together?"

"I don't know what you..."

"The hell you don't! You stood right in the lobby and told Ulrich that you didn't see the falls! You couldn't possibly have backed me up, no, not you! Don't talk to me about sticking together," he ground out, and then stalked away.

It was a hectic morning and an even busier afternoon. The checkouts were heavy, the new arrivals even heavier. Two of the maids were running behind, and everyone wanted their rooms now. The linen delivery was short, and when one of the maids reported a leak in the ceiling of 132, Manuel, the maintenance man, was still busy trying to get the cable on the TV in 212 working. Brian, who would normally have helped out, had disappeared about noon, and no one knew where to reach him.

And the phone just kept on ringing and ringing.

By midafternoon things had quietened down somewhat and Gabriela was able to check on Otto and Ellie, but Ellie was napping, so Gabriela didn't stay long. She took a break instead, going for a short walk past the pools and into the woods adjacent to the hotel where there were several well-trodden paths. One led past a clearing and small lake, while the other wound through the piñons and eventually led to a rock outcropping that overlooked the town of Apache Springs. Normally there would have been a guest or two in the area, but today Gabriela found herself mercifully alone as she sat on the red rocks and turned her face up to the sun, feeling the intense heat, letting it bake the tension from her muscles.

Almost three days since the accident, she thought as sweat collected on her skin. Three days and no end in sight. The worst part of the whole ordeal was Brian, though. Nothing in her imagination could have prepared her for her husband's reaction. Sure, she'd seen him stressed out before—mostly because of money problems—but never like this. He simply could not be reasoned with.

And that business about her not sticking up for him with the sheriff! How could Brian have even thought such a thing? All she'd told Sheriff Ulrich was the simple truth: she hadn't really seen a thing until it was over. No one, least of all the sheriff, had even questioned the accident until the media had gotten wind of the autopsies. Now Brian was making a federal case out of it because a couple of smart-alecky reporters had asked some stupid questions, trying to make a story out of nothing. And Brian was letting it get to him, blaming the sheriff, blaming her.

"Oh, damn it," she whispered and rested her forehead on her raised knees. If only she could wave a magic wand and turn the clock back, make everything go away. She and Clare would take that easy walk and pick wildflowers while the men continued their quest. And then Gabriela would stay with the party along that ledge instead of going on ahead. There would be no screams, no falls. If the rocky path started to give way, they all would scramble away quickly, getting past the danger. If she could wave that wand, the Whittakers would still be in room 101 in the hotel. The Whittakers would still be alive.

She sat there and tried to make it all go away, the way she would banish a nightmare. The trouble was, she kept seeing the scene over and over, hearing it, seeing the trail ahead of her, hearing the screams behind. She'd turned—maybe she'd frozen for a moment—and then she'd hurried back, around that bend in the trail. Another scream. And then she'd seen... What had she seen? Brian on the narrow trail, yelling, his face a mask of horror. Clare... Or had she seen Clare for that split second before she fell? Maybe she'd imagined it, because it's what had to have happened, and she'd heard Brian describe it so many times now, berating himself because he hadn't been able to reach Clare in time to save her.

Gabriela searched her mind, trying to sort out true images from imagined ones. Maybe, in reality, she'd only heard Clare's last awful cry and she hadn't actually seen Brian there with her in those last moments. Oh, God, she just couldn't remember!

The mind plays bizarre tricks when it's been shocked, Gabriela thought. It tries so hard to protect itself. Brian remembered it all much better, but then he'd been right there. How awful it must have been for him—she'd never, ever forget that look on his face.

Well, she'd told the sheriff everything she remembered, distinguishing carefully between what she was sure of and what could have happened. Maybe she'd left things out, but she'd tried her best.

But for Brian to blame her for her lack of memory when she'd been in shock was just too cruel.

Gabriela walked back to the hotel slowly, chewing on a blade of grass, mulling it over, trying to clarify her memories. Maybe if she talked to Sheriff Ulrich again, reread her statement to see if she'd left anything out ...

But why would she do that? This whole mess was merely the media trying to stir things up. It had everyone on edge. And most of all Brian, because he'd been the one with the Whittakers. He was feeling guilty. And no one was making it any easier for him—or for her.

Gabriela arrived back at the hotel to find Lorna Kessler there. Lorna was Brian's married sister, two years his junior—though Brian treated her more like a kid than a thirty-five-year-old woman with two children.

The women hugged each other in the lobby while Brian, who'd reappeared finally, stood looking on with a sour expression on his face.

"It's really good to see you, Lorna," Gabriela said. "Are John and the kids here, too?"

"No," Lorna replied. "They stayed in Payson. John's minding the shop, and Carla and Jill have so many summer activities, well, you know." She shrugged.

Of course, Gabriela didn't really know much about children and their busy summers. She'd like to know, though. If things were different.

"Anyway," Lorna was saying, "I just couldn't let Mom and Dad sit upstairs all alone in that dreary apartment worrying themselves sick. Sicker than they are, that is." She gave a weak smile. "I can't believe this whole mess. Every time I turn on the car radio or the TV it's the same. What a bunch of scum bags the press is! I just couldn't leave you and Brian here to face all this alone. I hope I can help out."

It was Brian who spoke first. "We can handle things," he said tonelessly. "So why don't you toodle on back to Payson and run your little knickknack shop or whatever you call it."

Lorna shot her brother a scathing look. "You know, Brian," she said coolly, "this is as much my home as it is yours. You wanted to run the place. You reap the profits, such as they are," she added pointedly. "I only drove up here to lend Mom and Dad moral support. I can help out at the desk, too, and take calls. But if you don't want..."

"We want you here," Gabriela interrupted. "We need you. We need all the help we can get, in fact, with so many calls." She gave Brian a look that said, Don't do this, not now, and turned back to Lorna. "Can you stay? Really?"

"Of course," Lorna said just as Gabriela was called to the phone.

"It's Sheriff Ulrich in Flagstaff," Margaret whispered in her ear.

Gabriela took the call in the office behind the front desk. She sat in the swivel chair with her back ramrod straight and braced herself, although she had no reason to feel apprehensive. She did have reason, however, by the time the conversation was over.

Brian came in and stared at her pale face. "Well?" he asked. "What does Ulrich want now?"

Gabriela swallowed and turned her eyes up to her husband's. "He told me that we're to keep ourselves available tomorrow morning."

"And just what does that mean?" he demanded.

"Something about a man coming here..."

"A man? What man?"

"I don't know what man," she breathed. "It's some kind of an investigator, someone from the government. He's coming all the way from Washington, Brian. What... What's going on?"

But all she got in reply were a few choice swear words before Brian stormed out.

SHERIFF ERIC ULRICH hung up the phone and nodded to Deputy U.S. Marshal Jed Mallory. "They'll be available all day tomorrow," the sheriff said. "I'm afraid my call upset Mrs. Zimmerman, though. Hope we aren't hassling these folks unduly."

Jed unfolded himself from the chair in Ulrich's office. "Well," he said, "if the medical examiner's initial findings are valid, then we've got a problem here, Eric. I'm headed over there right now, in fact. I understand that Jackson Many Goats is handling the autopsies."

Eric Ulrich rose also. "He's a good man. Apache. Real fine education down at the university in..."

"Oh, I know exactly where Jackson went to school," Jed said. "Tucson. We were roommates."

"No fooling?"

Jed laughed. "Have I ever lied to you? The truth is, I'm originally from Flagstaff. Born right down the road from here in the old hospital."

"No way."

"My dad was in law enforcement, in fact. Maybe you..."

"Mallory? You mean your dad's Max Mallory?"

Jed nodded.

"Well I'll be damned! And how is that stubborn old coot?"

"I'm afraid he passed away some years back."

"Sorry to hear it. A fine law enforcement officer. A real fine man."

"Yes, he was," Jed agreed. What he didn't say was that his dad was a helluva better lawman than a father. Ah, well, water under the bridge. "I'll be going on over to the medical examiner's now," he said. "I'll keep you posted." Then, at the door, he paused and added carefully, "Look, Eric, I know this is your turf out here, and I also know we feds can be a pain in the ass. But I do mean that. I'll keep you up to date on any developments. Okay?"

"That's good enough for me," Eric said. "Mallory, huh? I just can't get over it. You're Max Mallory's boy."

"Uh-huh," Jed said, and headed out.

Although Flagstaff had doubled in size since Jed had lived there, it was still an easy community to negotiate. In the old days before the arrival of the two interstate highways, everything of importance had been strung out along Route 66, which followed the railroad tracks. Now the downtown core still ran along Route 66 and the tracks, though the motels and supermarkets and malls were farther out, clustered at the interstate exits. It was a nice mountain town, filled with tourists in the summer, a lot of college kids during the school year, who took classes at Northern Arizona University, and a lot of Indian families: Navaho, Hopi, Zuni, Apache. The town was a hodgepodge of buildings from the Old West around the turn of the century and modern structures recently built to accommodate the influx of tourists and students and some retirees who preferred the cooler climate of the Arizona mountains to that of the desert floor farther south.

Jed stood outside the modern county structure that housed everything from the public works department to the sheriff's department and looked up and down the old route. Not much had changed since he'd been a boy here. Oh, there was the new county building he'd just left, and the state-of-the-art hospital complex to which he was headed. But the trains still rumbled through downtown along Route 66, and there were still twelve-dollar-a-night hotels and the bars—saloons—where the seedier side of the downtown population could be found.

He looked beyond the core of Flagstaff toward the pine-covered mountains. They hadn't changed, either, and few lived in the thick forests—the dirt roads were still treacherous, especially in the winter. The air was as pure as the day he'd left. No, Jed thought, tossing the keys to the borrowed car around in his hand, not much had changed. It was still a good place to live.

The hospital complex that housed the county coroner's office as well as many private doctors' offices was barely two miles from downtown in a suburban neighborhood adjacent to the university. Jed found the new complex easily and parked the sheriff's white Cherokee out in the visitors' lot despite the closer parking slots allotted for official cars, such as the one he'd borrowed. No point being pushy. He checked the directory in the main lobby across from the reception desk and noted the location of the coroner's office, where Jackson Many Goats worked. He found the wing easily and went into the offices, asking a receptionist where he might locate Jackson. As always, when Jed was in street clothes—today it was casual wear: jeans, boots and a button-down, light blue shirt and tweed sport coat—he showed his badge and ID.

"U.S. Marshals Service?" the girl asked. "Like Wyatt Earp?"

"Same outfit," Jed said, "different era."

"Um," she said, eyeing him appreciatively. "I'll buzz Jackson—Dr. Many Goats, that is."

"Thank you," Jed replied, giving her a once-over himself.

When Jackson opened a door to one of the labs and stepped through, his brown face underwent a series of changes. First there was nothing, then recognition, then surprise, finally delight. "Holy sh— I mean, holy cow! Is it really you, Jed?"

They embraced, stood back for a moment to look each other over and embraced again, Jed's head a full six inches above his old friend's.

"I can't believe it," Jackson kept saying, "*you,* here!"

Jed was as pleased to see his friend as Jackson was to see him. It had been too many years, way too many. He was pleased, as well, to find Jackson looking as young and cocky as ever—a handsome, thirty-four-year-old Apache Indian with short, straight black hair and a complexion as smooth as polished teak. He was short and reed-slender, though wiry, and Jed had seen him hold his own with guys twice his size. In school in Flagstaff when they'd been boys, there had been no getting away from the occasional racial brawls. That Jackson had come this far was a credit to himself and his family.

"You know," Jackson was saying, "you look as good as ever, Jed. The years have been kind to you."

"Why, thank you," Jed replied.

"Yep, you're still a handsome dude. The ladies still falling dead at your feet?"

"But of course," Jed said, "by the dozens."

"Uh-huh."

After they talked for a few more minutes and tried to get caught up, it was down to business.

Jackson led Jed through the door into the lab and nodded to the door beyond that. "You want to see the bodies?" he asked. "Then, of course, we can talk, look over my reports."

"Sure," Jed said, shrugging, grinning at his friend. "I've seen a few in my time."

The truth was, he had. Anyone who'd been in law enforcement long enough had seen corpses. It was procedure, and the experience could sometimes give an investigator a different point of view than he'd get from merely studying photographs.

Jed viewed both the judge and his wife, his face expressionless in spite of the churning in his stomach that he'd never, in a million years, admit.

"This is the wound I'm particularly interested in," Jackson was saying, holding the sheet away from the judge's head. "And this bruise here, on Clare Whittaker's shoulder." He pointed at the mark. "Of course," Jackson went on, "we'll never get anywhere with the bruise, too hard to prove it happened before the fall, and the actual cause of death is a broken neck. But that wound on the skull of Evan Whittaker..."

Back in his private office, Jackson got out the files and spread them on his desk for Jed to study. It was not Jed's job to make assessments or to speculate at this point. His job here was to listen to the scientific evidence as presented by the expert, and then to act on those findings. Speculation was for the courtroom.

And the fact that Brian and Gabriela Zimmerman were involved in this—*Gab,* he thought, *amazing*—well, he couldn't let that color his thinking, either. To Jackson Many Goats' professional credit, he never once mentioned Gabriela. Thank God, Jed thought as he scanned the pages of medical findings.

"Multiple contusions and abrasions to both the victims are consistent with the nature of the accidents," Jackson was saying, leaning over the papers, reading portions aloud to Jed. "There are large amounts of loose gravel and soil found in all the wounds that are also consistent with the geology of that particular canyon. In fact," he went on, "so far, I've only got two areas where there are inconsistencies, one being that wedge-shaped wound on the judge's skull, and the other, a large amount of human tissue found beneath the fingernails of Clare Whittaker."

Jed looked up.

"Could be she was clutching at either her husband or Brian Zimmerman," Jackson explained. "Why she was doing that is your territory, though. I've sent the skin samples down to the FBI lab in Phoenix for DNA analysis. It'll take weeks. Sooner or later they're probably going to want samples from the Zimmermans. I'll let you handle telling them."

"Right," Jed said. Swell. "Let's go back to the wound," he said. "Tell me about it."

He did, and the upshot was that due to the precise shape and depth of the head wound, he was of the belief that it had been caused not by a jagged rock, but most likely by a sharp, bladelike metal object. "You see," he pointed out, "there are no rock or dirt fragments in the wound, and like I said, the shape and depth of it appear to be caused by a man-made instrument."

"Such as?"

Jackson rubbed his smooth jaw. "I'm still measuring some objects, but the nearest I've come is a couple of camping tools. One's an axe, a small variety used to build campfires, you know. The thing is, the wound was inflicted by something that's quite sharp but then thickens."

"And nothing like it's been found at the scene," Jed reflected aloud.

"I doubt Sheriff Ulrich has sent anyone out there again," Jackson pointed out. "Up until yesterday there was no reason. Of course, this baby is yours now, buddy."

Jed smiled grimly. "Thanks to you, pal, it is."

"Had to get you out here somehow," Jackson teased.

They decided to meet for dinner after Jed got checked into a motel. While Jackson closed up shop for the day, Jed drove east along Route 66 till he found one of those old, cabin-style motels. He was sure the place had been there when he was a boy. The complex consisted of a Pan-Abode style office and fifteen detached cabins, single rooms with baths. It was antiquated but fit Jed's nostalgic mood. His own little cabin backed right against the woods and the river beyond.

He had an hour before he was due to meet Jackson at a steakhouse, so he showered and shaved and dressed in jeans and an old navy blue U of A sweatshirt he'd had since college. Jackson was going to get a smile out of that. In the meantime Jed spread out copies of all the reports he'd collected thus far on the round tabletop near the single window and went over them, page by page. The thing he hadn't mentioned to Jackson was Brian Zimmerman's statement to the sheriff that he hadn't been able to reach Clare Whittaker in time to save her from falling.

Jed reread the official statement from Brian. "I was ahead of both of them . . . the judge had already gone over the rim. . . . Oh, God, it happened so damned fast. . . . Tried to reach Clare, but she just went over . . . rocks and gravel sliding out from under her feet. . . ."

What interested Jed was the part about not being able to get back to Clare in time. So how, then, had flesh gotten beneath her fingernails? The judge's? Maybe. Maybe she'd tried to clutch at her husband to help him. Or maybe the flesh belonged to Brian Zimmerman. Had the man lied? Forgotten the details? And the results of the DNA testing were going to take weeks.

Then there was the wedge-shaped wound. That was the biggie.

The question was—Jed rubbed his newly shaved jaw—why? Why would anyone, least of all Brian or Gabriela, want to harm those people? What possible motive could there be?

He looked at his watch. Six p.m. He yawned. It had been a long day. Not that he wasn't looking forward to dinner with Jackson, but he was still working on East Coast time. Then, too, there was the added pressure of tomorrow's meeting with the Zimmermans. With Gab, damn it all. He might as well face it, this was going to be the hardest thing he'd done in his life. Harder than burying his dad, Jed realized. That love

had never been defined. His and Gabriela's love, that
had been clear. "Damn," he breathed.

He walked to the steakhouse, breathing in the cooling air of evening. Off to the northeast in the direction of the Navaho Reservation, thunderclouds still
loomed, but over Flagstaff the sky was clear, the kind
of clear that was so blue it dazzled your senses. Back
East, clear was a kind of white sky, hazy, the orb of
the sun never definite because of the humidity, and Jed
was never going to grow used to it.

By the time he reached the steakhouse he was awake
again and hungry. He spotted the official coroner's
station wagon in the parking lot in front of the long
wooden structure, and he grinned. Jackson enjoying
a few perks. Inside it was cool, air-conditioned and
crowded with summer tourists. A couple of babies
cried; kids were getting antsy in the waiting area. But
Jackson had a table for them, in the back by a window. He waved Jed over, then sat back down. Jed
threaded his way through the tables and joined him.

"This place here when you were growing up? I can't
remember," Jackson said, taking a swig of beer. Jed
knew he'd only have one, though; he'd never allowed
himself more.

"No," Jed said. "Must have built it after Pop
moved us to Phoenix." He, too, ordered a long-neck
beer from the waitress.

"I read about Max in the papers, about his dying. I
was real sorry to hear it," Jackson said. "A while ago,
wasn't it?"

"Seven, eight years," Jed replied. "A lousy ticker.
It ruined his life."

"Um," Jackson said. "And your mom?"

"In Tucson. The ultimate retirement. My sister, Hannah, lives close by with her family. I don't see them much. Once a year, maybe."

"But they're all well?"

"Perfect health."

"And you?"

"Me?" Jed laughed and took a long drink from the bottle. "I'm fine. Just a little creaky in the joints from all the humidity back in D.C."

"Still jog?"

"Yep. Every day. Well, almost every day." Then Jed said, "But what about you? Still married?"

"Oh, yeah. I've got three holy terrors running around the yard now. Susie wants me to get fixed, you know, but I'm not so sure. Hell, it might hurt!"

"I hear you," Jed said, laughing. "So how about your mom and dad? Your mom still at the library?"

"Head librarian now."

"And your dad?"

"A grumpy old retiree. He stayed with the railroad for thirty years and then quit. He fishes a lot now. Drives Mom nuts the rest of the time."

"It's hard to retire, I guess," Jed said, reflecting. "My father never got a chance to find out."

"Um," Jackson said. Then he asked, "So you were married? I mean, I never even heard about it till after."

"Yeah," Jed said, and shook his head. "It only lasted eighteen months. Eileen was a nurse in Arlington. We met when I needed a few stitches. Guess we were never right for each other." He shrugged.

"Didn't work out, huh?"

"No, it didn't."

"Any other prospects?" Jackson was asking, but Jed didn't answer; he was remembering that when Eileen left she'd said it was never going to work because he was still in love with his old college flame.

Gab, Jed thought. Tomorrow.

"So, you have anyone new yet?"

Jed shook himself mentally. "Ah, no, not right now."

"You aren't going out with anybody?"

"Oh, there are a couple of ladies I've dated. Nothing serious."

They talked for a long time. Over dinner and over three cups of coffee. They spoke little of the case that had brought Jed home, though, until Jackson finally broached the uncomfortable subject.

"Did you tell your boss you knew the Zimmermans?" he finally asked.

Jed gave him a lopsided grin. "Yes."

"Well, then, do you think you'll be okay with Gab? I mean, after all, you guys were quite an item for a while."

"That was years ago," Jed said. "One has nothing to do with the other."

"Strictly business, huh?"

"Sure it is." Still, Gabriela's face flew into his head, the mass of her dark hair, the tilt of her green eyes, that unusually pale, perfect skin with the honey-colored bridge of freckles across her cheeks and nose.... Gab. The way she always trusted everyone, the underdog's champion. He recalled that ugly, abandoned puppy she'd brought home. It had gotten run over, and she'd cried all day. Was Brian Zimmerman one of her souls-in-need-of-rescue? Had he, himself, been one? Interesting thought...

"Well, I'm glad to hear you can keep your perspective on this one," Jackson was saying as they paid the bill, "because I'm afraid the Whittakers' deaths were not accidental. Not the way the Zimmermans told it, anyhow."

"I've got a handle on myself," Jed assured his friend. "I really do."

But when he lay in bed in the dark cabin that night he wondered: did he really have a handle on this meeting tomorrow or was he kidding himself?

Sleep came slowly. Jed didn't mind, though, because outside his window the river rushed by and the branches of the pines soughed in the night breeze. The air was cold now, and fresh. He was glad to be here, glad they'd given him this case. Whatever difficulties he encountered, he'd handle. After all, he was Max Mallory's son and he could handle it all.

CHAPTER FOUR

PREDICTABLY, BRIAN disappeared the next morning. Gabriela asked everyone if they'd seen him, a little embarrassed that he hadn't even informed her, his own wife, where he was going. She finally got an answer from Herb, one of the pool boys. "He went to Flagstaff, Mrs. Zimmerman. Said he needed some parts for the pumps."

"Did he say when he'd be back?" Gabriela asked.

"No, not really."

Gabriela tried not to show her consternation to Herb, but she was really upset. Brian knew they were supposed to be there when the federal investigator arrived. He knew, and he'd gone to Flagstaff, anyway, even though the parts for the pumps could have waited. Lord, they'd already waited for most of the summer.

But, of course, Brian had to do it this morning. And what was this federal whatever-he-was going to think when the only eyewitness to the accident was gone? Guilty. Guilty as sin. Something to hide. What else could he think?

Guilty of what, though? Gabriela walked toward the office, passing the pools, not even noticing the familiar sulfur smell or the steam rising into a white mist over the dark water in the cool morning air. She was just being paranoid, she supposed. Maybe Brian's disappearance would appear to be casual unconcern to the investigator.

Oh, it was so hard to be objective when you were put on the defensive like this! What a terrible feeling—tried and convicted by public opinion, by rumor and innuendo, when you were perfectly innocent. Of course, it was all the fault of the media. Even as Gabriela walked toward the side entrance to the hotel she could already hear the phone ringing—all three lines simultaneously. The media had turned a tragic accident into a public circus.

The investigator... Well, he must have been sent out here to perform a routine follow-up to the death of a high-ranking government official. Sure. It was all routine. And when nothing out of the ordinary was discovered, the phones would stop ringing and life would return to normal at last. Sure.

But meanwhile there was work to be done, and Gabriela figured it would be better to keep busy than to sit around stewing about things over which she had no control. Lorna was with Ellie and Otto, and Margaret was at the front desk. Gabriela could catch up on some desk work. And Brian—well, he'd get back when he felt like it, and if he wasn't here for the federal guy, there wasn't much Gabriela could do about it.

She was almost afraid to go into the lobby. The local deputy had put up a barricade at the bottom of the hotel driveway and tried to ward off the press, so there weren't any more vans with satellite dishes, but she could still hear the phone ringing when she stepped inside. Margaret was getting good at fielding calls, though. She said, "No comment," and hung up. Simple.

She was hanging up as Gabriela approached the desk, and she made a face and rolled her eyes.

"God, Margaret, I'm sorry you have to deal with this," Gabriela said.

"It's no big deal. Kind of exciting, really, now that I know what to say. Makes the time pass real quickly. When I think of who I might be talking to on the phone... Wow! Bryant Gumble or Mike Wallace or Barbara Walters. Who knows?"

"You're being great about this, and we really appreciate it, Margaret. I'm going to be in the office working, but if Brian calls, please let me talk to him, okay?"

"Sure, Mrs. Zimmerman."

Gabriela went into her office, sat down and turned on the computer. She pressed some keys and got the monthly spreadsheet on the screen. July. She had to balance this month, get totals, close it out. Routine stuff, and a lot quicker with the computer Brian had purchased five years before. At the time, the hotel had been seeing an upsurge in business, and it had seemed a great idea, a good investment. Now Gabriela wasn't so sure it had been worth the expense. It had been just one more debt to pay off, and they were in such a hole....

She worked, tapping in figures, recording numbers, trying to concentrate on the screen and shutting out the ringing phone, Margaret's replies and her worry over Brian's whereabouts.

She was in the middle of totaling July's payroll figures when Margaret tapped on her door once and then came in. "There's a man here to see you, Mrs. Zimmerman. He's out in the lobby."

Gabriela's heart sank. It was the bigwig federal investigator, and Brian wasn't here.

She sighed. "Show him back here, will you please, Margaret?"

"Sure, Mrs. Zimmerman."

Gabriela brushed back her mass of hair and turned the computer screen off. She took a deep breath. She'd just tell him the truth, that Brian had gone to...

"Hello, Gab."

Gab. Only one person in her whole life had ever called her that. But no. That was impossible, it couldn't be...

Slowly she turned on the swivel chair and looked up. Time froze into absolute immobility for a heartbeat, then it rushed on as if to catch up for the lapse. Her body went cold, then hot. She could feel the stiffness of her pasted-on smile, and gears spun in her mind, spun but refused to mesh.

"Gabriela?" came his voice, and he stood there looking at her, his face solemn. She had to take a breath, had to answer, but needles of adrenaline shot through her veins, and she couldn't fit her mind around the reality of his presence.

"Jed," she finally managed to say, a whisper.

A small quirk tilted his lip. He nodded slowly.

Jed. Jed was there, standing right in front of her, lean and tall in a white shirt and sport coat and more handsome than ever, with the same generous nose and those artfully carved lips that could so easily curve into a smile. His hair was just as thick and unruly, still that dark-blond color that had caught and held the sunlight. And his eyes, deep-set and dark blue beneath straight brows, eyes that had always spoken so eloquently.

Jed Mallory. Here.

She felt a sudden dizziness sweep her, and she was so terribly afraid to stand up. Jed. "I...uh...I didn't expect..." What was she saying?

"It's been a long time," he said, and she noticed only then the unfamiliar maturity in his face, the lines, the slight thickening that masculinity lends to men past youth.

"Yes," she replied, fighting to recover. "A long time."

"You're looking well," he said, and it seemed as if that sentence held untold depths and layers of meaning.

"Thank you," she answered.

"How've you been, Gab?"

"Oh...fine, just fine."

"You have a family now? You know, kids and all that?"

She looked down for an instant. "No." She shrugged.

"Um," he said. "Well, I'm glad everything's going okay for you."

"It was," she said, "till the past couple of days. You know about the...?"

"The Whittakers, yes."

"Are you still with the Marshals Service, Jed?"

He nodded.

"Still in Arlington?"

"That's right."

"So it worked out." She averted her face. "I'm glad for you."

"As a matter of fact, that's what I'm here about. I really wanted to talk to your...husband, too."

She closed her eyes for a moment, then opened them.

"I've been sent to investigate the case, Gab."

His words finally sank in, and she looked up sharply and met his eyes. "You?"

"That's right. The Marshals Service has jurisdiction."

"You?" she asked again, her voice rising.

"They sent me because I'm from Flagstaff, Gab," he said quietly.

"Oh, my God," she whispered.

His voice changed timbre, became remote and impersonal. "Is Brian around?"

She looked down at her hands, still trying to digest the whole thing. Jed was the investigator. Impossible. And yet there he was, standing over her, waiting for her reply.

"Brian?" he asked again.

She couldn't meet his eyes. She simply could not. "He...uh... He had something to do in Flagstaff, parts to get. He'll be back soon, I'm sure."

"I was under the impression that he'd been asked to be here this morning."

She didn't answer. Her heart was beating like a captured bird. Her mouth was so dry.

"Well, all right," Jed said, his tone brisk. "I'll start with you. Is that okay?"

"Start what?" She licked her dry lips.

"I just want your statement about the accident. A few questions."

"I gave my statement to the sheriff," she said wearily.

"I need to get it again."

She finally found the strength to stand up and face him on equal terms. She'd forgotten just how tall he was, taller than Brian. She had to look up, and she wasn't used to that. "Do I need a lawyer?" she asked. "Am I being charged with anything?"

"No, of course not. This is only a statement. You can change it at any time. It isn't testimony, and it isn't legally binding." He paused. "Is there a problem?"

She shook her head, then gave a short laugh. "Problem? The Whittakers are dead and we're being hounded by the press and treated as if we're hiding something or we know something more than we do, and our switchboard is ringing off the hook and Brian..." She stopped abruptly, feeling the hysteria well up inside her and not wanting Jed to see her fall apart. She straightened her shoulders.

"Brian what?" he asked.

"Brian isn't here," she said quickly. "He had to get some parts in Flagstaff."

"Yes, that's what you said," Jed replied, and she knew he didn't believe her. "Look, I'm sorry about this, honestly. It must be hard for you. But I've been sent to do a job, and with your cooperation I'll get it done as soon as possible. Then I'll be out of your hair." He hesitated. "I don't want to make this any harder for you than it already is, Gab."

She gave him a searching look. "Is that what they teach you to say to all the suspects?"

His eyes met hers, but now she couldn't read behind the dark blue surface. "You aren't a suspect."

She put her hand on her forehead. "Sorry, I'm still pretty upset about the Whittakers, and then you appear out of the blue."

"It's been bad?" he asked.

"Awful," she breathed.

"I'm sorry," he said, and she believed him. And then they were both just standing there, and Gabriela thought she should say or do something profound, but her tongue was stiff in her mouth and her knees felt so weak.... The years fell away suddenly—she tried to stop them, but she couldn't, and there they were, she and Jed, back on the campus, and her sister's husband had just died and she had to tell Jed how afraid she was, how she could never marry him if he pursued this insane notion that he wanted to be a policeman....

"Gab?"

She blinked, shut off the memory and swallowed hard. "The statement, yes, sure. I can do that," she got out. "Is the office here all right?"

"It's fine."

"Right now?"

"Whenever you want."

"This is so horrible.... All right, let's get it over with."

He was all business then, a professional. He sat across from her and turned on a small tape recorder, giving the date, time and location before he gave her name, and asked her to relate the sequence of events in her own words.

Gabriela sat there, hands in her lap, and repeated her story. It didn't take long, but the whole time she was talking she was aware of Jed's eyes on her, neutral but implacable, as if he were noting every detail about her, every shade of tone, nuances of expression and body language. It made her unaccountably afraid, and she stumbled over her words a few times.

When she was done he leaned forward and stopped the tape recorder, then sat there in silence, as if thinking. She kept waiting for him to ask some more questions, to probe her story, but he didn't.

"I guess I'm not much help," she finally said to break the leaden silence. "But I really didn't see anything."

"Um," he said.

"Jed." She paused, wondering if she should say it. "You didn't ... ask for this case, did you?"

His blue eyes bored into hers. "No, I didn't. I was assigned to it, like I told you. It's helpful for me to be familiar with the area."

"I see."

"Why do you ask?"

"Well, it's obvious, isn't it? Maybe you wanted to come back here and question us. Maybe you were curious."

"Curious," he said.

"Did you tell them back in Arlington that you knew me?" she asked, her hands trembling a little.

"Of course I did," he said flatly.

She was going to press him further, but just then the office door opened and Brian strode in.

"Oh, Brian," she said, rising, relief flooding her.

"Margaret told me some guy was here to see us," Brian was saying.

"Yes," she said. "This is Jed Mallory. Remember him?"

Brian narrowed his eyes and looked Jed up and down. "Mallory," he said. "Oh, yeah, I remember."

"He's here to investigate the accident," she said.

"You're kidding." Brian's head swung to Gabriela. "Your ex-boyfriend is here to investigate us? You *must* be kidding."

Jed stepped forward. "I think Gabriela can go now. I have her statement. If you wouldn't mind me using the office for your statement?"

"What the hell?" Brian asked.

"I'm a deputy U.S. marshal, duly invested with the authority to conduct an investigation into the deaths of Evan and Clare Whittaker, Mr. Zimmerman. I'm sure I can count on your cooperation."

"I'm supposed to cooperate with you?"

"Brian," Gabriela pleaded.

The two men stood, practically chest to chest, Brian muscular and blond, bristling like a tomcat; Jed lean and alert, his eyes as distant as mountain lakes.

The standoff only lasted a second, then Brian Zimmerman backed off, his scowl changed to a rueful smile, and he pulled off his baseball cap and ran a broad hand through his hair. "Okay, okay, I'm sorry. This has been such a mess."

"I understand," Jed replied carefully.

"Gabriela, it's all right," Brian said, turning to her, and Jed saw the fear in her eyes subside. He clenched his teeth.

"Brian, you're okay?" she asked, and there was an edge to her voice. Jed wasn't sure what it was, but he didn't like it.

"I'm fine, babes. Go on. I'll talk to Mr. Mallory. Sorry I wasn't here sooner."

"No problem. I took Gab's statement while we waited."

Brian gave her a swift glance that Jed didn't miss. "Well, I guess we could get started. I mean, I'm pretty busy around here," Brian said. "And I already gave Sheriff Ulrich my statement, anyway."

"Yes, I've read it," Jed said.

"Oh?"

"I got all the papers before I flew out."

"Then why...?" Gabriela began.

"The Service needs to do its own investigation."

"That's what I don't understand," she said. "Why all this investigation? I mean, it was an accident, a terrible accident."

"It's routine," Jed lied.

She looked at him, and he knew she was trying to judge whether to believe him or not. It was godawful that he couldn't level with her, but he couldn't, and that was that.

"Well, I'll see you later," she said. "Or are you going back East soon?"

"When this investigation is over. A little while." He shrugged.

She turned to her husband. "I'll be up with your folks for lunch, Brian. If you have time, can you stop by?"

"Sure. See you later, babes."

Jed watched her leave. She was as tall and willowy as he remembered. She was wearing a tailored khaki skirt and a deep green short-sleeved shirt that matched her eyes. Her hair was loose on her back, curling wildly. He felt a pang in his belly at the memory of his hands in her hair, in the sweet perfume of it. She looked good to him, just right, with the air of self-confidence a woman acquires with maturity.

Brian was rubbing his hands together and sitting down at the desk. Jed dragged his attention back to him, and he wondered if Brian was a little too anxious to start his statement or if he, Jed, was reading things into every move this man made, if he was conjuring up signs of guilt.

"I'm going to record this," he said. "All right?"

"Sure, record away. There's really nothing more I can say. I told the sheriff everything."

Jed gave the time, place, identified the speaker, then leaned back in his chair and watched Brian Zimmerman. Watched more than listened, because a person's movements, his expression, his hands and other body language, were more telling than words. And besides, he'd already read the statements. He knew the story.

"So I was going ahead because it's a real nasty trail right there. Narrow with a big drop-off on the right side. The judge was about, oh, thirty feet behind me, and his wife a ways behind him. I didn't see exactly what happened because I was watching my step, let me tell you." Brian crossed his legs, looked up at the ceiling. "The first thing, I guess, was the rocks. I heard falling rocks, you know." He made a gesture with his hand. "Then the judge yelled and I turned, real fast, but all I could see was him going over. God, it was awful." Brian shook his head sadly. "Awful. Then Clare, that's his wife, screamed and ran toward him, grabbing for him, but he was gone, and she lost her balance and fell, too, and by then I was there, but it was too late."

"And Gab...Gabriela?" Jed asked, and he caught the look on Brian's face before the man deftly cloaked it.

"My wife," Brian said meaningfully, "had gone on ahead, around a bend. She ran back, though, and got there just about then. There was nothing we could do. Nothing. We did go down a ways, well, I told the sheriff this, and found a trail that goes to the bottom of the canyon. I went. Gabriela couldn't do it. She was a mess, you can imagine. I figured I had to check the bodies. So I did it. It was a hell of a long way down, but I found them. Both of them. Terrible. But they'd died quickly. It was over quick, at least.''

Brian sat back, uncrossed his legs and scratched at the back of his neck. ''That's it. We walked out to the truck and drove home, then called the sheriff and Mountain Rescue. The rest you probably know.''

''They were both dead when you reached them?''

''Oh, yes, no doubt about it. Head injuries. No heartbeat, no breath. I checked. Then I had to just leave them. I felt bad about it, but I couldn't get them out myself, you know?''

''Uh-huh.''

''And Gabriela was hysterical, so I had to get back to her. It was pretty late by then. What an awful day.'' Brian drew in a deep breath and toyed with the brim of his baseball cap, which lay on the desk.

Jed pictured Gab hysterical, saw the scene in his mind's eye: Brian holding her, comforting her, his hands on her. No. No, he couldn't do that. He was here on a case. That was all, a case.

''So, are we through?'' Brian asked.

Jed hadn't planned it, but the words came out before he could think. ''You know, I'd really like to see where it happened. Think you could take me there?''

''Well, I'm pretty busy....'' Brian hesitated, frowned. ''It's a ways, you know.''

''It'd take days to get someone official to take me there, and I'd really appreciate your help.'' He knew damn well he could call the sheriff and get a deputy to show him the spot right away, but he wanted some more time with Brian Zimmerman. The man's story was plausible enough, but there was that wedge-shaped wound to the judge's head that Jackson was convinced was man-made. Still, there wasn't even a sliver of a motive. So far.

"I'll have to let my wife know," Brian said, and Jed knew he was hooked. A man with something to hide felt more secure being close to the investigation. That way he'd know better how to defend himself against traps and tough questions. Of course, Brian could merely be a helpful kind of guy.

"Go ahead. We can go in my car," Jed said, rising.

"It'll take all afternoon."

"Hey, that's what I'm here for," Jed said, smiling, wondering if it looked genuine.

Brian dialed a number and got his father. He left a message for Gabriela, then stood, brushing his hands together. "All set. Say, you got good walking shoes on?" He looked down at Jed's cowboy boots. He had tennis shoes on himself.

"In my car. I'll change when we get there," Jed assured him. "You okay in those?"

"Sure."

They were cautious with each other on the drive, as if they were players on opposing sports teams. Polite but very careful. Jed's skin crawled whenever he thought of Gab with this man; he couldn't stop himself. And that loss of self-control came as a total surprise. She was nothing to him. A former lover. Most men had plenty of them. They never gave them a second thought.

But God, seeing her again had honestly been a blow. Hard. So familiar, yet so strange, and she didn't belong to him anymore. And even though he'd known that for years, the proximity had been devastating, had brought back all the pain and rage and betrayal.

He hoped he'd hidden his feelings. He hoped she hadn't seen what she'd done to him.

Put it out of your head, he told himself. And he looked out the window at the country through which Brian was directing him. Hills and canyons, dark green pines, piñon and juniper dotting the south faces. It was broken country, with even some cactus here and there. Drier as they descended, that pale, dust-colored ground appeared naked in the sun. Brush, heavy around streams, and bunchgrass. A blue sky, so dark at the zenith it was sapphire, the dry hills standing against it, like torn paper silhouettes. Too clear, like a trompe l'oeil painting. It was beautiful in a clean, sharp-edged way, the landscape of his boyhood. He steered along the road and drank it in.

Brian spoke more than Jed would have liked, really, requiring him to answer, to think of replies, to respond to this person who was Gab's husband. He didn't like Brian Zimmerman, although the man had done nothing objectionable. He had all of his lines right, his mannerisms down pat, but there was something... There were moments when Jed could have sworn Zimmerman was two people rolled into one, two personalities that didn't quite mesh. Was that assessment Jed's unconscious desire or was it a valid investigator's instinct?

It was a thirty-minute drive, north and east, toward the Fort Apache Indian Reservation. Then it would be a forty-minute hike, Brian told him, looking at Jed, assessing him, too. "Hope the altitude doesn't bother you," he said.

"Hope not," Jed replied.

He parked at the trailhead Brian indicated, just a wide shoulder of the road and a bridge over a deep, dried-up riverbed.

"That's the canyon." Brian pointed. "There's no water left in it this time of year. It gets steeper up higher where they fell."

Jed was tying up his running shoes, tossing his boots into the back seat. He was wearing tailored khaki slacks and a short-sleeved white shirt; he'd taken off his sport coat. Brian, however, was more suitably dressed for this trek, wearing jeans and a short-sleeved yellow polo shirt. Brian had brought along a day pack with water and light jackets. It was a short hike, but in the mountains you had to be prepared. Things happened.

They started out, Brian setting a good pace. He was probably dying for Jed to ask him to slow down. Jed wouldn't do it, though, not even if he puffed like an old steam engine. The path followed the riverbed, winding up, then it diverged, making sweeping switchbacks up a broad face until it rejoined the riverbed up higher. That was where the trail got narrow, its edge crumbling, the canyon far below now, a rocky ravine.

"You okay?" Brian asked, stopping for water.

Jed gritted his teeth. He smiled. "I'm fine."

They went on, and the trail narrowed even more. The path was dry and dusty, and dislodged stones tumbled over the edge and fell, bouncing, rattling. Jed could smell the dust that rose in puffs from his feet.

"How far down is it?" he asked. "What's your guess?"

"I don't know, maybe five, six hundred feet." Brian stopped and pointed. "See that? That's a deer trail that goes to the floor of the canyon. That's what I took to get down.''

"Looks tough."

"It was. I left Gabriela sitting on that rock." He pointed again. "She was too upset to follow me, and I was afraid to let her go down to the truck alone." He squinted at Jed under his baseball cap. "You want to go down there?"

"Not yet."

Fifteen minutes later, Brian halted again. "This is it," he said.

The trail hugged a rock face on the left side and dropped directly off on the right. The edge was crumbled, all right, only twelve inches across in places. Nasty.

"This part of the trail always scared the heck out of Gabriela. She hates exposure," Brian said.

Oh, Jed knew that. The Ferris wheel scared her, the chair lifts had made her nervous when they went skiing, the view of the Half-Dome in Yosemite Park had turned her putty-pale. Oh, yes, he knew all about Gab's fear of heights....

Without a bridging thought, an image sprang unwanted into his head. He and Gab at the Arizona State Fair—the Ferris wheel...stopping at the very pinnacle when the operator was letting people off below, loading new rides. "Oh, my God," Gabriela breathed, "I hate this! Make them start it up, Jed!" But he had held her close, the springing mass of her black hair tickling his cheek, and then he kissed her, long and hard, probing her mouth, his hand touching her breast, feeling the response. The ride started up. They never noticed. And that same night Jed made love to her for the first time. She had been a virgin....

"Frankly, I was surprised the Whittakers weren't more scared," Brian Zimmerman was saying. Her husband.

Jed had to shake himself. "Maybe they should have been."

"Yeah, maybe."

Jed stood on the edge of the trail, looking down. Scree, broken rock, a few dead branches. A fall would almost certainly be fatal here. There was nothing to stop you; one of those natural rock slides so common in the mountains. And the autopsies showed abrasions consistent with this kind of terrain.

"Not much to see, is there," Brian said. "But I'll never forget this place, never."

Jed craned his neck to look up the trail. It disappeared around the canyon wall. "Where does this trail end up?"

"Got me. I never followed it all the way. I've only been a few miles past there. The canyon widens out and the trail splits up where another stream comes into it."

"And you and the judge went farther along than the women, is that right?"

"Uh-huh. Clare got tired and Gabriela stayed with her. That was about a mile past here. Do you want to go up there?"

"No, no, not necessary. How far did you and the judge go?"

Brian thought hard. "Well, let me see. It took about an hour. Two miles, maybe. Evan was slow."

"And this was one of your treasure-hunt hikes?" Jed said.

"Uh, yes." Brian looked at him, surprised. "How'd you know about that?"

"I read one of your brochures in the lobby."

"Oh. Yeah, well, Evan liked to think there was some truth to the old story, you know."

"The Spanish gold?"

"That's right. Crazy."

"You don't believe in it?"

Brian laughed. "Hell, no. But we cater to our guests."

"Okay, I think I've seen enough here. But I'd like to get down to where you found the bodies."

"You sure? It's a hard descent."

"I'm sure," Jed answered.

They backtracked and started down the narrow game trail. Pebbles slid underfoot, the sun glared on the hillside, while across the ravine, the shadows inched up the far wall. Cactus jutted up and dusty bushes clung to the hillside like barnacles.

"You hanging in there?" Brian asked more than once.

"Fine, just fine," Jed answered.

Sweat dampened their backs by the time they reached the broken bottom of the canyon. Then it was a trek to the place where the bodies had landed at the foot of the scree field.

"Here, this is where they were," Brian said. He looked up, twisting his neck, taking off his cap, shielding his eyes with it. "See, there's the trail up there. Helluva way up."

It sure was.

Jed walked the area, starting where Brian stood, making concentric circles, checking the ground. Of course, it was pretty torn up by the rescue team who'd come to recover the bodies. He caught a metallic gleam and bent to pick it up. A silver gum wrapper.

"What're you looking for?" Brian called to him.

"I'm not sure. Just looking." He crushed the wrapper in his hand.

"The sheriff's men were out here already. They didn't find anything."

Jed didn't answer. He had hardly expected to find a blood-encrusted weapon up on the trail or lying at his feet, but he needed to spend time at the scene, to feel the place out, maybe only to satisfy his curiosity. No, not quite. It was to feel the vibes, to listen and breathe in the air and let his instincts deduce what they might. Sometimes he got answers that way. Sometimes victims cried out from beyond the grave.

Of course, sometimes they remained utterly silent.

He studied the terrain: rough, tumbled rocks from when the spring runoff flooded the canyon. The walls rose on either side, casting shadows on the floor of the ravine as the afternoon wore on. He turned slowly, shading his eyes, in a full circle. There was a lot of ground here, too much for one man to search. Even if there was some proof of a crime here—and maybe there wasn't—it might take a whole contingent of people searching with metal detectors and trained dogs to find anything.

It was too soon to order a full-blown search, but it was something he could keep in mind as a possibility. If Brian was guilty of something, he reasoned, then he'd had only moments to get rid of the weapon before Gab came on the scene, so he would have had to get rid of it right then and there. Toss it away.

That is, if Gab were telling the truth. But there was no way she'd lie, not Gabriela. She didn't have it in her, not even to defend her own husband. Unless she'd changed, totally changed, and he didn't know her at all anymore.

"I'd like to go up the other side there," Jed said, pointing. "It looks like there's a game trail."

"What for?" Brian looked up.

"To get another viewpoint. I like to be thorough."

"Mind if I wait here?" Brian asked. "We still have to climb back out, you know."

"I know. I'll try to hurry. Listen, I really appreciate your help. You've been real patient."

Brian found a rock to sit on. "My wife will kill me if we're too late getting back."

"Sorry. I'll explain to her...."

"I can handle her, don't worry." Then Brian looked up at the wall. "That other side's probably on the Apache reservation. The boundary's around here."

"Oh, think there's any problem?"

"Nah, not out here."

"Okay, I'll be back soon."

He liked being on his own. He climbed the narrow game trail on the opposite canyon wall until he was a few hundred feet above the floor where he squatted, winded. He could see the trail across from him, the rock slide, the spot where the bodies had been found. Above him, the bright sky arched, bridging the ravine, which was dulled with shadows now. He could even see Brian, moving around through rocks and brush. Zimmerman was probably growing restless.

Jed was rising to go back down when he sensed a presence behind him. The hairs on the back of his neck rose, and he pivoted, his body thrumming. There was a rock outcropping overlooking the canyon nearby, and it jutted out from the wall, a black silhouette against the sunlit sky, and on it...on it stood a figure, a black cutout of an Indian, bent and old, like those figures you saw all over the Southwest of the mythical humpbacked magician Kokopelli. Jed blinked and shielded his eyes. The figure was gone.

CHAPTER FIVE

VISITING HIS PARENTS was a distasteful chore to Brian Zimmerman. His mother was ill and his father was not much better—they had to live a quiet life. Their fourth-floor apartment was Victorian-dark and smelled moldy to him—all that old stuff they insisted on hoarding.

His mother, Ellie, he felt a certain fondness for, but Otto was a pain in the butt, had been ever since he was a boy. Pushing, questioning, disapproving. Not once in his thirty-seven years could Brian recall doing anything right in his father's eyes and, if he had, Otto had sure never acknowledged it. His sister, Lorna, on the other hand, was Otto's little darling. No matter what she did, it was okay with the old man. And for that Brian disliked her intensely.

He sat in the living room with its drawn curtains after returning from the site of the accident and frowned at his parents, thinking with no guilt whatsoever that when they were gone it would be a relief. Well, maybe he'd miss his mother a little, but not for long. It would be Gabriela who mourned.

"So what did that U.S. marshal expect to find out there?" Otto was asking his son. "I get the feeling we're not being told everything."

Brian sighed. "How should I know?"

"He didn't say anything?" Ellie asked, and took a sip of her tea.

"Not to me."

"Why did they send a U.S. marshal, for goodness' sake?" Ellie asked.

"Well, I can tell you why they sent this particular one," Brian said. "He's an old friend of Gabriela's."

"Is that so?" Otto glanced up.

"Oh, I do remember Gabriela saying something about him once. Didn't he...? Oh, I must be confused," Ellie said.

"He was here once," Brian told her, "a long time ago."

"And they sent him out from Washington?" Otto said. "Well, good, he'll be on your side, then, an old friend like that."

"Oh, sure," Brian said sarcastically.

"What do you mean?" his father asked.

"God, I'm tired of this. Can we talk about something else, please? It's been made into such a big deal."

Ellie shook her head sadly. "You're right. This whole thing is being blown out of proportion. I wish there was something we could do to help...."

"Well, there isn't." Then Brian's head came up. "You could keep Lorna out of my hair. That would help."

"Now, look here," Otto began. "Your sister was very thoughtful to come all this way to pitch in. The least you could do..."

The conversation went on, Ellie treading on eggshells, Otto's face tight and red. But Brian didn't notice. There were too many other things pressing on him. For one, he'd had a call from the casino in Las

Vegas where he and his buddy George Lemming did most of their gambling. The bottom line was, pay up now. He could just see himself lying in a hospital room in Flagstaff with both his legs in casts. Then there was the bank that carried the paper on the latest remodeling job at the hotel. Bankers didn't break legs, but their collection departments could get downright nasty. Hell, in thirty days they could file foreclosure papers and the hotel could be history.

If Brian hadn't been so stressed out, he might have laughed. Wouldn't Otto love that! The Apache Springs Hotel, gone.

"Got any beer in the fridge?" Brian asked, rising, his mind flitting from one potential disaster to the next.

"There's a can or two, isn't there, Otto?" Ellie said.

Brian headed into the kitchen, opened the refrigerator door and rolled his eyes. Wall to wall health food. His father couldn't really believe he was going to save Ellie's life with broccoli and bean sprouts!

He found a single can of beer, popped it open and leaned back against the sink, thinking, his mind pivoting this way then that.

Out in that canyon this afternoon with Mallory he'd damn near had a heart attack. Mallory circling the land, searching, circling some more. But he hadn't found anything—thank God. Still, the man had been looking, and that meant something. Questions raised by the autopsies, probably. What else could have brought him here?

Brian took a swig of beer and tried to assess the situation. It wasn't good. Most likely the autopsy on Evan had turned up that wound to the head. Then again, there had been a dozen contusions on the judge's head. Brian had seen them. He'd figured that no medical examiner on earth could be positive, not one hundred percent positive, that a sharp rock hadn't caused the first one. He *couldn't* be positive.

So Mallory was feeling things out, probably looking for a reason why someone would harm the judge. And Deputy Marshal Jed Mallory wasn't going to find one. Brian's own wife had no idea why. But she had almost seen his struggle with Clare. Oh, yeah, Gabriela had come back around that bend just a little too soon....

"Did you find a beer, honey?" Ellie called out.

"Uh, yeah. Be right there, Mom."

Brian grimaced. Gabriela. He just hoped to God she didn't make any connections. She might be a nag, but stupid she was not. And what had she meant when he and Mallory had gotten back a few minutes ago and she'd asked if they'd found anything? What had she thought they were going to find?

It seemed to Brian just then that the whole world was conspiring against him. He could barely comprehend it. Gambling debts, a streak of the worst bad luck ... then this. People had accidents in the mountains every day. Why was everyone on his back?

It happened then—as it had been happening more and more frequently of late—a sudden burst of light and pain that exploded behind his eyes, a surge of sensation, and for a minute Brian didn't know who he was or where he was. He leaned against the fridge, floundering in the sea of light and hurt until it abated and reality returned. There was an instant of panic— what was happening to him?—and then a calming. No big deal. Just too much stress lately. No big deal.

"Son?" Ellie was calling.

"Coming, I'm coming," Brian muttered.

He left the apartment shortly after, making his way down the stairs, which he preferred to the slow old elevator, coming out in the lobby, where he nodded absently to guests. He never noticed the decor that his mother and his wife had agonized over: the rose-peach walls; the Victorian-patterned carpet in leaf swirls of green and rose and peach; the stuffed chairs and sofas and benches in coordinating shades; the heavy green drapes pulled back with swags from tall windows; the restored walnut moldings and horizontal panels of flowered wallpaper below the ceilings; the potted palms and lush, restful atmosphere, as if the hotel existed in a different time.

He took it all for granted, his mind on other things. He was tired and strung-out, but there were a few details he still had to take care of. For one, he'd better go and make sure Gabriela had locked up last month's financials. If that snoop Lorna ever saw them, she'd rat to Otto. But mostly he had to get in touch with George, get the ball rolling before the ground crumbled beneath him. Yes, George Lemming was just the man he needed. He had all the Las Vegas connections—his brother being a manager at one of the largest casinos there. Of course, it meant splitting the profits from his find with George, but what the hey? There'd be more than enough for both of them. Don't want to get too greedy, Brian thought as he locked the financials in the safe.

Before going into town to locate George—George always stopped by the Tippler Bar after work—he checked in with Gabriela, finding her in the kitchen as she put together tomorrow's food orders with the head cook.

He nodded to his wife. As she approached he couldn't help but notice what a knockout she still was, all long limbs and that mass of hair, a face that was classic in its beauty no matter how tired or angry or hurt she was. Desire stirred him. Gabriela was his. His to do with as he pleased. That talk of hers about divorce—all women threatened divorce when they wanted their own way. It meant nothing. She was his and would always be his. The notion made him feel powerful, and he thought about Mallory, Deputy U.S. Marshal Jed Mallory—eat your heart out, pal. And now soon it was all going to be good between him and Gabriela again, no more fights over money, no more tearful recriminations. Damn it, he'd never meant for his wife to suffer. He loved her. It was just this streak of lousy luck he'd been having....

Gabriela smiled at him. "How are the folks?"

"Fine, fine, you know. Listen, babes, I've gotta meet George for a few minutes, but when I get back maybe we'll leave the place in Lorna's capable hands and grab some stuff from here and cook out at the cabin. How's that sound?"

"I'd like that," Gabriela said. Then she added, "You know, Lorna really is perfectly capable of handling things, Brian. In fact, she's been better at handling all these newsmen than I am. She's probably on the phone right now. I do wish you'd cut her a little slack."

"Sure, sure," he said, checking his watch. "I'll be nice as pie to my sister if it makes you happy."

"It would," she said, and he kissed her cheek, something he hadn't done in a long time, but she stiffened a little, embarrassed in front of the help, he guessed.

He did find George at the Tippler. It was a hangout for miners and loggers, a real workingman's saloon at the edge of town. The room was dark and smoky, and the jukebox boomed country and western from five in the afternoon till closing. There was at least one fight a night in the place, and hard-core women hung out at the bar in pods. Brian had always thought they were the biker types, real tough, real seasoned. He gave them a wide berth, preferring a gentler, more malleable woman.

"Hey, Brian," George said from his seat in a booth along the far wall from the bar. "Didn't expect to see you out and about. How's it going? The radio's been full of news about those accidents."

"It's been grim, George," Brian said. "I'm pretty uptight."

"I'll bet you are."

Then Brian, who hadn't sat down, scouted the saloon for an empty table. He spotted one and said, "Got a minute? I have something private to discuss."

"Sure," George said, curious as he rose and told his buddies at the booth he'd be back in a minute.

George was a big man, six-foot-two, two hundred and twenty pounds, with a ponytail and tattoos. In his twenties he'd gotten into logging, and now he owned his own company, had his own contracts with the U.S. Forest Service, lucrative work. His base of operations was about ten miles northeast of town in tall timber country, where some fifty local men were employed by him. He was known to be a good man to work for; Brian knew him to be the luckiest man alive with a pair of dice. They'd met right out of high school at a local dice game and taken their first trip to Las Vegas together as soon as they were twenty-one. For Brian it had been years of ups and downs at the dice tables. For George it had been mostly ups.

"So what's happening?" George asked as he seated himself across from Brian, an oversize beer mug clasped in those lucky, beefy hands.

Brian wasn't sure where to begin, so he just jumped right in. "You know the treasure hunt at the hotel?" he asked.

"Yeah, sure, everyone in town gets a real kick out of it. Spanish treasure."

But Brian waved him off. "I found it, George. I found the goddamned treasure."

"You are, of course, putting me on."

Brian grinned and sat back, folding his arms.

"You aren't kidding? You're serious?"

Brian nodded.

"No shit," George said, and whistled softly.

"The best part is that no one but me knows it. Of course, now there's you."

"Yeah? So what's the hitch?" George asked, then shook his head in amazement.

"The hitch is, it's on reservation land."

"Fort Apache?"

"Uh-huh."

George thought a minute. "Oh, I got it," he said. "Belongs to the Apaches, then. So big deal. Ninety percent of the res is unoccupied. Go in at night and haul it out. I take it the loot's not in the middle of a village or something."

"Hardly," Brian said. "In fact, it's so inaccessible I could never get a vehicle in there. But that's only half the trouble. Once I do get it out, I gotta find a buyer, someone who collects stuff under the table. Now, where in hell am I going to find some rich, unethical dude like that around here?''

Then George grinned. "I see," he said. "You're thinking about my brother, his connections.''

"Is he still the manager at that ritzy casino?''

"Sure is.''

Brian leaned forward and clasped his hands together on the tabletop. "And I bet he still knows all those Fortune 500 high-roller types.''

"Probably.''

"So he could maybe introduce us to one, you know, a collector, someone who doesn't mind buying under the table.''

"That's possible.''

"I sort of thought so," Brian said and he smiled, but just then the barmaid came by and interrupted them. "Can't you see we're having a conversation here?'' he snapped.

When she left, shooting Brian a nasty look, George said, "Fifty-fifty. That's the split I want, buddy.''

"Done," Brian said, feeling better than he had in months.

GABRIELA WAS AMAZED and relieved when Brian returned an hour later looking ten years younger.

"Well," she said, "seeing George certainly perked you up.''

"Guess I just needed to get out of here for a few minutes," he said. He headed to the kitchen and put dinner for two together: trout steaks that they'd grill outside, coleslaw, new red potatoes.

Gabriela stood by the swinging doors, still marveling. This wasn't like Brian at all. Usually he ate on the run, and never did her husband cook dinner for them.

She knew, of course, or suspected, that he was jealous, that Jed's sudden appearance in their lives was at the root of her husband's newfound attentiveness. It had to be that. And the idea made her nervous.

It wasn't ten seconds later that Brian said, "I hope Mallory doesn't think we're going to put him up at the hotel."

"Oh," Gabriela replied, "I'm sure he must have gotten a room in town." She shrugged. "He isn't checked in here, anyway." She'd tried to sound matter-of-fact, but the truth was she knew precisely where he was spending the night. When Brian had gone to find George a short while ago, Jed had stopped at the hotel and told her where he'd be—just in case. In case of what? Gabriela wondered. Still, seeing him again had been a shock, and she was too afraid to examine the reasons.

While Lorna fended off a reporter who'd driven in from Albuquerque, New Mexico, Gabriela and Brian slipped out the back kitchen door and took the foot trail to their cabin. The sun was well behind the red rocks now, casting warm golden shadows on the tops of the pine trees. It was cooling off at last, as it always did in the evenings here, and she was grateful for the respite, anticipating a meal alone with Brian, a break from the frantic pace of the last few days. Lorna said she was happy to watch the desk and dining room and had promised not to disturb them. Gabriela walked next to her husband and thought that maybe tonight would be for the two of them, no talk about the Whittakers or money or gambling. Maybe they could relax.

They cooked outside on the gas grill and sat on the tiny porch and ate. Then Brian leaned back in his chair and propped his feet on the rail, looking young and satisfied. When it was too cool to stay outside a minute longer, they went in and sat in the living room, Brian in his favorite chair, Gabriela stretching out on the couch, one arm behind her head. She stared up at the log beams in the ceiling and half closed her eyes.

"I enjoyed tonight," she said lazily, keeping at bay the image of Jed that seemed to lurk just at the corner of her mind's eye.

"Yeah," Brian said, one leg thrown casually over the arm of the chair. "I just wish we could get away for a week or two. Maybe Hawaii."

Gabriela didn't say that with his mom's health so poor, and with the balance in their checking account, not to mention her constant thoughts about divorce, it was unlikely they'd ever vacation together again.

She thought about that and her heart constricted. Her feelings were so painful: she knew that reconciliation was a pipe dream of Brian's. Even those rare moments when her husband showed her he still cared, she knew how much he'd truly changed. It was as if the man she'd once loved was lost, replaced by a stranger, a man who had no true feelings for her, whose former spontaneity had become a desperate compulsiveness, a search for something she didn't understand.

"What about Hawaii?" he said.

Gabriela didn't want to burst his bubble, so she replied, "That would be great. Hawaii . . ."

"Maybe we will," he said. "Yeah, maybe in a few weeks we'll just get away."

"Um."

"Mexico's nice this time of year, too. Hot though. But a little heat wouldn't be so bad. What do you think?"

"Well, I like Mexico. Maybe later in the fall."

"Why wait?"

Gabriela held back the reasonable reply that formed in her mind. "Because we don't know how long this investigation is going to take."

"Harassment is what it is."

"I suppose they're just dotting all the I's and crossing all the T's. They have to do that. Evan was up for the Supreme Court, after all. They have to be sure."

"Yeah, well," he said, "they don't need us for that."

"Maybe," she said carefully, and Jed's image came out of its corner. *Go away,* she thought. *Just go away.* But it wouldn't. Jed, so tall and well built and boyishly handsome. Yet that morning, when she'd given him her statement, he'd been so businesslike, mature, she'd barely known him. Could he be the same man to whom she'd given herself so long ago?

Gabriela tried desperately to dispel the image of that first time with Jed, but it was there in her head, as clear as a bell. Her shyness, her nervous reactions, the infinite care he'd taken with her. A little pain. And then, later that night, he'd pulled her close and they'd begun the age-old ritual all over again, but that time she'd no longer been afraid. How young and innocent and fresh they'd been. . . .

"I don't believe that Mallory," Brian was saying as if to himself. "You don't believe that crap about him being assigned this job, do you?"

"Well . . ."

"I'd lay a hundred-to-one he begged for it. The minute he saw our names..."

"Brian, we don't know that."

"You don't think he didn't want to see you again?"

Oh, God. "That was ten years ago. In college. I'm sure I don't mean any more to him than he does to me. We're not even friends."

Brian stood and shook his head, going to turn out the light on the porch. "Sometimes you're so naive it's pathetic," he said.

"Why, thank you," she said. "You know what they say—if you don't have something nice to say..."

"Well, it's true. He still had the hots for you that summer he came up here and we were just married. Remember that?" Now he was standing over her, his arms folded.

"Wounded pride. I don't know and I don't care."

"I think you'd go to Hawaii with me if you were sure he wasn't still going to be hanging around," Brian stated flatly.

"That's ridiculous," she said, and came to a sitting position.

"So let's just do it. Let's get out of here."

Gabriela sighed heavily. "I don't really want to get into this right now," she said.

"What're you going to say? Money? My parents? It's always the same with you. You never let me do the thinking around here."

"It's hard.... What I mean is, I do trust you, Brian. I just wish..."

"What? Say it."

"I just wish you'd get some...help."

"Help."

"With the gambling." There, it was out. He'd forced the issue.

He was silent for a long moment, then said, "Go to hell."

Gabriela put her face in her hands. "Don't you see what you're doing to us?" she groaned, and then he did a rare thing, he sat down next to her and drew her against him.

"You've got to trust me," he said, putting his mouth against her hair. "I'm going to take care of everything."

"How? How are we ever going to get out of this hole we're in?"

"Trust me," he whispered. "Pretty soon it'll be all right again."

He brought her face up with a hand against her cheek and she fought back tears. He didn't know what he was saying, he was in denial; there was no way out, not unless he stopped his gambling and they could somehow make arrangements with the bank to rewrite the loan. And then there were his debts with the casino in Las Vegas. How were they ever going to pay all that money back? Trust him? She couldn't.

He kissed her cheek and her nose and her forehead. She closed her eyes and desperately tried to go with it. He kissed her lips and put a hand on her breast, gently kneading, then tugged her green cotton shirt out of the waistband of her skirt and slipped his hand up against her warm skin, nudging her bra out of the way as he slowly forced her down onto the couch. His lips were on her breasts, his teeth against her. She could feel the evidence of his desire against her thigh, and something inside Gabriela quickened. But it was different, something she'd never before experienced. It was a kind of fear, almost panic, a sense of claustrophobia.

He's my husband, she cried to herself even as she stiffened against him.

"Come on, babes," he whispered. "I know it's been a while. Relax . . . relax . . ."

But she couldn't. There was just nothing there. And then when his hand slid up her thigh and he tried to pull her underwear away, she thought she was going to scream. She went totally rigid and tried to sit up.

Brian swore, rising on an elbow, his eyes locking with hers. "What in hell's the matter with you?" he demanded.

"I . . ."

"It's him, isn't it! It's that goddamned Mallory!"

"No! It isn't that! I swear it isn't!" she said, and rose to her feet, adjusting her clothes.

Brian muttered something under his breath, then grabbed her arm. "You're a liar, Gabriela," he said. "Either that or you're a fool." And then he went to the door, tugged it open and slammed it behind him.

She stood in the middle of their living room—a place where they'd once been happy—and knew he was right. She was lying. If she'd let him make love to her it would have been Jed's face she saw behind closed eyes—Jed's face, his body joined to hers.

CHAPTER SIX

JED AWOKE EARLY the next morning, still unused to the two-hour time difference. He lay there in the generic motel room in Apache Springs, hands behind his head, and reviewed the previous day.

Gabriela. She came to him awake as she had when he was asleep. She had a few more lines on her face, and her figure was a trifle heavier, but then she'd been so skinny in college. She looked good, all in all. Wonderful, in fact. There was that look in her eyes sometimes, though, an expression.... What was it? Fear, apprehension, disappointment—not quite any one of those. The look swept across her features whenever her husband was mentioned, though she took pains to hide it. Jed felt a renewed spurt of dislike for Brian Zimmerman.

He considered the man, shutting off his emotional reaction to him. An ordinary guy, a hotel owner. Obviously he liked the outdoors, knew the country around here. He was in good physical condition, hardly winded by their hike yesterday. Jed couldn't decipher Zimmerman beyond that, but something didn't ring true, although he couldn't have said what it was. Not yet, anyway.

So, was he capable of sinking a weapon into a man's head? It wasn't as if it was self-defense or some kind of physical fight. It had been a hike, that's all, with a

Washington judge who'd wanted to get out into the wilderness, smell the air, stretch his city-bound muscles. To look, half seriously, for legendary Spanish treasure that was supposed to have been left in a cave somewhere around this area.

The scenario made no sense. Brian Zimmerman, out of the blue, abruptly swings a weapon at the judge, pushes him off the trail and then shoves his wife off, too. No reason, no motive. The Whittakers were wealthy people and spent a good sum every year at the Apache Springs Hotel. Why would Brian kill the goose that laid the golden egg?

Jed sat on the edge of the rumpled bed, his head in his hands, scrubbing at his hair. Damn. Too many unknowns.

He pulled on shorts and the tattered Redskins T-shirt, put his room key in his pocket and went for a run, going by time rather than distance, because he didn't know the area. Up the main street of Apache Springs, a typical small western town, with some old false-front wooden buildings, a new gas station, a yellow-brick post office, a hardware store, the Coyote Café with the day's special on a placard in the window. The only vehicles in sight were five battered pickup trucks parked in front of the café. Early breakfast customers, he guessed. Ranchers or loggers. The aroma of coffee wafted out of the café's open door, and quiet voices rose and fell inside, conversation in the rhythms of his youth.

The only jarring note was the "WestNews" van with its signal disk parked on the empty, dusty street. *Bloodsuckers,* Jed thought.

There was a grocery store, a drugstore and a souvenir shop full of Indian arrowheads, silver jewelry, sand paintings, the usual. Two bars, closed now, their neon beer signs unlit, their interiors dark. A barber-shop with an antique spiral-striped barber pole by the door.

Everything was closed except the café, the town cool and silent, lying still under the pale morning sunlight. As Jed ran, he breathed in the clear air, even shivered a bit at first. Hell, it couldn't have been much more than fifty degrees.

A truck drove past him, and the driver threw a pile of newspapers tied in string in front of the drugstore. Probably from Flagstaff. He waved to the driver as the truck came back down the main street; the man waved back.

Ten minutes into his run, his muscles were warm-ing up, his breathing settling into a rhythm. He fol-lowed the road up past the entrance to the Apache Springs Hotel, its red stone bulk brooding over mist-enshrouded sulfur pools at the top of the driveway. Gabriela was up there, probably still asleep. Was she lying in bed, her arms around her husband, her long legs entwined with his, her head resting on his shoul-der, the way she used to sleep with Jed? *Stop,* he told himself.

Maybe this had been a real bad idea, him taking this case. He should have told Gish just how well he knew the Zimmermans and that he couldn't take it, should have let Gish send Taylor. He almost laughed out loud. Sure, let someone else go and investigate Gab and her husband! Not too likely.

He ran up the road for fifteen minutes, then turned at a collapsed wooden barn and started back. He strode out for the last mile, really pumping, then pulled up to the motel and stretched his legs while his breathing slowed.

An hour later he was showered, shaved and dressed in jeans and boots and a short-sleeved cotton shirt. He called Gish to report on his progress, which up to now was zilch.

"And the medical examiner's still certain the wound on Whittaker's head was made by a metal object?" Gish asked.

"Absolutely," Jed replied.

"But so far you don't have a weapon, this metal object?"

"No, sir, I was out at the site yesterday. Nothing."

"Um," Gish said. "Well, I suggest you concentrate on finding it."

"Yes, sir."

"A motive, what about a motive?"

Jed sighed. "Nothing on that, either."

"Well, Judge Whittaker didn't hit himself in the head, and presumably his wife didn't do it, so this what's-his-name and his wife..."

"The Zimmermans, sir."

"Right, the Zimmermans, have to be involved. And unless they're real psychopaths, there's a motive."

"Yes, sir," Jed said.

"So get to work, Mallory. Next thing you know the FBI will be on my case again. Let's get the job done."

"Yes, sir."

Jed formed a plan of action. He was probably going to have to call in dogs to search for a weapon—but this morning he was going to concentrate on that motive. And that was going to take a little legwork.

Breakfast first. The pickups were gone from in front of the Coyote Café, but it was full—the second contingent of customers, the local business folk, the retirees and a few others.

He sat at the long counter on a round stool covered with patched red vinyl. The middle-aged waitresses wore aqua nylon uniforms and rubber-soled shoes. Jed ordered eggs over easy, hash browns and whole wheat toast. He got it fast, with a side of chunky red salsa that made him smile, and his heavy tan mug was refilled with coffee every time he set it down. "You're new here," his waitress said as she wrote up his bill.

He decided it was best to tell the truth. If he lied, told them he was a newsman or reporter, they'd find out in a town this size.

"Uh-huh. I know the Zimmermans from a long time ago, though."

"Awful thing, that accident," she said, tucking his check under his plate.

"Actually, that's why I'm here. I'm a U.S. marshal investigating the accident."

"A marshal? Like Wyatt Earp?"

"That's right. I'm looking for some background on the Zimmermans, routine stuff."

"You talk to them yet?" she asked suspiciously.

"Uh-huh. Took statements and all. But, you know, sometimes you can get a different viewpoint from other people, so I'll be asking around. Do you know them?"

"In a town this size? How could I not know them? Well, I'll tell you this, they've had bad luck lately, lots of it."

"Oh?"

"Well, Ellie got cancer. She's real sick. That's Brian's mother. And Otto is getting on. I happen to know they're in financial trouble, 'cause my son works up at the hotel, and they're using a smaller staff nowadays.''

"That's too bad. A real shame."

She leaned on the counter. "It's Brian's fault. Now, I love the old couple, and Gabriela's a nice, sweet lady, but I'm not fond of Brian. He's, well, kind of thoughtless."

"Um."

"And he gambles. I hate gamblers, divorced one twenty years ago and I say good riddance." Then she picked up the coffeepot and filled someone else's cup.

Jed left her a five-dollar bill; his breakfast had been $2.99.

The barbershop was next. He'd get himself a trim, even though he didn't really need one. He entered the narrow, wooden-floored building and smelled shaving lotion, hair oil and the pungent scent of a lady getting a perm.

A short, wiry man rose from behind a newspaper and peered at Jed over reading glasses. "Stinks, don't it?" he said.

"Well..."

"My wife does hair in the back room. It's Mary's day for her perm. Sorry about that."

Jed smiled. "That's okay. How about a trim?"

The barber walked around Jed. "You don't need one."

"Sure I do."

"It's your ten spot." The man shrugged.

He sat Jed down, wrapped him in the striped cape, started snipping, a little here, a little there. "You're a stranger here. You come specially for my haircut?"

Jed laughed.

"Well, then you're here because of that there accident that killed the judge and his wife. Your boots look like you come from here, but your haircut and your shirt come from some big city. You a newspaperman?"

"No. I'm with the U.S. Marshals Service, and you're right, I'm here to investigate the accident."

"Seems like maybe somebody don't think it was an accident."

"It's just routine. Whittaker was a federal judge, a personal friend of the president."

The barber snorted. "If I fell off some cliff and broke my damn-fool neck, nobody'd investigate it."

"True."

"That's the way it goes, I guess."

"Do you know the Zimmermans?"

The barber snipped. "Sure, I know 'em. Knew Brian when he was a little kid. Played poker with Otto for thirty years."

"They're real shaken up over this accident."

The barber shook his head sadly. "Ellie don't need that grief. None of 'em do. But it'll pass."

"I suppose so."

"Brian's gambling won't go away, though. He's got the bug bad. Vegas is too damn close by."

"He goes to Las Vegas to gamble?"

"Sure, flies out of Flagstaff. Used to go once a week, but he's been staying home lately. Either his pretty wife got on him, or he just owes too much money."

"He's in debt, huh?"

"Real deep, so I hear." The barber undid the cape and swirled it off with a toreador's flourish. "There, got the sides a little."

"Thanks, it looks good."

"Looked good before," the barber said dryly.

Jed left him fifteen dollars and walked down the street, nodding to people, looking in store windows. So, he'd found out a few things that frankly didn't surprise him. Brian Zimmerman was a compulsive gambler, in debt. Well, there was a motive, all right, but it wasn't a motive in *this* case, as far as he could see.

He went back to the motel and called Eric Ulrich up in Flagstaff.

"Mallory, here, Sheriff. I'm afraid I'm going to need a team of dogs to do some searching in that canyon."

"Oh, boy," Ulrich said.

"There aren't any local handlers?"

"Maybe in Phoenix. I can check."

"Would you do that, please? And also, I could use some names. Friends, close acquaintances of the Zimmermans."

"Hold on," Ulrich said, and Jed could hear him shuffling papers. "Here it is. I had a deputy compile a list for you. Figured you'd ask sooner or later, and I sure don't want you going back to Washington saying we're a bunch of hicks out here."

Jed laughed. "You forget, I'm one of you hicks, too."

"Uh-huh," Ulrich said, and he read Jed his list, beginning with Brian's sister, Lorna Kessler, who lived in Payson, some friends, his banker, Keith Long, and his best gambling buddy, George Lemming, who evidently ran a logging outfit nearby.

Good man, Ulrich, Jed thought, just like his father. Max would have done the same thing.

He scribbled the names down, tried calling Lorna Kessler. Her husband, John, told him she was in Apache Springs, helping out. Her husband was not happy about it, either, because he had to stay home with the kids, and besides, Lorna and her brother didn't get along at all. "Brian's a real bully," Lorna's husband said, "and I told her she was crazy to go."

George Lemming. Jed had written down the directions to the base of his logging operation, where he could be found most of the time. He decided to go out there—it was only ten miles away.

He drove, turning off the highway onto a dirt road that wound up to a plateau. There it was, a silver trailer on blocks, various behemoths of logging equipment and some pickup trucks parked in the shade of a stand of pine trees. Around the site the mountains rose, crowned with almost black pines, tall timber, George Lemming's livelihood. In the distance, he could hear chain saws.

Lemming was there, a big man with his hair combed back in a ponytail, an earring in his left lobe and tattoos on his arms.

"Yeah?" he said. "Can you make it fast?"

Jed pulled out his billfold with his badge and ID. "I'm Deputy Jed Mallory, U.S. Marshals Service. I'd like to ask you a few questions about Brian Zimmerman."

"What for?"

"It's part of a routine investigation of a federal judge's death."

"Routine, my foot."

"Do you have any reason to believe the judge's death wasn't an accident, Mr. Lemming?" Jed asked.

"No, do you?"

"Has Mr. Zimmerman spoken about the accident?"

Lemming shrugged.

"He's said nothing?"

The big man turned on Jed belligerently. "What can he say? Just because the judge was some big-deal political guy, there's this furor over it. Now I ask you, did this happen when those two hunters were found frozen to death last fall? Hell, no, they weren't important enough."

"It certainly was unfortunate, though, a terrible thing for Mr. Zimmerman to go through."

"I'll say. Listen, Mr. Marshal, Brian is a great guy, the best friend a man could have. I'd trust him with my life."

"Uh-huh. I understand you go to Las Vegas with Mr. Zimmerman from time to time."

Lemming shrugged. "We used to go a lot. Lately Brian's had bad luck. I still go, though."

"Is Brian Zimmerman in debt to any of the casinos in Las Vegas?"

"Hey, what the hell business is it of yours? Ask Brian if you want to know!"

"Thank you, Mr. Lemming. You've been very helpful."

He drove back, musing. Pieces were beginning to form a picture, but they brought Jed no closer to solving the crime, if indeed there was one. He was learning about Brian Zimmerman, and he didn't much like what he heard. His instincts had been right on—Brian was not a particularly wonderful person. That, however, did not make him a murderer.

Why had Gab married him? She must have loved him, or at least she must have *thought* she loved him to do it. Did she still think so, or did that fleeting look in her eyes mean that she felt differently now? She'd stayed with Brian for nine years, though, a whole lot longer than she'd been with Jed.

Why didn't they have any children? Gab had loved children and wanted lots of them. Or she *had* wanted them. Maybe she'd changed and he was making all his judgments based on another person entirely. He didn't know this Gabriela Zimmerman, not really, and ten years was a lot of water under the bridge.

Back in his room there was a blinking message light, and when he called the desk he was given Jackson Many Goats' number. He dialed and got through to his friend right away.

"Get your butt on up here," Jackson said.

"Did you find something?"

"Neil Skadway's here—he's the chief forensic pathologist from the police lab in Phoenix, a real expert. He's got something to show you."

"I'll be there in less than an hour," Jed said.

It was just under forty miles to Flagstaff, along a winding, two-lane highway that climbed toward Humphrey's Peak and its snow-covered summit, then met up with the interstate that took him into Flagstaff. He knew the route by now and let his mind roam at random, although it always came back to Gab, like a bee to its hive.

Maybe she was protecting her husband, lying for him. That would be natural, wouldn't it? Her story was good—she'd seen a little, but not enough to say what had really happened. The best lie is one that's as close as possible to the truth. So maybe Gab and Brian had concocted the story together, cleverly leaving out only one small detail.

His mind rebelled. No. He knew Gab, had looked into her eyes, those emerald green depths that had always shone in innocence, that still did. An accessory to murder? Never.

She was beautiful still, and good. In the past he'd faulted her for being too generous, too trusting, too soft-hearted. But she was no weakling. She'd always had her own mind, a core of independence that he'd admired and come to rue.

He drove west along the interstate, elbow on the doorframe, ascending gradually, the sheriff department's Cherokee rolling smoothly, window down, the fresh, piney air in his face.

Sure, he'd felt betrayed when she wouldn't go to Arlington with him; he'd been stung by her words about his father. He'd felt betrayed when she hadn't trusted his judgment because of her brother-in-law's death. It had hurt a lot. He'd toughed it out, though. And then there'd been that abortive visit to Apache Springs when he'd heard she was married. Even now his jaw clenched in humiliation and anger at the memory.

It had been over then, and he'd gone back to Arlington almost with a sense of relief. There were woman all over the place, good women. He'd find another one, love another one. The trouble was, Jed had been wrong about that. Even his own wife had known it.

He arrived in Flagstaff when the town was in the full swing of the August Festival of the Arts. Traffic, tourists, banners and signs proclaimed the many events. There were cars from California, Oregon, Illinois, Michigan and Florida. Most of the people had no doubt already been to see the Grand Canyon, only

eighty miles northwest, or if they hadn't, they would
go soon.

He drove past downtown Flagstaff to the county
coroner's office in the suburban hospital complex and
went straight to Jackson's office.

"You made good time, Jed," Jackson said, coming out to greet him. "Come in. I want you to meet
Neil."

A very round, fair man sat in Jackson's office,
punching keys on a computer. He turned and pushed
thick glasses up on his small nose.

"Neil, this is my old pal Jed Mallory. Jed, this is Dr.
Neil Skadway, a very talented gentleman from Phoenix."

The pathologist turned off the computer, stood and
shook Jed's hand.

"Okay, so what's this you have to show me?" Jed
asked, leaning back against Jackson's desk.

Skadway began pacing the small office, his arms
folded, raising a finger from time to time to make a
point. "I examined the bodies of the Whittakers,
okay? And their injuries were consistent with a fall
from a cliff in this area—contusions, abrasions, some
internal bleeding. Mrs. Whittaker's cause of death was
a broken neck between the second and third cervical
vertebrae, okay? Mr. Whittaker, on the other hand,
had a wound to the back of his head, as Jackson de-
scribed. Clean, caused by a sharp steel blade that
penetrated 2.4 centimeters into this part of his brain,
here." He touched the back of his own head.

"And that caused his death?" Jed asked.

"No question. It's the only wound on his body that
was antemortem—that is, before death. All the others were after death."

"How can you tell?"

"Because there was little or no fresh blood in the lacerations he incurred from the fall. In other words, there was no blood pressure, so bleeding was minimal."

"The wound couldn't have been caused by a rock, a natural object?"

"Absolutely not. Its clean edges, the incised nature of it, makes that impossible. Also, when a natural object punctures the human body, there's debris left inside, dirt. It's not clean like this wound, okay?"

"You'd testify to this, Dr. Skadway?" Jed asked.

"Certainly." He unfolded his arms and reached for a bag on Jackson's desk. "I took the liberty of going to some stores, hardware stores, outdoor equipment places, okay? I bought these as items that might have caused the wound to the judge's head. They're the right size and so on." He took out a heavy meat cleaver, the type used by butchers, and a couple of small axes, the kind hikers carry to cut firewood at a campsite. One had a wood handle, the other was stainless steel with a rubber grip. Both had blades that were four to five inches long and three or so inches wide at the sharp edge, curving in toward the handle.

The men examined the tools, turning them over in their hands, silent for a time.

"Now," Skadway said, "the cleaver would inflict a wider wound, I believe, so an ax like this really is the most likely instrument involved."

"And a man used to the outdoors would be likely to have one of these," Jackson said quietly.

"Yes, the salesclerk at the camping store said that you could even carry it on a belt holster."

"Uh-huh," Jed said, hefting the steel ax.

"It seems to me that you might want to find out if Brian Zimmerman owns an ax like this," Jackson said, and his eyes met Jed's.

Skadway cleared his throat. "Then there's the tissue under Mrs. Whittaker's nails. Even though some got broken, she had long, very well-taken-care-of nails, so there's plenty of tissue. I would recommend you get the Zimmermans in here to provide skin samples so we can try to get a match, okay? Jackson's already sent the stuff to our lab, but we won't have results for some time."

Jed's heart sank. Not Gab, a murder suspect. No. "I may need a court order for that," he said. "Neither one of them needs to submit to tests. Not yet."

"That's true," Skadway said, "but often innocent people cooperate."

"And just as often they don't," Jackson said, and his gaze once again met Jed's. It was clear that he knew what was in Jed's mind.

"I'm going to finish up my report, Jackson," Skadway said, settling his bulk into the chair in front of the computer. "It'll be ready this afternoon, okay?"

"Thanks, Neil. We appreciate your help." Jackson put a hand on Jed's shoulder. "Come on, let's get out of here for a while." He shrugged out of his lab coat and hung it on a hook. "You hungry?"

"I don't know." Jed looked at his watch: two o'clock. He tried to grin. "I guess so."

"Well, I'm starved. I haven't been out of this place since eight this morning. I work too damn hard. Pretty soon I'll have a heart attack like Hank did."

"Hank?"

"The ex-medical examiner. A good guy. Retired now."

"Oh." Jed thought of his dad and other men who worked too much, pushed themselves too hard.

They walked out of the building, and the fresh air reminded Jed of how stale and medicinal the lab had been.

"You mind fast food for lunch?"

Jed strode along, his brow furrowed. Jackson poked him with an elbow. "Do you...?"

Jed stopped short and gave him an intense look. "Well, at least I know what kind of weapon to look for," he said.

"Jed, forget it for now. Let's go to lunch."

"Sure, all right. Sorry."

Halfway across the lot, Jackson put a hand out and slowed Jed down. "Well, well," he said, "look who's here."

Jed followed his gaze and saw an old green-and-white Blazer, and a woman in white slacks and a blue workshirt with rolled-up sleeves getting out of the driver's side, a familiar figure with curly black hair pulled back into a ponytail. She started around to the passenger side.

"That's Gab," Jed said, surprised.

"Go on. I'll be in the restaurant," Jackson said dryly.

Jed strode up to her, but she was leaning inside the car, helping someone out of the passenger seat, and didn't see him.

"Gab," he said, behind her. Then, louder. "Gab."

"Oh!" She turned quickly, startled, and her eyes opened wide, her hand going nervously to her hair.

"Sorry, I didn't mean to..."

"Oh, Jed," she said, a little breathlessly, "I have to get Ellie to her doctor's appointment." And she turned away, helping an elderly lady down from the Blazer's high seat.

"Ellie, this is Jed Mallory. He's, ah, investigating the accident. Jed, this is Ellie Zimmerman, my mother-in-law."

"Nice to meet you, Mrs. Zimmerman." She was a pretty lady, gray-haired but fair, with a fleeting resemblance to Brian. But she looked ill, her skin gray, and she moved slowly, obviously in pain. "Here, let me help you."

"I could get a wheelchair in the clinic," Gab said, "but she won't let me."

"There'll be time for that later," Ellie said. "I can still get around."

Jed walked her inside, taking most of her weight, which was frighteningly slight. Gab walked on her other side, and she didn't say a word until they were in the clinic and Ellie was sitting down, then she went to the desk to check Ellie in.

"That was very nice of you, young man," Ellie said. "Now, how do you know Gabriela?" she asked when her daughter-in-law was out of earshot.

"I, uh, took her statement the other day. Your son's, too."

"Awful thing, just awful. I always liked the Whittakers."

"Yes, it was a terrible accident."

"Brian and his treasure hunts. Well, the judge loved them, too...."

"I must confess, Mrs. Zimmerman, I knew Gabriela a long time ago, too. In college."

Faded blue eyes, surprisingly sharp, met his. "Oh, you're the one. You even stopped by the hotel once, several years ago. I see."

Fortunately Gab came back then. "You can go right in, Ellie."

"Oh, good. I hate to wait. It takes so darn long, anyway." She pushed herself laboriously out of the seat, and Jed hastened to help her up; her frail bones felt like those of a hurt bird he'd once held.

They helped her into the doctor's office, and she put her cool, paper-dry hand over Jed's. "Thank you, Mr. Mallory."

"That was really unnecessary," Gab said once they were back out in the waiting room. "I bring her here every week, and I can manage just fine."

"She's a nice lady," he said, ignoring her pique.

"Yes, she is."

"Very sick, too, isn't she?"

Gab looked away, stricken. Her voice came, choked. "Yes, very sick."

"I'm sorry."

"We all are."

He stood there, feeling awkward, not knowing quite what to do next, but realizing he couldn't leave her. He cleared his throat. "Uh, Gab, can we go somewhere while you're waiting?"

"What for?"

"To talk."

"About what, Jed?" Her green eyes met his, challenging him.

"Well...it's been a long time, Gab. I'd like to, you know, catch up. Just talk."

"I have errands to run."

"A few minutes, Gab. Why are you being like this?"

"Like what? Look, I'm busy. I have a list of things to do, then I have to get back and work at the desk. I..." She stopped abruptly.

"Gab." He dared to put a hand on her arm, and she left it there. "Please." He could feel her tension through the thin cotton of her shirt; she was practically vibrating. But she was upset, he knew, about Ellie, and then he'd startled her. He couldn't seem to say the right thing around Gab. She took everything the wrong way. She was prickly and defensive, but he should have known how she'd react—she'd always been that way when she was disturbed.

"Come on, Gab, a few minutes." He tried to make it light. "I'm no threat, and it's all off the record."

She pulled her arm away from his hand, looked down and shook her head silently as they walked outside together.

"Come on over and have something to eat with Jackson and me."

"I can't."

"I'd just like to find out how you've been, that's all."

She raised her head, and she looked angry, her eyes swimming in moisture. "A little late, don't you think? Ten years late. Well, I've been fine, everything's fine. Or it was until you came and tried to blame that accident on my husband."

"I'm doing a job, that's all."

"Yes, Jed," she said bitterly, "I know. You're doing your job and still trying to live up to the reputation of the great Max Mallory."

"Gab."

"Please." She looked away and shook her head. "Don't make it hard for me, Jed."

"Make what hard?"

"Staying away from you." She turned and walked to the green-and-white Blazer, and he could swear he saw one of her hands wipe at a tear, but he must have been mistaken. The parking lot was hot and smelled of asphalt, and the heat waves rose up around him, suffocating him. He watched Gab climb into the car and drive away, and he felt as if he'd lost something valuable, just let it slip out of his grasp.

Damn, he thought. *Damn.*

Jackson was almost finished with his lunch when Jed got there. "I couldn't wait," he said. "I was too darn hungry. I ordered you a burger."

"Thanks, Jackson."

"So, she left?"

"Yeah." The waitress placed a plate in front of him, and he realized his stomach was growling. "She doesn't like me much."

"Can't blame her," Jackson said, wiping up the last of his ketchup with a french fry. "You're trying to put her husband in jail."

"It's hardly reached that point yet."

"It'd be the way she sees it."

"I guess so."

"And the fact that you used to go out, well, that makes it pretty bad, at least in her eyes."

Jed contemplated his burger. "Yeah, I'm a real rotten SOB."

"Right," Jackson said.

Jed took a bite. Maybe there was something else he could have said, something that would have convinced her to stay and talk to him. Just talk.

"What're you going to do next, Jed?" Jackson was asking.

"Look for the murder weapon. Try to get skin samples."

"From Gabriela?"

"From her, too. And Brian."

They were quiet then, gazing out the plate-glass window toward the west where thunderheads were building into an afternoon storm.

"Storm brewing," Jackson said lightheartedly. "The spirits will be dancing in the mountains."

"Uh-huh," Jed said, distracted.

CHAPTER SEVEN

GEORGE LEMMING SQUATTED down and shone his flashlight on the floor of the cave, and for a minute he couldn't say a thing, then he whistled softly. "I never believed it till now. Goddamn, I really never believed it."

"I told you so," Brian said smugly from where he stood close to the entrance.

"Holy cow," George said wonderingly, while outside a sudden, violent thunderstorm rumbled across the land.

Wind touched Brian's back, a cool wind slashed with rain, but inside the cave it was bone-dry, chillingly so, which was the reason the treasure had remained so well preserved for four hundred years, lying there unseen and untouched in the high desert climate.

"Look at this." George reached for a sword that lay next to a pile of leather-clad bones. The hilt was inlaid with jewels. "Would you look at this," he said again, awed, and outside a bolt of lightning flashed and thunder cracked in the pewter sky.

"I see it," Brian said. "I've looked at all of it."

"When did you find this cave?"

Brian thought a minute. "Oh, before all that mess with the judge and his wife."

"How many times have you been up here? Has anyone seen you?" George shone the light across the floor, stopping at a helmet, a lance, strips of leather, another beautifully inlaid sword, more bones. Then the beam of light touched a gold cross that glittered in the dry dust, a hand-worked crucifix on a gold-link chain, entwined with the small, glaringly white bones of long-stilled fingers. A priest, no doubt.

And there was a leather bag, gleaming golden coins spilling out of its neck, lying amid the bones in silent irony. George drew in his breath and stooped to touch the coins with a finger, to wipe away the layer of powdery dust that shrouded everything.

"This is only the second time I've been here," Brian replied. "I'm real sure no one saw me. Way too remote, even for the Apache."

"Amazing," George said, still looking around. "I swear I never believed a word of those old Indian legends. Not a single word. And would you just look at this stuff! What do you think it's worth?"

"I haven't got any idea. A million. Twice that. More. I mean, the rubies and emeralds on that hilt alone must be worth a fortune. And those pieces of eight... Well, it's gotta be invaluable."

"I'll call my brother when we get back to town. Sorry I had to wait until I saw it myself, but Glenn's a real careful guy. If I asked him to get us the names of some collectors, and we didn't produce... Well, he'd have been pretty ticked off. You understand."

"Yeah, sure," Brian said, dispassionately eyeing one of the scattered piles of bones that had once been a living being. "But now that you've seen it, you can make that call."

"You bet I will."

"And tonight."

"Sure, sure. I wouldn't worry, though, this stuff has been here for centuries and no one's found it."

"Tonight," Brian said. "I mean it, George. Tonight."

"Yeah, sure. Just for godsake don't let any of the TV and newspeople get wind of this, Brian."

"You think I'm nuts?" Brian snorted.

"No, I never said that. It's just that the town is still packed with them. You never know where in hell they might be snooping around."

"Bunch of vultures," Brian muttered.

Outside thunder rumbled again, rolling across the dry land, echoing in the canyon. "We'll hire a helicopter to get it out," George was saying. "Yeah, a chopper. We can bag this stuff, and the pilot will never be the wiser."

"A helicopter would cost a lot of money," Brian said doubtfully.

"Yeah, but we'll be able to afford it," George said, then laughed, slapping his thigh. "Maybe I'll just goddamn retire."

Another bolt of lightning split the sky above the canyon and lit the rim of the cliff like a strobe light, and in the sudden glare there was an Apache Indian, an old man whose back was bent under the weight of many years and this new burden that lay on his heart like lead.

GABRIELA COULD NOT believe it when Jed drove up the circular drive to the hotel the next morning and flatly asked if she and Brian would accompany him to Flagstaff and agree to give skin samples at the lab there.

She stood on the stone veranda and stared at him in disbelief while next to her Brian's face drained of blood. "You're joking," she breathed, her eyes locking with Jed's.

"Not in the least," he said tonelessly.

"But...but why?" she stammered. "What in God's name is going on?" And then she could feel anger rising beneath her shock. How dare Jed ask that of them!

But Brian put a hand on her arm, as if to tell her to say nothing more. "Skin samples," he said, his voice as even as Jed's, though Gabriela could sense just the slightest tremor in it. "Kind of an odd request, isn't it? I mean, what do we need here, a lawyer?" Brian was obviously trying to make light of it, but he had made a point.

Gabriela said, "*Do* we need a lawyer, Jed? I think you owe us an explanation. You're acting as if we're criminals or something. You'd better tell us what's going on."

Jed still stared at her. He seemed to be deciding something, and then he said, "There was human tissue found beneath Clare Whittaker's fingernails."

Gabriela shook her head in disbelief. "Well, it's obviously the judge's. They were together. This is ridiculous, Jed. We told you, neither of us got to them in time."

"The skin tissue samples would help answer some questions," Jed replied. "Of course, if you want me to get a magistrate to write up a court order, I can. It would be better if you both came along voluntarily, though. It's your call."

Gabriela glared at the man she'd once loved. How dare he do this to them, how dare he? "This isn't fair,

Jed," she said tightly. "You're abusing your position."

"I'm doing my job," he said without inflection.

"Okay, this is bull," Brian said. "I'm going to get a lawyer. I'm going to sue you for harassment!"

"You can try," Jed said matter-of-factly.

Brian went down the stone steps and stood close to Jed, his angry face only inches away. "You're really stepping over the line this time, Mallory."

"Okay, I'll head on back to Flagstaff and have a court order here by one this afternoon if that's the way you want it, Mr. Zimmerman."

The air sparked with tension as the two men glowered at each other. Gabriela looked from one to the other, from Brian's furious red face to Jed's hard expression, and suddenly she couldn't stand it for another second.

"All right, all right," she bit out. "We'll go and give the tissue samples. We have nothing to hide. And when you find out the skin belongs to Judge Whittaker you can damn well leave us in peace! Brian?" she said, turning to him. "Let's just go get this over with. I can't stand it anymore, I honestly can't."

"Goddamn it, Gabriela . . ." Brian said furiously.

"I know, I know, but we're innocent. How can it hurt?"

"He can't make us do this, you know. I think I should call a lawyer," Brian said loudly, but his anger had turned to bluster.

"Oh, it's not worth it, Brian," she said, thinking of the cost. Once you start with lawyers... She hated for Jed to see this family wrangling, to witness Brian's temper. It was embarrassing. She was terribly aware of his impassive scrutiny while he waited for their decision.

Finally Brian shrugged and said harshly, "Okay, for God's sake, I'll do it, but this is a royal pain, Mallory."

"I appreciate your cooperation," Jed replied smoothly.

"I'll go tell Lorna where we're going. How long is this going to take?"

"Travel time and just a couple of minutes at the lab," Jed replied.

"Okay, okay, I'll be right back."

The minute Brian was gone, Gabriela swung around to face Jed. "Why are you doing this to us? Why, Jed?" Her voice was full of the anguish she'd hidden from her husband. "It isn't fair. It isn't right. The accident was bad enough, and now you're torturing us. Brian's right. You're way over the line."

"I'm not out of line with this, Gab, believe me. There's a lot more to this than you know."

"What?"

"Well, the flesh under Mrs. Whittaker's nails. She obviously grabbed at somebody. It's important. Something happened out there on that trail, something that doesn't fit with the statements you've given. I wish to God it was simple and straightforward, but it isn't. And I have to do my job."

"Oh, right, I forgot for a second. Hassling innocent people is part of your job, isn't it?"

"You know that's not true."

"I thought, I really thought, you had integrity, Jed. I believed you did, but now I'm beginning to think I was wrong. I don't think you're just doing your job, no matter what you tell yourself. I think you're picking on us, on Brian especially, because of what happened between us in the past.''

"I disagree. I'd do the same thing regardless of who was involved.''

She narrowed her eyes and put her hands on her hips. "No, you wouldn't. Your judgment is tainted, and whatever case you're trying to make will be tainted, too.''

"That's my problem, not yours,'' he said coolly.

"Oh, God, you haven't changed a bit! Always right, always so superior!'' She took a deep breath. "Up till now I was trying to give you the benefit of the doubt, but this skin sample business... Hasn't it ever once occurred to you that we had no reason whatsoever to harm the Whittakers?''

"Yes,'' he said. "Every minute of every day since I arrived.''

They drove right past the gaggle of media people who were waiting, as usual, at the entrance to the hotel driveway. Gab sat straight and tall, eyes ahead; inside she cringed in humiliation as the cameras swung toward the sheriff's department car, hoping for a new angle, a new glimpse of human misery.

"Damn newspeople,'' Brian muttered.

Flagstaff was less then forty miles away, but the drive seemed to last forever. Gabriela hadn't taken the time to change her clothes, and as the day grew warmer she was hot and uncomfortable in the jeans and long-sleeved shirt she'd put on that morning. She sat in the back seat behind the two men and vacillated between anger and an overwhelming sense of helplessness. A dozen times she told herself that she should have talked to Jed yesterday at the clinic in Flagstaff and tried to sort out this whole crazy mess. Maybe he was feeling rejected—again—and he was concocting ways of tormenting her. Could he have changed that much?

Just stay strong, she told herself as hot air from the open windows buffeted her face. She and Brian were going to get through this. And then she thought about the other night at the cabin, Brian trying to make love to her. Her rejection of him. It wasn't, it couldn't be, the sudden reappearance of Jed in her life. For months, years now, she hadn't been in love with her husband. They'd made love—occasionally—but it wasn't the same as earlier in their marriage. It was more as if they went through the motions. And when she'd talked to Brian about getting a divorce she'd meant it.

No, Gabriela thought, Jed was not at the root of her marital troubles. Still, she was going to stand by her husband through this ordeal, and Brian would stand by her. Together they would both defy Jed Mallory. The divorce? Well, she'd have to put that on hold until this was over.

She switched her gaze from one man to the other. Both were attractive. Both were proud. Both were vulnerable and had brought out her nurturing side in one way or the other. With Brian, of course, it had always been his compulsive nature. When they'd first met, he'd hiked and camped and bicycled furiously—even pursued her with that same compulsiveness—but then his trips to Las Vegas had increased, and he'd redirected a part of his boundless energy into gambling. It happened to a lot of people; Gabriela just wished Brian wasn't one of them.

She studied her husband while the silence stretched out with the miles. Once he had loved her completely and worked at their marriage, but then so much of him had pulled away from her. There was his love of the dice tables, and then, a few years ago, he'd started up the treasure hunt at the hotel, advertised it in travel magazines, really made a success of the venture—until the other day. If only he hadn't pushed so hard, pushed the clients as much as he did himself. Judge Whittaker had to have been tired out....

No, she thought, looking down at her lap, it hadn't been Brian's fault, not one bit of it. No more than it had been her fault. She refused to accept guilt for the accident.

She looked up at Jed, at the sun-browned back of his neck and the curling light hair that swept around the back of his ears. His skin glowed a little in the heat, and she could even see the sheen collecting on the forearm that rested casually on the steering wheel.

Jed had always taken over every situation. Unconsciously but single-mindedly. He'd always been on track, his eyes always focused on his goal. He got that from his dad, the intense, unquestioning drive, yet for all his attempts at perfection there was the flaw of not being in touch with his true self, of trying too darn hard to emulate the wonderful Max Mallory. She wondered if Jed had ever recognized that aspect of his personally.

When they turned onto the interstate, Gabriela tore her gaze away from him. How humiliating this was, finding herself between those two men, forced to compare them, forced to take sides. It was ugly, and on top of the Whittakers' accident, it was close to undoing her. Why, oh why, did it have to be Jed? Why couldn't she be left in peace to mourn?

She knew, somewhere deep inside, that Jed had come on this investigation because he couldn't stay away—because of her. Oh sure, he'd denied it, but she knew better. And that skewed the odds, as Brian would say. It raised the stakes.

Jed had to win this one.

But then, so did Brian.

They arrived at the hospital complex shortly before lunch. Jed got out first, then Brian, and Gabriela swung her door open last, wondering whether giving these skin samples voluntarily was the wise thing to do. Maybe Brian was right and they really should have consulted a lawyer, despite the cost.

They began to walk toward the main entrance of the hospital, and that was when Brian seemed to hesitate. "What?" Gabriela said, striding alongside him behind Jed.

"I'm not sure," he began, and then he stopped suddenly, his head cocked to one side. "The whole way up here I've been thinking and thinking."

Jed, too, had stopped. He turned and faced them. "Something wrong?"

"I don't know," Brian said again. "The more I think about the accident... The thing is," he said, and he began to push up the sleeve on his plaid shirt, "I've got these scratches...."

"Brian? What are you saying?" Gabriela asked, staring at the long red furrows on his arm that had scabbed over.

Jed was staring, too. He looked decidedly grim when he took off his wire-rimmed sunglasses.

"It's just that... Well," Brian went on, "I'm always out in the woods and always covered with scratches, so I never gave these ones a second thought until just now in the car.''

"Go on," Jed said tightly.

"Well, the more I think about me trying to get back to Clare when she screamed, the more I'm convinced that I reached for her and she had hold of me for an instant. I think maybe her nails did make these marks." He studied them, his brow furrowed, the sunlight dancing on his hair. "It's so hard to remember.... Everything happened so damn fast.''

Gabriela could see Jed clench his teeth and a muscle working furiously in his jaw. "Are you changing your statement?" he asked.

"Well, I don't know," Brian said, looking perplexed. "I mean, if there's skin under Clare's nails, well, it may just be mine. The whole thing was such a shock, and it happened so fast.... I guess I should change that part." He stared at the scratches and shrugged.

Jed was also staring, but at Brian's face, trying to read him. The whole thing made complete sense to Gabriela, though. It was logical. And suddenly she could see it in her mind's eye, a flash of Brian reaching for Clare, Clare clutching at him but teetering. Yes! It was all coming back now.

She was about to tell Jed that, corroborate Brian's story, but Jed was talking. "It's real convenient that you remembered this right now," he was saying.

"What do you mean by that?"

"It doesn't take an idiot to figure out what you just pulled."

"Are you calling me an idiot?" Brian said in a long, hard voice.

"I wouldn't dream of it," Jed said coolly. "Come on, let's go get this farce over with."

"You mean you still want the samples?" Gabriela asked.

"Yes," Jed said, and he ushered them inside to the lab, where Jackson Many Goats was waiting.

Brian submitted to the test first, rolling up his sleeve, watching while Jackson used a tiny scalpel-like instrument to take a scraping from the crook of his elbow. He then put a small Band-Aid on it and said that was it, and Brian got up from the stool, saying, "Wasn't bad at all."

Then it was Gabriela's turn. She looked Jed square in the eye and sat down in the sterile white lab, offering Jackson her right arm.

"Wait a minute," Jed said suddenly, and he took a step forward. "Gabriela...Mrs. Zimmerman, that is, doesn't need to do this."

Jackson looked at him curiously, the scalpel poised above her arm.

"Mr. Zimmerman's changing his story—his statement, that is," Jed said meaningfully. "It's pointless for his wife to..."

"Take the sample," Gabriela interrupted sharply. "If Brian did it, I will, too," she said icily, her eyes flashing.

He could say nothing, obviously, and Gabriela felt as if she'd won a small victory. It seemed terribly important. Now Jed would know how loyal she was to her husband. Somehow, as Jackson did the scraping, she felt less disloyal.

The medical examiner was gentle, and the scraping barely hurt at all. He talked while he did it, which took Gabriela's mind off the procedure.

"Results won't be in from Phoenix for several weeks," he was saying. "Takes the technicians a while to do the DNA work. But we will have results back on the blood enzymes more quickly and they can tell us a lot. Of course, we can already pretty much assume now that the flesh found beneath Clare Whittaker's fingernails will be a match with Mr. Zimmerman's." The whole time that he talked, Gabriela kept her gaze on the white-tiled floor. She and Brian were being treated as suspects, and it was so bizarre she had trouble believing it.

If the drive to Flagstaff had been uncomfortably silent, the ride back was worse. Gabriela could feel the tension in the air take on a malevolent quality. She was afraid to speak or even think too much in case she made matters worse.

If only Brian had remembered Clare scratching him earlier, Gabriela thought, but then she stopped herself. He hadn't. And that was that.

And Jed's reaction! He'd behaved as if Brian had suddenly pulled the story out of a hat just to spoil whatever crazy scenario Jed had imagined. Well, if Brian had insisted that he'd never reached Clare and the flesh under her nails tested out to be his, okay, then there was a definite discrepancy in his story. That's what Jed had hoped for. But Brian had ruined that chance.

Sure Clare had his flesh under her nails! She'd been scrambling for her life! The memory flashed in her mind again like a scene from a familiar movie. You knew what happened but couldn't remember the exact details, the precise order of events. But now, clearly imprinted on her mind, was the picture of Brian's hand outstretched toward Clare as she clutched at him. There was nothing odd about the fact that Brian, too, had only just recalled the details.

She looked from one man to the other. Brian was staring out the window, a fist tapping against his mouth. He was deep in thought. Jed, though, could have been on a Sunday drive, contemplating the scenery. But she knew him—had known him as intimately as any two people could know each other—and he was not as easy in his skin as he appeared. The proof of it was that small, almost imperceptible tick in his jaw. He was angry and frustrated. He'd been foiled by Brian.

They arrived back at Apache Springs at the hottest part of the day, early afternoon. Only a few wilted newspeople still lingered. By then Gabriela's blouse had rings under the arms and her bra was sticking to her. It was due as much to nerves as to heat, and she could hardly wait to get out of that car, away from Jed.

Her hand was on the handle, and Brian had already opened his door. They'd both had enough of Jed Mallory for one day. All she wanted to do was escape. But Jed had other plans. "Just a minute," he said. He'd put an arm on the back of the passenger seat in a deceptively casual manner and was leaning toward Brian.

"What the hell now?" Brian asked.

"Oh, just one more question," Jed said.

"Go on, get it over with."

Jed smiled amiably. "Just one of those little details, you know."

"Sure, ask away."

Gabriela saw it all from the back seat, saw Jed pin Brian with those blue eyes, heard the change in his voice, the intensity, the false mildness of his look.

"Tell me something," Jed said. "Did either you or the Whittakers carry a camping ax that day?"

Brian sat there for a second, thinking, looking as cool as a cucumber, and then he said, "No, not that I can recall," and Gabriela felt herself start. Then she clamped her mouth shut and sat there weak and dizzy with shock.

MOISTURE CLUNG to the tin-and-canvas sides of the enclosure, and then single drops slid down the metal, slowly, steadily.

The humpbacked old man reached over from his cross-legged position and poured water on the hot rocks, causing steam to rise above the sizzling coals, until the makeshift sweat lodge was filled with the hot mist.

He groaned and closed his paper-thin eyelids and felt the moisture collect on his skin while he cleared his head of thoughts, inwardly seeing only an empty sky, a blank blue screen. He allowed nothing to invade this privacy; no hawk or eagle or screeching magpie would he permit to wing across his blue expanse.

For a long time the Apache Indian sat there, alone in the universe of his making. His name was Two Bears, and no one in the tribe knew his age. Some guessed he was one hundred years old; others said he was older. It did not matter. He had been born on a cold winter's day, and he could remember his mother suckling him. He also clearly remembered the white man's celebration of the turning of the century. He remembered the wars that had spanned the earth—his older brother had died in the first one. He remembered his wife and his son, who were both now gone although he had grandchildren, and he remembered the old stories that had been passed down through the millennia. Age was of no account.

Two Bears considered himself a true conduit for the spirits. For all his very long life he'd told his tribe his closeness to the spirit world, his power, came through Kokopelli, that mythical figure so well known to the Pueblo and the Navaho and the Ute, who had been in the Southwest long before the Apache had emigrated from the north. His picture was in the rock paintings dating from the Anasazi, the Ancient Enemy Ones, who had lived on the land a thousand years ago. The Apache had seen these paintings and had accepted the flute-playing magician as one of the significant spirits.

His mind still a blank, Two Bears reached out again and poured more water on the hot rocks. Although he appeared stooped and frail, he could survive the dehydration as well as the next man. After all, he'd been coming to the sweat lodge since before these mountains had been peopled by anyone but the Apache. Dehydration did not trouble him. Nor had hunger ever troubled him. Most things did not trouble him, in truth, because his life had been long and good.

But today he was troubled.

Slowly, calculatingly, he allowed his problems to appear on the blank expanse of his mind, and he examined them, asking the gods for guidance and answers.

It had begun when the evil spirits of the Spanish cave had been awakened by the white men. Two Bears himself had dreamed that night of Kokopelli, who came with a warning: there had been deaths; the spirits of the cave had risen and would need strong medicine to be put to rest again.

Two Bears had been visited by the magician before, of course, and the dreams were not always to be believed because Kokopelli was, after all, quite a trickster. But the next day in the village he heard news of these deaths—so near the reservation—and his old heart had quickened dangerously. Someone had indeed found the cave.

It was beginning again. The greed, the deaths. The whites, the Apache. Two Bears did not understand the irony of it; he knew only that this greed was evil and must be stopped.

As the visions of the problems came to him one by one, he examined them and prayed for guidance from the spirits. The heat and smoke buffeted him for longer than he normally would have tolerated, but still he stayed in his sweat lodge in the heart of the reservation. After a very long time he began to see a solution. He saw the face of an Apache, someone familiar, but Two Bears could not grasp who it was. This Apache person-vision was the key to the problem, because he was somehow the bridge between the Apache and the white men. It was through this unknown man that the evil could be stopped and the greed put to rest.

The trouble remained: who was this man who walked with one foot in each world?

Two Bears left the lodge when the sun was setting before him and the faint lights in the heavens were growing at his back. The answer to this mystery would come. And so would the answer to Two Bears' role in this. But for now he was too exhausted to continue the search.

Old and bent, he crossed the broken land of his ancestors and made his slow way home.

CHAPTER EIGHT

GABRIELA GOT INSIDE the cabin just before she broke down completely. She closed the door behind them very carefully, leaned back against it and wiped sweat from her upper lip. Her nerves were twitching, her stomach churning with nausea. Brian flopped down on a chair and rubbed the back of his neck. "Wasted the whole day," he muttered.

"Why did you say that?" she breathed, trying to keep her voice under control.

"Say what?"

"That you didn't have a camping ax."

"Oh, for God's sake," he growled.

"Brian, you lied," she whispered.

"You're as bad as he is, Gabriela. Will you lay off?"

"You deliberately lied, Brian. You have an ax. You always carry it. I've seen it a thousand times."

He shrugged. "I guess I lost it."

She walked toward him, her chest so tight she could barely breathe. "You lost it."

"I must have lost it that day, you know, when I left you and went down to check out the bodies. It was quite a scramble."

"But you lied. You said you didn't have one. Why?"

Brian stood and faced her. "Because I don't want that damn marshal bugging us anymore. I lost the ax and that's that. I wasn't about to go into a long explanation, for God's sake."

"But all you had to say was you lost it. Why didn't you?"

"I just told you." His voice was rough, he was losing patience, but she couldn't stop. She put a hand to her forehead and closed her eyes.

"What if they find it, Brian?"

"How in hell can anyone find it? I don't even know where I lost it!"

"I don't know, I don't know!" she cried. "But what if they do?"

"Drop it, Gabriela. I'm sick of the subject. I've had about enough today."

"And that scratch on your arm," she went on. "You never noticed it until now? You got scratched reaching for Clare Whittaker and you couldn't remember?" Her voice rose shrilly.

"Okay," Brian said in a deadly quiet voice, "so what are you getting at?"

She turned her back on him; her hands were shaking. "I don't know. I don't even know. It's too awful to think about."

He turned her around to face him, and he stood close, his face cold and hard, utterly unrecognizable. "Tell me what you're thinking, Gabriela. Come on."

She stared at him, wide-eyed, and a kind of terror shook her soul. "No," she whispered.

His hand tightened painfully on her shoulder, and his mouth stretched in a bizarre rictus. She watched, horrified, suddenly realizing he was trying to smile.

"Come on, babes," he said. "What's got you so upset?"

"You lied," she repeated.

"I explained that."

She shook her head. "Will you call Jed and tell him the truth?"

Brian let her go with a muffled curse, and she sagged against a table. He whirled on her so that she shrank back even farther. "Ever since that Mallory got here you've been like this! Now you're on his side again! Oh, sure, I can see it! Get me locked up, behind bars for murder, and the two of you can go on your merry way. Well, it's not going to work! You're mine, and you're going to stay that way!"

"No," she said, "you're wrong, Brian."

But he wasn't listening. He stalked around the living room, cursing. He raised an arm and swept a lamp off a table, and it shattered, making her jump. "You disloyal bitch!" he shouted. "Who do you believe, huh? That federal patsy or me? I'm your husband, and you better remember it!"

Frightened, she stood there watching him, her heart leaping in her chest. Her mind refused to propose any more questions, even to herself. She could only watch and react to this stranger, this wildman. She had to get him settled, she had to.

"Okay, Brian," she said. "I'm sorry. I was upset. Please, please, calm down."

"You want me to calm down? After what you just said?"

"I'm sorry," she breathed.

"The hell you are!"

"I am. Please, Brian, you're scaring me."

He came up to her and thrust his face into hers. "How dare you question me. After nine years, you act like this!"

She stood stock-still, her back against the table, quaking. Her lips trembled.

"And the minute my back's turned you'll be off to him, won't you? Running to him, telling him everything about us!"

"No, no, I'd never . . ." She tried to sidle away, but he grabbed her wrist and held her still. His grip was like iron. "Let me go, Brian."

He tried to pull her close then, as if to embrace her, to seal his ownership, but she couldn't bear it. She gasped and pulled away, wrenching her arm from his grasp, even as he pinned her against the table with his body. She struggled, suffocated, panicked, then got a hand free and grabbed at the first thing she could reach—his hair. She held on and yanked, and his head snapped back.

She got away then, but he turned and swung at her, his open hand cracking against her cheek, flinging her across the room, stumbling, falling, hitting her head on the coffee table with a sharp crack that made her see stars. Sobbing and panting she lay there, too weak to get up.

Then Brian was kneeling next to her. He was white-faced and scared-looking. "Gabriela," he kept saying. "Gabriela, babes, please, answer me."

But she couldn't. She was crying too hard, and something in her heart was broken beyond repair. Even as Brian stroked her hair back and held her hand, it was as if she was removed from the dreadful scene they were enacting. This couldn't be happening.

"Gabriela, I'm sorry. I didn't mean it. Please, talk to me. Are you okay?" Brian's voice was full of concern; somewhere her consciousness registered that, but still she couldn't stop the sobs that tore at her.

His face disappeared for a time and then was back, and he laid a cool wet cloth on her head. "There," he said, "that's better, isn't it?"

The sobs finally slowed, although Gabriela couldn't have said why or how. They slowed, and she could finally get her breath, and then she was quiet, with only an occasional hiccup of grief. She rolled over on her side and curled up in a fetal position.

"Babes, you okay?" came Brian's voice. "Let me see your head. I'm sorry, God, I'm so sorry. Gabriela?"

She couldn't answer, not yet. Nothing seemed to matter except to gather the strength to put this from her mind. She ignored Brian, unable to deal with him, not now. Her mind shut off like a door closing.

Finally, finally, she felt strong enough to sit up. A wet rag fell into her lap and she saw blood on it. She put her hand up to touch the spot and winced.

"Babes, please, talk to me," Brian begged, but she had nothing to say.

Slowly, painfully, pushing herself up, she stood.

"Gabriela? Come on, say you're okay. Say you forgive me. Please."

But still she ignored him, and, straightening her shoulders, she walked into the bedroom, shut the door and locked it.

She must have slept then, because when she next looked at the bedside clock it was after 10:00 p.m. and dark outside. She was alone, and she felt a little better, although her head hurt and she was weak and shaky.

Sitting on the side of the bed, she took a deep breath. She wouldn't think about it, she wouldn't.... Eventually she got up and looked into the mirror. Oh, God. Pale, haggard, her eyes red and swollen, the marks of fingers on her cheek, a knot on her forehead.

No sound came from the living room. Still, she didn't want to face Brian now, she couldn't. Carefully, she opened the bedroom door. The cabin was empty. There was a note on the kitchen counter.

I'm sorry. Please forgive me. I'm leaving you alone and going into town for something to eat. See you later and we'll hash this all out.

                                        Love, Brian

Reading the note, she felt a spurt of relief. It was as if she'd planned it all out. She simply walked out of the cabin empty-handed, then made her way along the path, past the steaming vapor pools and into a back door of the hotel. She walked quickly upstairs to an empty room, one that she knew was undergoing repairs, and locked the door behind her.

She took a long hot shower, letting the water run over her head, splashing, cleansing, washing away the horror, letting the water flow until it ran lukewarm, then cool. Naked, she lay between the clean sheets, smelled the faint turpentine smell of the newly stained woodwork, curled into a ball and cried herself to sleep.

JED'S ALARM SOUNDED, and he reached out and shut it off. He lay there thinking over the previous day and frowned. It had all gone badly. First Brian had defused the one piece of evidence they had, and he had hurt Gab. She'd been torn between loyalty to her husband and Jed's investigation, and he'd pushed until she gave.

He was more sure than ever that she was innocent; no guilty person would have reacted the way she had over that skin sample business. And she'd inadvertently backed Brian into a corner, so that he had to go along or look guilty as hell. Well, he'd slid out of it neatly, good old Brian had.

He rose and pulled on his running shorts and the old gray T-shirt, socks and shoes. He stretched a little, breathed in some of that cool, pine-scented air flowing in the open window. Today, after breakfast at the Coyote Café, he'd go back to the site in that canyon—the murder site, he called it in his head—and take a better look around so he could plan a search for the missing ax. He'd have to use dogs, and they'd have to scour the whole area, the trail the Whittakers fell from and the whole canyon floor. He'd have to ask Sheriff Ulrich up in Flagstaff to find a team of dogs. He hoped it wouldn't be a problem.

Gab, he thought. He'd seen her face yesterday when he'd asked about an ax. It had frozen in shock. She'd clearly known her husband was lying. He wondered if she'd said anything later to Brian about it. If he knew Gab she had; he'd lay money on it. And maybe that was good. Maybe it would cause Brian to make a mistake.

He was reaching for his room key when there was a soft tap on his door. Who? The tap came again, quietly, hesitantly. He glanced at his watch; it wasn't even seven yet. He went to the door and pulled it open.

"Jed," Gabriela said, standing there on his threshold wearing sunglasses and the same clothes she'd worn to Flagstaff yesterday. "Jed, oh, thank God. I was afraid you were still asleep." Her voice was hurried and breathless, and he pulled her inside and shut the door and simply stood there looking at her.

"Oh, Jed," she said again, and her voice was full of heartbreak.

"What is it?" he asked. "What happened?"

She started crying then, tears rolling out from under the sunglasses, her shoulders shaking. There was nothing to do but pull her close, hold her, try to still her trembling.

She put her hands flat against his chest, but not to push him away; she leaned against him, her forehead against his breastbone, and he smelled the floral scent of her hair. He stroked her head and mumbled soothing words, and his whole world fell into place with a quiet and satisfying click.

She stopped shaking after a while, then sniffed and put a knuckle up to her nose, sniffed again and gave a weak laugh. "I wasn't going to cry, really I wasn't."

"You want to tell me now?" he said very softly.

"Yes . . . no."

"Come on, Gab. No games, not between us." He tilted her face up and gently took her glasses off. He saw them then, the red marks on her cheek and the bump on her forehead, and a white-hot rage ignited in him so suddenly, so overwhelmingly, that he dropped his hands and stepped back as if pushed.

"Did Brian do that?"

She looked at him from swollen sea green eyes and said, "Would you believe it if I told you I fell?"

"No, goddamn it!"

"Okay, then I won't."

"Has he ever done this before?"

She shook her head. "We had a fight, a bad one."

"He hit you, Gab! There's no excuse, fight or not! Goddamn it, where the hell is that son of a—"

She put a hand out and held him back. "No."

"Why the hell not?"

"Because what happened was between a husband and wife. It was private. Brian's pretty upset."

"He has reason to be," he said, and swore again.

She looked away and sighed. "That's why I'm here, I guess, Jed. I need to know what's really going on. I know you, and I know you're not telling us something very important. I need to know, Jed."

"Look, Gab, I can't tell you."

She didn't answer but looked around the room and sat down on a chair. "I'm not leaving till you do tell me, Jed. This isn't the Dark Ages. You can't burn people at the stake for no reason. I'm not stupid. You asked Brian about an ax. Obviously you have reason to believe the Whittakers' deaths were not accidental. I know in my heart that's impossible...it's insane. But I'm trying to be objective."

For a long minute Jed assessed her, then finally he sighed, sat on the edge of the bed and scrubbed a hand through his hair. "You know I can't discuss the case with you. Especially you."

She leaned forward and put her hands on her knees. "Jed, you have to tell me what evidence you have."

"No, I don't. I can't."

Her voice was calm, her eyes steady, luminous. "You know as well as I do that my husband had no motive. You know he didn't do it."

"Gab, please, don't push me on this."

She grimaced. "This is so horrible, so awful, you don't know..."

"I know," he said softly. "I've seen a lot of these situations. It's hard."

"Will it get better, Jed?"

"Sure it will."

He got up from the bed and walked over to where she sat. He squatted down in front of her and took her hands—they were cold and limp. "I'm so sorry, Gab. I wish I could have spared you this."

"Do you really, Jed, or are you enjoying our torture?"

He dropped her hands and turned away, suddenly angry that she could still defend her husband. "I'll tell you the truth. I don't care much for your husband, and I like him a whole lot less after what he did to you."

"You bastard."

"You asked me." He turned and faced her. "But it doesn't matter. I'd do my job the same way even if he was the greatest guy on earth."

"I'm not so sure."

"Believe me, Gab, if I felt that I was jeopardizing this case in any way, I'd ask to get off it and turn my records over to a new man."

She leaned back in her chair and smiled grimly. "You know, I believe you just might. Following staunchly in the footsteps of Max Mallory, as usual."

"There are worse footsteps to follow."

"Brian's innocent until proven guilty, Jed, isn't he?" she asked suddenly, desperately.

"Oh, yes, he is that." He hesitated, then decided to go ahead. "Will you go back to him now?"

Her head snapped up. "Back to him? I haven't left him. He's my husband, Jed. I won't leave him during this mess. What kind of a person would I be then?"

"A smart one."

"You don't understand," she said sadly.

"No, I don't. This man beat you up."

"He was under a lot of pressure. I pushed him," she said defensively.

"That's what they all say."

"No, really, Jed. He was sorry the minute he did it. He tried to apologize."

"Uh-huh."

"Jed . . ."

"Look, Gab, you're married to this guy, I know, but I don't have to like it. I don't think he deserves you, and I don't believe you're really happy with him."

She stared at him, white-faced.

"I wish you'd stay away from him for a while, go somewhere."

She gave a short laugh. "Do you realize how that would look? Man involved in accident, wife leaves him. The timing couldn't be better."

But he only shrugged.

"My marriage is none of your business, Jed, and I don't want advice from you."

"Then why did you come here?"

"I told you, to find out why you were after Brian."

"And that's all?"

Gab stood up, ignoring the question. "I'm sorry, I'm keeping you from your run."

"Never mind that. Can I take you to breakfast?"

She smiled wanly. "Oh, I don't think that's such a good idea, Jed. The newspeople will probably see us and..."

"No, I guess not." He wanted her to stay, though, couldn't bear the thought of her going back to that man.

"What will you do today?" she asked.

"I was planning on going up there, to the canyon," he said carefully, "feel out the area some more."

"Oh." She averted her face as if he'd hit her, and he couldn't stand the pain she was suffering. And now she'd go back to that lout and wait and worry and go out of her mind wondering when someone would come up with proof that Brian was a murderer. Proof she wouldn't believe.

"Come with me," he said.

"What?"

"Today. You said you had a fight with Brian. Well, let things cool off and come with me. We'll take a hike, that's all." Suddenly it was imperative that she stay away from Brian. He wanted her with him, to comfort, to talk to, to protect. He wanted to be alone with her at last, to study her at his leisure, to know what she was like now.

She was quiet for a minute. "I don't know," she finally said.

"It'll just take a few hours. You can just relax. You know how you always used to go for a walk when you were upset. It'll do you good."

"But you're on the job. I know you, you'll be up in the canyon trying to get vibes. I know how you work."

"You're wrong," he said, then caught himself. "Anyway, how could I get vibes from anyplace with you around screwing up the signals?" He allowed a smile to tug at the corner of his mouth.

"Brian will wonder where I am...."

"Let him," Jed muttered.

She smiled without humor. "Straight from the mouth of someone who's got no wife."

"He doesn't deserve you, Gab," he said.

"Never mind that now." She sighed. "I really don't want to face anyone looking like this." She put a hand up to her cheek. "Maybe I should..."

"Please come."

"I..." She sighed. "We'd be back this afternoon?"

"Yes."

He yearned to go to her and hold her again, to make everything all right, to turn back the clock to when they were both innocent kids and loved each other without complications.

"Can we stop by the hotel? I'll grab some food from the kitchen and tell someone that I'm going on a hike. I mean, I can't just disappear."

"Okay, sure." He hesitated. "What if you run into Brian?"

"I won't. He never goes into the kitchen."

"Can you deal with him when he finds out that you went with me?"

"Yes," she said tiredly. "You know, I just don't care about that anymore."

Jed's heart swelled.

BRIAN WAS IN THE OFFICE checking Lorna's figures from the day before. He shouldn't have had to do it, as it was his wife's job, but he couldn't find her, and he was too embarrassed to ask around to see if anyone had seen her that morning.

It had been a hell of a night. He'd left Gabriela locked in the bedroom and gotten something to eat at the bar in town. He could have gone to the hotel kitchen, but the staff would have wondered why his own wife didn't fix him dinner.

Then, after a few beers, he'd gone home, expecting a contrite wife who'd listen to his apologies and forgive him. Instead the cabin had been empty, the front door wide open, and Gabriela had been gone.

He hadn't slept well and had worried all night. What if she was angry enough with him to go to that righteous jerk Mallory and blurt out what she knew about the ax?

She wouldn't. No, not Gabriela. She'd never do that. Of course, he'd never hit her before, and he'd never seen her so hysterical before, either. Damn. It was just that she'd pushed and pushed, and he'd already been so damned stressed out.

He left the office, spoke to Margaret for a minute, then went up to see his folks. Maybe Gabriela was there or maybe she'd called them—not that he'd ask.

He heard the blender as he approached their door. Every morning, every darn morning, Otto fixed a smoothie of fresh organic fruit for breakfast, with wheat germ and yogurt and God knew what else. No one could hear his knock above the blender's noise, so he walked in, putting a cheery smile on his face.

"Oh, Brian, I didn't hear you," Otto said.

"Yeah, I know. I heard that thing going. How's Mom?"

Otto shrugged. "No worse. Still feisty."

"Uh, good, good."

"What brings you up here so early?"

"Not much. What's going on?"

"Well, your mother called the cabin last night and no one was there. She needs to talk to Gabriela about going into Flagstaff. Can you tell her to stop by?"

"Sure I can, no problem. Yeah, we were out last night."

"Well, I'm glad to hear the mess with the Whittakers hasn't made you into a recluse."

"Not much chance of that," Brian said, then he made an excuse and left.

No Gabriela. Not in the office or the cabin or out by the pools. The car was still in the parking lot, her purse was still at home. She had to be around.

He discovered where she was when he went to the kitchen to grab some coffee, and the breakfast cook told him that Mrs. Zimmerman had been going on a picnic.

"Where's she going?" Brian repeated. "What do you mean?"

"She just came in and got some food and stuff. I figured you two were going on a picnic, but I guess she's with someone else."

"Gabriela was just here getting food?"

"Uh-huh, not five minutes ago."

"Oh, sure, that's right," Brian improvised. "She was going on up to the lake, uh, that fishing lake, with a friend."

"Oh, well, I bet she needed a break about now," the cook said sympathetically.

"She sure did."

Brian got out of there fast and headed back to the cabin. His hands were shaking. He dialed the Pines Motel and asked for Mr. Mallory's room. The phone rang and rang and rang, and when the desk clerk came back on the line to find out if he wished to leave a message, he asked her to pop outside and tell him if the white Cherokee was there.

It wasn't.

He put the phone down carefully, then swore under his breath. He should have known. Who else would she have run to? Anger built in him, and he started to shake again. Right this second, his wife—his wife— was going somewhere with Mallory, no doubt spilling her guts: the ax, his debts, the fight last night—everything. Panic took over from the anger, a deep, seething panic that twisted his gut and made his heart pound, then he caught himself.

Gabriela was his wife. She'd never betray him. It would be the end of her, too. No, she'd never do it. Sure, she was worried about this situation, as he was, but when the money was in the bank she'd be as content as a pig in a poke. Security, that's what she wanted, and he'd give it to her. He was going to tell her he hit it big gambling. There was no reason for her ever to know the truth. He'd tell his parents the same thing. He'd promise never to gamble again. He'd let her remodel the hotel again, use one of those fancy decorators she was always wishing they could afford. She could have a free hand. It would all work out.

Brian got himself under control, took a few deep breaths and decided what to do next. He'd call George, yeah, and get his butt moving. It was more important than ever to get that stuff out of the canyon. He called the trailer at George's base camp and luckily found him in. In the background he could hear voices and some big machinery grinding away. George's voice lowered the minute he heard Brian's.

"You got the helicopter lined up yet?" Brian asked.

"Hey, buddy, take it easy. There's no rush," George replied.

"Easy for you to say," Brian grumbled.

"Relax, it'll get done," George said. "Man, you're a mess."

"Yeah, I am. In debt up to my ears. Let's get on the stick, George," Brian said, putting down the phone and wondering again what in hell Gabriela was doing with her old flame Mallory. He remembered her hysterical reaction to his lie about the ax, too, and had to tell himself over and over that Gabriela would never in a million years betray him. No way. But what, then, was she doing with that jerk?

The familiar explosion of light and pain assaulted him, without mercy, and he stumbled backward, palms pressed to his temples, searing agony the only reality. He shook his head to keep the voices at bay. He couldn't give in, not now.

CHAPTER NINE

TWO BEARS STOOD stock-still and watched the man and woman step out of the white Cherokee. They couldn't see him, he was sure, positioned as he was behind a juniper. But the old Apache could see them clearly, and he recognized Mrs. Zimmerman from the hotel at the hot springs. He recognized the man, too, from the day he'd been down in the canyon with the woman's husband. The man had climbed up the far side of the canyon, alone, as if searching for something, and he had seen Two Bears.

The man represented the law. Two Bears knew that instinctively, without even seeing the official car, and it was good that he was here at the trailhead with the pretty woman, investigating again, the Apache reasoned. Yes, this was a good sign.

The man and the woman, carrying a small day pack, began to head along the old trail up the canyon where those people were murdered. Two Bears followed at a safe distance, not wanting to be seen, for now only wishing to feel out their intentions. The woman was, after all, wife to the greedy one.

It was rough going, keeping pace with these two, who moved steadily up into the ponderosa pine forest. He was winded, and after a time he stopped in the middle of the trail, forgetting to take cover. He knew at once that stopping was a mistake when he heard the

1
3 WAYS TO PLAY see inside
for big CASH prizes and FREE GIFTS!
First play your "Win-A-Fortune" game tickets
to qualify for up to
<u>ONE MILLION DOLLARS IN LIFETIME INCOME</u>
– that's \$33,333.33 each year for 30 years!

FOLD ALONG DOTTED LINE AND DETACH CAREFULLY ▶

WIN A CASH FORTUNE

GAME TIX NO. **1a**

Game Ticket values vary. Scratch GOLD from Big Money Wheel to determine the potential cash value of prize you will receive if the sweepstakes number assigned to this ticket is a prize winning number.

DO NOT SEPARATE—KEEP ALL GAMES INTACT

WIN A CASH FORTUNE

GAME TIX NO. **1b**

Game Ticket values vary. Scratch GOLD from Big Money Wheel to determine the potential cash value of prize you will receive if the sweepstakes number assigned to this ticket is a prize winning number.

DO NOT SEPARATE—KEEP ALL GAMES INTACT

WIN A CASH FORTUNE

GAME TIX NO. **1c**

Game Ticket values vary. Scratch GOLD from Big Money Wheel to determine the potential cash value of prize you will receive if the sweepstakes number assigned to this ticket is a prize winning number.

DO NOT SEPARATE—KEEP ALL GAMES INTACT

WIN A CASH FORTUNE

GAME TIX NO. **1d**

Game Ticket values vary. Scratch GOLD from Big Money Wheel to determine the potential cash value of prize you will receive if the sweepstakes number assigned to this ticket is a prize winning number.

DO NOT SEPARATE—KEEP ALL GAMES INTACT

WIN A CASH FORTUNE

GAME TIX NO. **1e**

Game Ticket values vary. Scratch GOLD from Big Money Wheel to determine the potential cash value of prize you will receive if the sweepstakes number assigned to this ticket is a prize winning number.

DO NOT SEPARATE—KEEP ALL GAMES INTACT

(U-H-SR-08/95)

Follow directions below to find out!

With a coin, carefully scratch off the three gold boxes. Then check the chart below to learn how many FREE BOOKS will be yours!

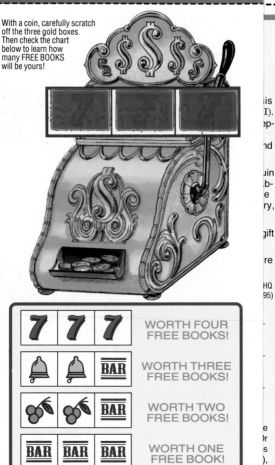

7	7	7	**WORTH FOUR FREE BOOKS!**
🔔	🔔	BAR	**WORTH THREE FREE BOOKS!**
🍒	🍒	BAR	**WORTH TWO FREE BOOKS!**
BAR	BAR	BAR	**WORTH ONE FREE BOOK!**

You'll receive four brand-new Harlequin Superromance® novels. When you scratch off the gold boxes and return this card in the reply envelope provided, we'll send you the books you qualify for <u>absolutely</u> free.

Harlequin
Reader Service®

Dear Reader,

Get out a coin—kiss it for good luck—and go to work on the WIN-A-FORTUNE tickets enclosed. You could end up a <u>million</u> <u>dollars</u> richer!

By returning these tickets you'll also be in the running for hundreds of other cash prizes we'll be giving away. It costs nothing to play this game—there's no fee, and no purchase is necessary!

We're holding this sweepstakes to introduce you to the benefits of the Harlequin Reader Service®. Scratch off the gold boxes on the enclosed Lucky 7 Slot Machine Game and we'll send you <u>free</u> <u>books</u>!

How many FREE BOOKS will you get? Play the Slot Machine Game and see! These books are absolutely free, with no obligation to buy anything!

The Harlequin Reader Service is **not** like some book clubs. We charge you nothing—ZERO—for your first shipment. And you don't have to make any minimum number of purchases—not even one!

over, please

FOLD ALONG DOTTED LINE AND DETACH CAREFULLY

► FOLD ALONG DOTTED LINE AND DETACH CAREFULLY ►

BEFORE MAILING DID YOU...

1. Play your Win-A-Fortune tickets? Don't forget to fill in your name and address in the space provided on the back of your game piece!

2. Play your Lucky 7 Slot Machine game for free books? If you have played your Slot Machine game, you may also play your Ace of Hearts game for a free gift.

woman's voice from below. "Two Bears? Is that you?" Quickly he scurried into the scrub oak and hid himself, not even certain exactly why he did not want to speak to these people. He knew only that these two were mixed up with the awakening of the evil spirits.

He watched carefully, unseen now, as the woman gave up and shrugged, and the pair began to walk on. His old heart was beating too hard, and he could sense peril ahead in the pine-scented air. It was true, these people were involved in the awakening, and he sensed they were in danger. He wondered if he should warn them, but something held him back. It was not his destiny to speak to them yet. He knew then that he must find the one who would be the bridge between his way and the white way. Now, more than ever, this messenger must be found.

"WEIRD," GABRIELA SAID over her shoulder, "I know that was Two Bears. He's usually very friendly. He used to work as a gardener at the hotel, in fact."

"I wonder why he didn't answer," Jed said from behind her as they moved on.

"Who knows? Maybe he didn't hear. He's got to be a hundred if he's a day."

"Yeah, well," Jed said, "I hope I can still hike at a hundred."

"Don't we all."

They walked along the trail, leaving the ponderosa and juniper and scrub oak forests behind as they ascended, following the dried-up gorge. The land never ceased to amaze Gabriela, an ever-changing land that was formed by the subtle differences in altitude. No sooner had they left the stunted oaks than they entered cactus country, strewn with rocks and boulders and occasional clumps of bunchgrass that eked out an existence in this arid climate.

The temperature seemed to climb immediately, too, once they were out in the open, and Gabriela wished she'd had time to change from jeans and shirt to shorts, but Jed had wanted to get started, and she would have had to stop back at the cabin, and Brian... She just couldn't be near him right now.

Where had it all gone awry? She reached up unconsciously and touched her forehead, felt the swelling. And then she quickly dropped her hand, all too aware of Jed striding along just behind her. What must he think? She felt humiliated and strangely guilty. No wonder women were so reluctant to report abuse. God, it was mortifying!

And just how was her husband feeling? she had to wonder. He'd been so sorry, genuinely ashamed. Now here she was on a hike with Jed, and Brian was surely going to find out about it. How was he going to take it?

"How are you feeling?" Jed asked, and she stopped and took a breath in the heat.

"I'm okay. A drink of water, maybe." Then, after drinking deeply and passing the water bottle back to Jed, she said, "You're wrong about Brian. You'll see." She watched as his sinewy throat worked when he, too, took a drink of water, and then she quickly looked away.

He wiped his mouth dry with the back of his hand and put the bottle back in the day pack, zipping it up. "You aren't going to believe this," he said, "but I hope I'm wrong. For your sake, I honestly do."

The land was broken here, slashed by deep ravines and wide gulches, and the trail wound up along the dried-out cut. It was rough going, their feet sometimes sliding on loose, gravelly dirt, cactus catching at their clothing now and then, insects buzzing around their perspiring faces. But Gabriela noticed little of the discomfort. She was too consumed with awareness of Jed. He'd gone ahead, leading the way, helping her where the trail was broken and precipitous, taking her hand, his strong, sun-browned forearm taut and muscular, the blond hairs catching the light.

She was crazy to look at him like that, but she couldn't help it. And a part of her knew that was really why she'd come along, to be alone with Jed, to test her feelings, to study him, to dare to remember those hands on her flesh and the way they'd been together. How could she ever have forgotten the feel of Jed next to her, naked, inside her, loving her, whispering against her hair things that were wonderful and loving and tender.

Jed was as handsome now as he'd been in his youth. Maybe more so with the maturity that was beginning to line his face. There was just something about him, masculine competence, yes, but underlying it all was that vulnerability that had initially attracted her, a need to be recognized for who he was, a need to be appreciated. Max's legacy.

She watched her footing but she couldn't help watching him with equal care, the roundness of his buttocks, the curve of thigh and calf beneath his jeans. The gliding movement of muscles in his back and shoulders under the light green polo shirt, whose short sleeves rested on the swell of his biceps. She took in the strong line of his jaw and the generous curve of his nose, the golden tan of his skin. The touch of silver now showing at his temples... How could she have ever forgotten Jed? How could she have put from her memory the ease with which he moved and spoke and the beautiful blue of those eyes that were fringed with incredibly dark lashes?

If she couldn't stop herself from looking at Jed, she knew in her heart that he was having the same trouble. They stopped for a break just before reaching the place where the Whittakers had fallen, and she felt Jed's gaze settle on her reluctantly as she knotted her hair at the nape of her neck. She closed her eyes and let him look, half of her withering in guilt, the other half melting in the hot sun beneath his stare. In Apache Springs men occasionally still eyed her despite knowing both her and her husband. It had been a very long time, however, since anyone had looked at her the way Jed was looking at her right now. Even Brian had stopped admiring her years ago. She'd felt and acted like an old married woman. She'd hidden from everyone her unhappiness with her marriage, and now she felt a crazy kind of freedom again, despite the horror of the past week. It was so wrong. But there was a hot stirring in Gabriela that she could no more control than her breathing or the quickness in her heart.

"More water?" Jed asked, and she opened her eyes and met his gaze. There was a stabbing sensation deep inside her.

"Jed, why didn't you ever marry?" she blurted out.

A rueful, crooked smile formed on his lips. "I did."

"Oh," she said, her heart leaping treacherously.

"Didn't take," he said.

"Oh. Well how long were you married?"

"Eighteen months." He shrugged.

"Were there children?"

He shook his head. "Probably better there weren't."

"Um." She sighed, aware that her reaction to the news of his marriage had been far too strong. She felt terribly anxious. "Do you still see each other?" she had to ask.

Again he shook his head. "No. But it wasn't a nasty divorce. I guess we'd be friends."

"I'm sorry," Gabriela found herself saying, "I mean about it not working out."

"I'm not," he muttered, and she wondered if she'd heard him correctly. She looked down at her sneakers, her cheeks burning in the sun.

They took the same trail that Brian had taken him down to the floor of the canyon. Jed helped her all the way, his golden hand on hers, on her elbow, her arm. Once her feet skidded on the gravel and she came up sharply against his chest, but neither of them dared react; they both quickly disentangled themselves and went on.

It was blazing hot on the canyon floor, and above not a cloud showed in the perfect blue bowl of sky. "God, it's hot," Jed said, and she noticed the wet spots on his shirt and sweat dripping from the short, curling hairs at the nape of his neck.

Gabriela was hot, too, but the heat inside her was all mixed up with her emotional state. She knew she shouldn't have made this trip—she knew how it was going to look to Brian, but she told herself that what she was doing was absolutely innocent. She was merely getting away from the hotel to calm herself.

It wasn't working.

"I'm going to walk around the area," Jed told her. "Why don't you take a breather?"

Gabriela sat on a boulder and tried not to look around. She knew she was sitting very close to where Evan and Clare had met their deaths. She knew, as well, that there'd most likely be blood on rocks and on the ground. And she knew, also, that if she saw it she'd scream.

For a time she shielded her eyes and studied the sky. Two hawks circled lazily in the sky overhead, one occasionally screeching to its mate. She wondered, idly, if hawks mated for life, and then she thought about Jed and their relationship of so long ago—were humans supposed to mate for life? If so, she mused, then their brains too often got in the way of their hearts. Too much thinking. Perhaps those two hawks winging overhead were a whole lot smarter than she was.

She watched Jed across the canyon. What was he thinking? How did he regard her and Brian? Did he know about Brian's ax? Was that the evidence he wouldn't discuss?

No, the whole thing was ridiculous. Jed had nothing on Brian. There *was* nothing.

She opened the pack and took out the water bottle and began to feel better about the whole thing. Everything she and Brian had done since the accident was perfectly logical. Lord, she thought, if Brian had any reason at all to feel guilty, he'd have hired a lawyer by now. But he hadn't. He'd cooperated. And as for hitting her, well, she'd pushed him too far. He was already under so much stress; she should have been supportive instead of accusatory.

Gabriela took a long drink of water and then wiped the sweat from her neck and brow. Why was she making excuses for Brian's behavior? For years he'd been treating her more like an object than a person;

for years they'd been growing apart. They were going to get a divorce as soon as this was over. She still felt, though, that she owed him loyalty. Just as you'd owe any friend or family member loyalty. She couldn't sever her emotional ties to Brian as if they'd never existed. He'd been her husband for nine years, their lives intertwined. Wasn't it natural to try to think the best of him?

She hung her head and felt the sun pounding on her neck and suddenly felt like crying. Everything was so sad. It had been for a long time, and the deaths of the Whittakers had only brought it all to a head.

She wished fervently that Jed hadn't appeared just at this time. It complicated everything so much. But he'd be leaving soon, she was sure. He'd have to close the case soon, when he couldn't find anything to incriminate Brian. He'd return to his job and their lives would take separate directions again.

She contemplated that: Jed leaving, going back to his job in Arlington. What did he do there? Who were his friends? She'd been so terribly frightened of losing him because of his choice of career that she'd never even considered the rest of her life without him.

Now, though, he'd come back. And he wasn't hurt or wounded, never had been, apparently. Somehow her furious objections to his choice of job didn't seem so clear in her mind anymore.

So without him around she could divorce Brian without feeling guilty. It was a scary thought, and it would hurt so to leave Ellie and Otto. Oh, she could hardly bear that part of it! And what would she do? Where would she go? Back to California? Well, she'd have to wait till this ordeal was over before she could do anything. She owed Brian that much.

Jed was getting closer, and she could see his face. What had he expected to accomplish here? Nothing, it seemed. Then she had an errant thought: maybe this trek had another purpose. A part of her sprang to life with the notion, while another part cringed in guilt.

"Well?" she said when he returned, his shirt soaked, a sheen of sweat on the lean angles of his face.

He shrugged. "I needed to get the picture."

"Did you?"

"Pretty well."

Gabriela stood up and sighed. "We should head back," she began, but he reached out and held her arm.

"This hasn't been easy for me, either," he said quietly.

She gave a short laugh.

"Believe me, it's true."

She looked down at his hand on her arm. He let her go. "You're obsessed with this. You're trying to punish Brian for something I did to you ten years ago."

"I'd never do that."

"You *are* doing it."

He looked at her with ineffable sadness. "I don't want to fight with you, Gab. It never got us anywhere."

She felt as if he'd slapped her. As if ten years were gone in the snap of a finger and they were back in his student apartment in Tucson arguing about him taking a job with the Marshals Service. Only this time the argument was about her husband. Her husband. She took a deep breath but her voice was tremulous when she spoke. "The Whittakers were killed in an accident. It was an accident."

He was quiet for a long time, and then he said, "You don't really believe that, Gab."

"No," she breathed, "you're wrong. Of course I believe it. For God's sake, Brian is my husband!"

"I know that," he said somberly. "Oh, I do know that."

The hike back out to the road seemed even longer than the walk in had taken. Part of it was the afternoon heat, of course, but Gabriela was also growing more uncomfortable around Jed by the minute. She was so terribly confused. If Jed Mallory had turned up on her doorstep before the accidents, it would have been different. Her knight on a white horse coming to save her from a marriage gone sour. But now he was a wedge between her and a husband who needed her support, and his presence was making her crazy.

Still, she couldn't deny the effect his nearness had on her, and with each step she took she could feel his eyes resting on her, walking on her skin like a thousand tiny feet, stroking her like a hundred pairs of hands. And neither of them could talk about it or acknowledge it in any way. The feeling was too dangerous. If they gave voice to it, it would be empowered.

They rested in the cool ponderosa forest and sat in the shade together, drinking the last of the water, eating sandwiches. Both were very quiet, very careful.

When Jed did speak it was about the mundane. "I'd forgotten how much I enjoy the West," he said, leaning back against a boulder, his hands behind his head. "You've never lived in the East. The heat and humidity are hell. And in the winter, I swear it's twice as cold as here. A damp cold. It goes right through to your bones."

Gabriela said something about how she'd heard that. She didn't dare ask why he didn't try to get posted to the West.

"It's crowded, too," he reflected. "Traffic's as bad around Washington as it is in L.A."

"Do you ever go on assignments somewhere else?" she asked casually. That was a safe subject, anyway.

"Sure," he said. "Marshals are charged with all kinds of duties. We transport federal prisoners that come under our jurisdiction. We work with the Drug Enforcement Agency and often run auctions for them when they sell off a convicted dealer's assets. We work a lot with the judiciary...." He shrugged.

"So that's why you're on this assignment," she said, and then wished she hadn't.

"Yes" was all he replied. "And I was glad to be sent out here. Arizona... I get home to see my mother and sister about once a year, is all. And then it's in Tucson. I haven't been in these mountains for... Well, you remember the last time I was here."

Gabriela gave a shy nod. Yes, she remembered. And she remembered that seeing him in Apache Springs had almost torn her heart out.

She looked down at her folded hands. She'd been so young then, young and cocksure. But deep down where dreams lay hidden, she'd known that she'd always have a place in her heart for Jed. Brian, well, her husband's life had suited her. He'd been young and handsome and fun, so easy to be with. He'd pursued her for a year. He was settled. And in a small, clean town. She loved his family and his life and the hotel. She'd adored him. It had been enough. But now she knew with a strange clarity that Jed had never really left her thoughts. It was as if he'd always been someplace in her soul.

She continued to stare at her hands, unfocused, and felt the heat of tears building behind her eyes. But she'd never cry in front of him, and she'd never, ever, let him know how close she was to ending her marriage.

"You know," he said, watching her, "I told my boss I knew you and Brian. I told him about...us."

"Don't," she whispered. "Please."

"I'm going to say it. Sorry, Gab, but I've never lied to you, and I've got to tell you I wanted to see you again. I didn't know it, though, until the other day when I walked into your office."

"Jed, don't." God, if he said another word, she'd scream!

Quickly she got to her feet and stuffed the sandwich wrappers and water bottle into the backpack and pushed it toward Jed, fighting for control. She could feel her breath coming hot and quick, and her head was swimming. She started out before he was even ready, striding along the trail at double pace, her chest heaving. Then she could sense him behind her, and she thought she might go out of her mind with images of Jed stopping her and turning her into his arms and kissing her forever and ever, making it all go away, making everything right.

Neither said another word until they were in the Cherokee and almost back to the hotel. Jed stared straight ahead and said, "I've got to ask.... Do you ever, have you ever, thought that we made a mistake ten years ago?"

Gabriela felt that stabbing sensation deep in her belly. She licked her dry lips and tried her voice. "No," she said. "When it was over that was it."

"Sure," Jed said. "Sure it was."

CHAPTER TEN

GABRIELA WAS THERE that afternoon waiting for Brian when he got back to the cabin. She looked pale and tired but composed, and the moment he saw her he was sure she hadn't said anything about the ax to Mallory. Relief washed over him with such force that his anger with her drained away as if it had never been.

"Gabriela, babes, you had me worried," he said. "And then going off like that today..."

"I should have told you, but I..."

"I understand. I'm really sorry about yesterday. You know I didn't mean it, babes. I guess this accident thing has me more uptight than I thought." He gave a little laugh. "I wasn't exactly Mr. Cool, was I."

"No," she said cautiously.

"I'll never do it again, I swear. Never. You have my absolute promise on that. Let me see your head." He walked to where she was sitting on the couch and tilted her head up, touching the bump with a finger. "God, I'm sorry. But you're okay, aren't you?"

"I'll live," she replied.

"So where did you go today?"

"Jed and I went back to the canyon," she said, meeting Brian's gaze with clear eyes. "He wanted to look around some more."

"And he needed you for that?"

"No, but I thought I should get away for a while."

"Well, I wish you'd picked someone else to get away with," he said.

She stared at her folded hands and said nothing, and Brian pretended not to notice.

"He's really after me, Gabriela, you know? Really has it in for me."

Gabriela didn't say anything at all, and Brian knew he was on thin ice. Losing his temper like that had been a terrible mistake. He needed Gabriela, needed her on his side, committed to him, running interference for him with Mallory. He needed whatever information she got from her old boyfriend. She was important to him right now, real important.

"Babes, we're going to start all over. Yeah, that vacation I talked about. Mexico, Hawaii. I'm turning over a new leaf, I swear. And when we get back, we'll think about having a kid. I know you want kids. And, well, it's time to do something about it." He sat beside her and pulled her head onto his shoulder, stroking her arm with his other hand. "Just think, little kids running around. Wow." He turned his face and kissed her on the temple, then on the bump on her forehead. "I'll never lay a hand on you in anger again, Gabriela. You believe me, don't you?"

"Yes," she said, "I believe you."

But even though she said she believed him, even though she did not resist his embrace, she was unresponsive. Upset, sure, she was still upset, and he didn't blame her a bit. "It'll be better, babes, I know it will."

"Will you do one thing for me, Brian?" she finally asked.

"Anything."

"Will you promise to stop gambling?"

He squeezed her close to his side. "Of course I will. I promise. It's over."

She smiled wanly as he caressed her shoulder.

The very next morning Brian told everyone he was going up to Flagstaff on an errand. He was going on an errand all right, but not to Flagstaff. He had to get that damn ax. With Mallory nosing around out there, he just might find it, and that would be bad. Brian had known from the instant he'd flung it into the canyon that he'd made a mistake. Well, it was time to remedy that, make good and sure no one ever found it.

It took him more than two hours in the broiling sun to find the damn ax once he was there, but he did find it, wedged neatly between two large rocks. Sweating, he held it and stared dispassionately at the dried blood on the blade.

A half hour later, some distance off the trail that led back to his pickup truck, he dug a hole behind a clump of scrub oak. He had an odd sensation that someone was watching him as he scraped away at the dried earth, and for a moment he paused, looking around, but who would be out here?

He shook off the persistent feeling, chalked it up to nerves and imagination, and finished burying the ax, confident that no one in a million years was going to find it now.

No weapon, no motive, no case. "Screw you, Mallory," he said, rising, dusting himself off. And the whole way back to the truck, he whistled a cheerful tune.

That afternoon Gabriela was polite and accommodating, trying as hard as he was to find a level of emotion they could both sustain. It seemed to be working, that precarious balance in a relationship be-

tween two people when one has been hurt too badly to
merely kiss and make up.

They worked together, they spoke, they smiled.
They talked courteously and managed to coexist
without too much strain. That night Gabriela slept on
the couch, and once when Brian took her into his
arms, she turned her face away and said, "Please,
Brian, I need some time."

Anger rose in him, hot and heavy, but he squelched
it. He needed Gabriela. And at least things were getting back on an even keel. Even the press had ceased
its vigil, since nothing at the moment was happening.
And George had set up a meeting with his brother in
Vegas for the next day. A real important meeting.

Brian figured he had it made.

IT WAS THAT SAME DAY that Jed Mallory and a team of
dogs and handlers from Phoenix went into the canyon. Jed, who'd worked a couple of times with
bloodhounds, wasn't as keen on the team of German
shepherds mixed with the purebred bloodhounds, but
their trainers assured him they were the top team west
of Macon, Georgia.

"If there's an ax down there, they'll sniff it out,"
one of the handlers told him.

Jed was feeling good; at last he was doing something. The ax would be found that day, he was sure.
Soon, in fact, and then he could make his case, signed,
sealed and delivered—the Mallory Touch, his col-
leagues called it.

He put aside thoughts of how this was going to af-
fect Gab, what the discovery of her husband's ax, with
the judge's blood and Brian's fingerprints on it would

do to her. He couldn't think about that; he had to do his job.

Jed, four handlers, eleven dogs, Sheriff Ulrich and four of his deputies went along on the hunt. Ulrich also brought with him the vital piece of Judge Whittaker's clothing that was going to provide the scent for the dogs. Three reporters even followed them out to the accident site, having gotten wind of the dog search.

The newspeople, with their city shoes and heavy video cameras, were a laughable lot as they tried to follow the dogs along the main trail and then down the steep game trail onto the rough canyon floor. One lady even fell and slid into some rocks and had to be helped out by a deputy.

They sweated and cursed and got underfoot so badly that Jed ordered Ulrich to escort them back out of the canyon.

"You can't do that!" one of them said, his face lobster-red from effort.

"Oh, yeah?" Jed replied. "Watch me." And he got another deputy to shoo them all the way back to their vans.

He almost missed it when the handlers loosed the dogs, getting there as they were straining on their leads, their bodies quivering with anticipation, excitement, the love of the chase. The handlers went among them, letting each dog smell the piece of Judge Whittaker's bloodstained clothing, patting their heads, talking to them, crooning, saying their names. The dogs panted and pulled, shuddering with energy. The bloodhounds bayed soulfully; the shepherds strained at their leashes silently, paws scraping at the rocky ground.

Then they were off, noses to the dirt, tails wagging frantically, hackles raised. The men followed as the entire team of canines instantly turned the same direction, barking, howling, baying. It was bedlam, the day scorching hot, choking dust rising from beneath the scrabbling feet of men and dogs, whose howls and whines echoed off the steep rock walls.

The dogs searched the trail and canyon for a long time, whining, baying, barking, crisscrossing the rough ground, stopping every time at the place where the bodies had fallen. They whined and scratched and howled there until their handlers directed them away, but they kept circling, returning, knowing only that was the right scent.

And then, Jed noticed with a spurt of excitement, three of the dogs kept returning to another site—two large boulders on the canyon floor. The dogs put their paws on the rocks, scratched and sniffed at the crevice furiously, tongues lolling, baying, tails flapping madly. But there was nothing there.

After two hours one of the handlers approached Jed. "Sorry," he said, "but we aren't going to find anything. My guess is that there may have been something, right around here, but whatever it was is gone."

A great and heavy disappointment settled on Jed, then anger took over. "Zimmerman," he whispered harshly. "Damn it."

"What do you want to do?" the man asked. "I charge per hour, and it's your dime."

"Keep at it for a while," Jed said. "Widen the circle."

"Okay, sure."

But Jed knew they wouldn't find it, not now. It was too late. He swore under his breath and kicked at a loose rock. Max Mallory would have had dogs in the canyon the moment he knew a weapon existed, and he wouldn't have cared if it was his own mother who was the suspect! Damn.

The search wound down; the dogs were leashed, panting, and taken out of the canyon, and silence settled over the land once again. Jed was one of the last to leave, frustrated, furious with himself, hot and sweaty and tired, and as he followed the now-familiar path down to the road where his car was, he passed without noticing a clump of scrub oak, behind which was a newly dug spot of stony earth covered over with dead leaves.

Jed spent the next day writing up his report to present to Gish in Arlington. Often he got up and studied the pictures he'd tacked up on his motel room walls when he'd first checked in: newspaper pictures, police file photos, pictures from Jackson Many Goats, ones of the murder site, the Whittakers' bodies in the canyon and in the forensic lab. He studied them and wrote himself lists with question marks after key phrases. Motive? he'd written. In debt, he'd put under Brian's name. Scratches, DNA. Murder weapon?

And he added to his lists of things to do. He crossed out "dogs."

He barely left his room, telling himself he needed time to think, but he finally admitted that it was because temptation was only a mile away at the hotel, and it would be much, much too easy to give in, to go up there on some pretext to see Gab.

That afternoon he left Apache Springs to drive to the Phoenix airport, his report neatly stowed in his leather duffel bag. He wasn't looking forward to this trip—he was worried about Gab, and he knew Gish was going to chew him out but good.

Jed sat on the plane with a muscle ticking angrily in his jaw—if he'd gone into that canyon with dogs in the first place, Zimmerman wouldn't have had time to retrieve the weapon. But no. Instead, Jed had been screwing around with forensic experts and with Gabriela. He could have kicked himself in the butt and saved Gish the trouble.

JED'S PLANE WAS OVER New Mexico, flying east, when Brian Zimmerman announced to his wife that he was going to Las Vegas with George Lemming the next day.

"You promised," she said. "Brian, you sat right there and promised."

"Babes, I told you, I'm not going to hit the tables, I swear. I have some business to take care of, that money I owe the casino. I'm just going along with George to fix things up."

"I don't believe you. Brian, I'm sorry, I just don't believe what you're saying. Do your business by phone. You don't have to go!"

"I do, really. Trust me."

"I can't!" she cried.

"I trusted you with Mallory," Brian said. "I never held that against you. I never said a word!"

"How can you compare those situations?" she asked, aghast.

"I trust you, you trust me," he said, shrugging.

"Don't go, Brian." Gabriela was doing the dinner dishes, but she kept turning around to face him, dripping suds and water all over the floor in her agitation.

"I have to go."

She shook her head slowly. "You have to change. You're kidding yourself. You're in denial. Can't you see how you're hurting me, your family, the hotel, yourself?"

"I'm not going to gamble, babes. Really I'm not. I promised you and I won't."

"Oh, Brian, you're lying to yourself and don't even know it," she said sadly.

"I don't believe this!" Brian finally shouted. "I have business to take care of! A phone call will not work. I have debts and I've got to take care of them."

"With what, Brian? How are you going to pay those debts?"

"I'll manage, don't you worry. This is business. I can handle it."

"Like you've handled it before?"

"Gabriela," he said warningly.

"Don't go, Brian," she repeated.

"Goddamn it, Gabriela!"

She turned from the sink again and leaned against it, facing him. There was something white and pinched about her face that scared him. "If you go, I won't be here when you get back," she said quietly.

"Don't issue me any ultimatums."

"I'll move out, Brian. I mean that. This time I mean it. I can't take any more."

"I don't believe you," he said.

"Believe me, please."

"It's because of Mallory, isn't it. I was too damned nice about that, I guess. Maybe I should have called him out on it!"

"No, it's not because of him. This has nothing to do with him. It's your gambling. I'd do anything if you'd just tell me how to help you stop."

He narrowed his eyes. "Oh, well, you sure are one terrific person, aren't you. Big of you, Gabriela. You can mess around with your old boyfriend but I can't go to Vegas?"

"I did not mess around with Jed."

"Well, you wanted to. I know that look in your eye. I know you only too well. I saw how you two looked at each other. It made me sick!"

"You're disgusting," she whispered.

"You're not exactly the Virgin Mary yourself!" he said, and left, slamming the door behind him.

In the morning Gabriela was in the kitchen making coffee when Brian got up, headachy and crabby from the beers he'd had with the guys last night. She was very quiet, her eyes holding such a world of accusation that he couldn't meet them. He was sick of fighting with her and sick of feeling guilty. A man had to do what a man had to do, and he couldn't let his wife take control. He wished he could tell her that everything was going to be okay in a few days, a week at the outside. But he couldn't, not yet.

He went into the bedroom and packed a small bag, just a change of clothes and a toothbrush, because they'd be back the day after tomorrow, and when he got out to the living room, Gabriela was there, her arms folded, just looking at him.

"You're actually going," she said, her voice shaking just a little.

"I told you, I have to go."

"I meant what I said last night, Brian."

"Sure, sure."

"Please, don't go."

"I'll be back the day after tomorrow early. We'll talk about it then."

"I won't be here. Don't you understand, Brian?"

"We'll talk about it then, babes. Take care. Keep an eye on Lorna, will you? 'Bye." And he went out, threw his bag on the seat of his pickup and drove off to meet George. He thought once, briefly, that his wife wouldn't dare leave him, not now, and then his mind switched to much more important matters, such as the meeting in Vegas and what George's brother had to say, who he'd lined up to buy the stuff and just how much they could bilk him out of.

He met George finishing up some work out at the base camp, and they drove to Flagstaff together in George's car. They talked about the treasure, about what they'd do with the money, about the timing, when to hire the helicopter and other details.

"Yeah, I have a line on a couple of charter services. I thought I'd tell them I'm working for some museum and we've found some artifacts, just in case the pilot gets curious and looks in the cave."

"Good idea."

"I'll make sure it's a big-enough machine to carry us *and* the treasure. I got us some canvas bags, too."

"You told your brother it had to be soon, didn't you?" Brian asked.

"Sure did. He understood. He gets ten percent, by the way."

"Absolutely."

They drove along in companionable silence for a time, passing the familiar scenery on the way to Flagstaff. Brian felt free for the first time in days, weeks even. He leaned back against the seat and sighed.

"You know, that investigator from the U.S. Marshals Service was out to see me," George finally said.

"Oh, yeah?"

"Asking about you."

"That jerk was everywhere, talking to everyone. What a pain. I hope he didn't bug you," Brian said.

"Nah."

"What'd he want to know?"

"He asked about us going gambling, stuff like that. He knew you owed money."

"What'd you say?"

"Nothing. I told him to ask you if he wanted to know."

Brian laughed. "You're a pal, George."

"So what's there to tell? Nothing." George shrugged.

They were almost at the airport when George broke the silence again. "You know, I've been thinking, Brian."

"Yeah?"

"I sure as hell hope you finding that treasure doesn't have anything to do with those 'accidental' deaths."

"Oh, for crying out loud, not you, too, George."

"I don't take much stock in coincidences."

Brian looked at his friend coldly. "I told you once already, I found that cave before the accident."

"I know what you told me."

"Listen, you have more important things to worry about than crazy accidents, pal. Like whether your brother has dug up a good-enough buyer to handle our merchandise real expeditiously."

"I'm not worried about that."

"He better have big bucks, George," Brian said, turning to stare out the car window.

GABRIELA MOVED OUT of the cabin that afternoon. She cried a little as she packed, but she tried not to let it get to her. This had been coming for a long time, and she knew she'd reached the end. She sat on the side of the bed and looked around the room she'd fixed up herself and shared with Brian for nine years. She tried to be objective, searching her mind, asking herself whether she'd be doing this right now if Jed hadn't reappeared.

Yes, she would have. She'd been planning to divorce Brian for a long time. This had been inevitable, she supposed. If not today, then next week or next month. The timing was bad, that was all.

He'd hit her in a fit of anger, and he'd lied to a federal investigator, never mind his excuse, and she simply couldn't live with a man who did those things, not even for one more day.

Wiping her eyes angrily, Gabriela thought about the past two days. While Brian had been oblivious, she'd been anguished, her mind weighing and questioning and testing her feelings. Jed was gone, so she had no one to run to, and she knew she'd had to give her marriage this one last chance. She'd imagined for a moment it might work out when Brian had promised never to gamble again, but reality had set in last night—final, irrevocable reality.

She finished packing, just what she could carry, figuring she'd get the rest later. When she took her comb and brush and toothbrush out of the bathroom, it hit home again, and the utter finality of her actions made her cry. But only briefly.

Hoping no one would see her, she loaded her bags into the old Blazer and drove around to the hotel's rear service entrance, dragging them into the service ele-

vator without encountering anyone except one clean-
ing lady who looked at her askance but didn't say
anything. She carried her luggage down the hall to the
same room she'd spent the night in before, the one
undergoing repairs. It couldn't be given to a guest, so
she knew she could use it for a while. What she'd do
after that she had no idea.

Panting, she dropped the bags and sat on the side of
the bed, putting her face in her hands. All her hopes,
all her dreams and youthful enthusiasm, all her love,
and it had come to this: failure and humiliation, pain
and loneliness and a broken heart.

Gabriela straightened and put her shoulders back.
"Okay," she said aloud to the fresh white Sheetrock
walls, "a new leaf, Gabriela, and quit feeling sorry for
yourself." Then she stood up and headed for the door,
ready to face Otto and Ellie.

It didn't make it any easier that Lorna was there.

"Oh, come on in, Gabriela. Join us for lunch?" she
said.

"Uh, no, really, I only came to tell you something.
All of you."

"Sounds serious," Lorna said. "Is that investigator bothering you again? The reporters . . . ?"

Gabriela shook her head. "It's not about that.
Lorna, I've left Brian."

Lorna drew in her breath, then put her arm around
her sister-in-law's shoulders. "Come in and sit down.
Tell us about it."

"Wait," Gabriela said, panicking for a moment.
"Do you think, I mean . . . will Ellie . . . ?"

"She's going to find out," Lorna said quietly.

"Yes, I guess so. I just wish I didn't have to . . . not
now."

186 APACHE SPRINGS

"I know, but these things never happen at convenient times, do they?"

Gabriela tried to smile and let Lorna lead her into the kitchen, where her in-laws were sitting at the table, eating bowls of fruit with yogurt topping.

"Hi, Gabriela. Sit down. Want some fruit?" Otto asked.

"Hello, dear," Ellie said. "You look tired. Have some of this good yogurt."

"She doesn't want to eat," Lorna said. "Gabriela has something to tell you." She kept her arm around her sister-in-law's shoulders, giving her support.

"Oh?" Otto said, his bushy gray eyebrows rising. Ellie only looked up, putting the spoon down carefully.

"Oh, this is so hard," Gabriela said. She looked from one to the other. "You know I love you both very dearly."

"Gabriela, what...?"

"I've left Brian. I moved out of the cabin and took that unfinished room on the third floor," she said, her words tumbling over one another.

"You what?"

"I'm sorry, I'm so very sorry, but I can't stay with him. I need to get away for a while. I know this is a bad time—the accident and all, so I won't leave right now. I'll see him through the investigation, and then..."

Ellie said, "It's a quarrel. All couples have them, dear. You'll make up."

Gabriela shook her head. "I've tried and tried, but I can't anymore." Her voice broke. "He went to Las Vegas with George Lemming this morning."

"It's just a quarrel," Ellie repeated, patting Otto's arm.

"Is it this accident thing?" Otto asked.

"No, really, it's not. I'd spoken to him about a divorce earlier, but this came up, and I thought I could stick it out, but I...I just couldn't."

"I don't blame you a bit," Lorna said firmly. "My brother is not a very nice person, and he doesn't deserve you. He never did."

"Lorna..." Ellie began.

"It's true, Mom. He never appreciated Gabriela."

"Is it that nice young man you used to know at school?" Ellie asked suddenly.

"No," Gabriela blurted out. "Oh, no." She went to Ellie and held her hand. "It's not because of another man. It's me and Brian and our marriage."

Ellie's eyes filled with tears. "What will you do? Where will you go?"

"I'm not sure what I'm going to do," Gabriela replied. "I'll stay and work if you want me to, until you get a replacement. It won't be easy now, in the middle of the summer season. Or if you want me to go right away..."

"Stop being foolish," Otto said. "You'll stay however long you need to."

"I should get a room in town."

"I won't hear of it," Otto said. "I won't listen to this. You stay right here at the hotel. Not another word about it."

"Thank you," she said. "I'll never stop being your daughter-in-law, you know. Wherever I go, I'll always visit. I'll come back. I'll call. You'll never really get rid of me." Her eyes were brimming and her heart was full.

"Stop that," Otto said. "You're not going anywhere for a while. We'll take it one day at a time, all of us. It'll work out. These things always do, one way or the other."

Gabriela sighed.

"Does Brian know?" Lorna asked.

"He knows that I told him I wouldn't be there when he got back, but he didn't listen."

"Maybe you'll make up," Ellie said faintly.

Gabriela only looked away miserably.

She dreamed of Jed that night, alone in her hotel room. She dreamed they were young again, happy and carefree, and there was no Brian and no accident. They held each other and kissed and laughed. She could hear him, feel the smoothness of his skin and smell his special, sweet-musky scent.

"I love you, Gab," he told her solemnly in the dream.

"I love you, Jed," she answered.

And then the place they were in turned dark and she reached out for him, but he was gone, and somehow it was all her fault. She tried to scream but she couldn't make a sound. She tried and tried until with a start she woke up; it was dawn, another day, but it was still all there: Brian and the lie he'd told, the fact that she'd left him, and she had to carry the burden all by herself.

CHAPTER ELEVEN

BRIAN WAS GONE and so was Jed, and Gabriela spent the morning feeling oddly as if she'd been deserted. There was no one hounding her about what she'd seen at the accident site, no one accusing her of disloyalty or unfaithfulness. Of course, Brian wasn't around to nag and nitpick. It was too calm, too normal, and except for calls from a couple of TV stations and one from the loan officer at the bank that held the paper on the hotel, she was able to sail through the entire morning feeling less stress than she had for a week. The lull before the next storm, she mused. Lorna was handling the hotel exceptionally well, leaving her free for her morning visit to Otto and Ellie.

Even they were politely quiet—at least on the subject of her new living arrangements. It was as if everyone needed this break. She wondered, though, if Brian's parents were both in a kind of denial over her divorce plans.

Back at the front desk, she spoke to Lorna about that. "I'm really getting worried about your parents and this whole thing with Brian."

"They can handle it," Lorna said. "You've got to live your own life, Gabriela. And frankly, I don't know how you've put up with Brian for so long. You're my hero, anyway." And then she brought up the subject of the hotel's finances. "You know, I'm not blind or as stupid as my brother thinks I am. It looks as if every time the hotel's a little ahead of the game, Brian drains the account.''

Gabriela looked at her sister-in-law in surprise. How did she . . . ?

"I looked at the books in the safe," Lorna said, shrugging. "Brian thinks I'm so dumb I don't remember the combination. If he doesn't get some help with his gambling, this place is going to go on the auction block within the year.''

All Gabriela could do was nod.

"Maybe," Lorna went on, "well, maybe my husband and I could take over for a while. I don't know. We talked on the phone last night, and we'd have to rent out our house in Payson, move the kids to the school up here. . . . Anyway," she said, "it's a thought.''

"Brian would never let you." Gabriela sighed.

"We talked about that, too. Dad is still the owner of the place. It would be a battle, but someone's got to do something.''

"Yes," Gabriela admitted. "Yes, I know you're right. It's just that, well, this is Brian's whole life. He'd be lost.''

"Gambling is his life," Lorna was fast to point out.

The rest of the morning Gabriela spent doing busy-work in the kitchen and out at the vapor pools. The hotel was quite full, and of course guests still had questions about the Whittakers. At least ten people wanted to know if they could go on the treasure hunt and see the spot where Evan and Clare Whittaker went over the cliff. But Gabriela was firm; the treasure hunt had been discontinued.

She did some thinking, too, while she kept her hands busy. This investigation, she was sure, was far from over. Jed was as tenacious as a pit bull—once he got hold of something, he wasn't going to let go.

Maybe the whole thing was about Brian's ax. Maybe someone had actually found it and that was the evidence that pointed to Brian. Well, Brian had explained that to her—he'd lost the thing. He should have been honest about it, but he hadn't. So she'd tell Jed and clear up the whole matter. That would end the investigation, because Brian had no motive whatsoever for harming the Whittakers. And then Jed would leave for good, return to Washington and be posted somewhere else. She'd never see him again.

Gabriela tried to tell herself that was all right. Ten years ago she'd made the decision to end the relationship. Maybe she'd made a mistake. Maybe she'd been so afraid of losing him, as her sister had lost her husband, that she'd blown her chance for a happy life. But that was all water under the bridge. Jed was not really interested in her anymore. That trip they'd taken into the canyon together... Well, he'd only felt sorry for her. Curious, maybe, to see what she was like now. And hadn't she felt curious, too? Sure she had.

Gabriela told herself that a dozen times. Even as she and Lorna took a lunch break together, her mind kept returning to that trek with Jed and to his real motives. No, she convinced herself, he couldn't really still care. It would be best, in fact, when he finally was forced to close the file on this case and leave for good. She had to get on with her life—a new life—and so did he.

The thought led Gabriela to a decision she realized she'd been flirting with all along. If Brian wasn't going to come clean about losing his ax, she'd tell Jed herself, even tell him why Brian had been less than honest. Together they'd all pitch in and find the stupid thing and put an end to this ridiculous investigation. She'd be free then to sort out her life, to decide which direction to take. Free of Jed and all those memories and free of Brian, free of a marriage that had been over ages ago.

It was ironic. But the very thing that might have brought them back together—the accident—was now doing exactly the opposite. The deaths of Evan and Clare were making her see a lot of truths she hadn't wanted to examine.

Right after lunch she telephoned Jackson Many Goats in Flagstaff. She knew what he was going to think. She didn't care. "When is Jed due back?" she asked casually.

"Ah...tonight, I think," he said. "A United flight from Washington if I recall correctly."

"You don't know the time?" she asked.

"No, not exactly. Late, I think he said."

"Thanks, Jackson," she said, and hung up.

Gabriela made a second call, to United Airlines, and found out that there was an evening flight due into Phoenix from Washington at 10:30 p.m. She could, naturally, wait till tomorrow morning and contact Jed then, explain about Brian being afraid to tell the truth about losing his ax. She could wait. But something inside her was pushing to end this whole thing, get it over with and get on with her life.

She left the office where she'd been making the calls and found Lorna chatting on the porch with some guests. "Can you mind the store if I drive down to Phoenix this evening?" she asked.

"Sure," Lorna said. "Is there something . . . ?"

"No. It's just an errand," she said, lying, "something that's needed doing for a while now."

All afternoon her determination ebbed and flowed, though, and she had to tell herself over and over that her motives were sound. She had to tell Jed about the lost ax, no matter how bad this second omission looked. She had to do whatever it took to get this investigation over with. She was not being disloyal to Brian. She was, in the long run, helping him out of a jam.

Never once, that whole long, hot afternoon, did Gabriela allow herself to think she was meeting Jed's flight for any other reason.

THE DRIVE DOWN to the desert floor took Gabriela two hours. The air conditioner in her Blazer didn't work, and the heat made the trip seem even longer, despite the fact that she hadn't left until seven. With each hundred-foot drop in elevation, the temperature seemed to rise a few degrees, and by the time she was winding down through saguaro cactus country to the east of Phoenix it had to have been close to 100 degrees. Her crisp blue shirt and tan linen skirt were hopelessly wrinkled. She didn't care, though. She was not meeting Jed's flight for any reason other than to set the record straight.

Gabriela drove through the heavy traffic of Scottsdale and on toward Sky Harbor International Airport in south Phoenix. The sun had set already, leaving behind a western desert sky that was splashed with reds and oranges and purples against a bank of black thunderheads. It was August, monsoon season in the Southwestern United States, when late summer rains moved north nightly from the Pacific off Mexico's Baja California peninsula. In the desert no one complained about moisture, though. Maybe it was going to rain tonight, Gabriela thought as she pulled into a parking lot. Great, the roads heading home would be hell, the drive twice as long.

But even as she crossed the still-hot asphalt and lightning began to streak the western sky, she put the tedious drive from her mind. Once she told Jed the truth and they found the damn ax, a terrible burden was going to be lifted from her shoulders. She couldn't have waited till morning.

The storm moved in quickly, however, and the ten-thirty United flight was put in a holding pattern to the east of Phoenix as strong winds and slashes of lightning moved over the airport.

Then the rain came, blurring the runway lights from where Gabriela stood staring out the plate-glass window of a concourse. Finally the flights began to land, after a half-hour delay. She didn't mind the wait, though, because this was something that needed doing. Damn Brian, she thought, watching the planes touch down every few minutes.

JED WAS ANNOYED as he pulled his leather duffel bag from the overhead luggage compartment. He hated delays, and he was tired. But mostly he was annoyed with himself and his own bad judgment.

Gish hadn't been happy about the dogs not finding the weapon, and he had trouble with Jed's failure to find a motive for the murder.

"And the wife, this Gabriela Zimmerman? You putting pressure on her, too? Maybe she knows something," Gish had said.

"I've tried. She's pretty loyal, though," Jed had explained.

"Where's the old Mallory touch?" Gish had asked. "We need some results here."

"Yes, sir, I know. I'm doing my best." Was he? Was he really?

And what was the last thing Arthur Gish had said before Jed had left his office? Something like, "The president himself called me and wanted to know when arrests were going to be made! The president!"

Jed had explained, "I don't have a motive, sir, and I don't have the murder weapon. If I made an arrest at this point, no DA in America could get a conviction."

"Then find a motive, goddamn it, and find that weapon! A nominee to the highest court of this land was murdered and I want results! Get the hell back out there and get the job done, Mallory, or I'll have your ass!"

"Yes, sir," Jed had replied.

Gish, of course, was right. Jed needed results, and he'd been waiting too long, letting the case drag out, worrying a little too much about Gabriela's feelings getting hurt.

This was a homicide he was investigating, and Gabriela... Well, he was sure she knew more than she was saying. If he had to, he'd drag her to Phoenix and interrogate her until her head reeled. She must have seen something, and he'd get it out of her. Maybe she even knew where that damn ax was. What an idiot he was to have let the past influence his judgment!

As he walked down the jetway, he was also thinking he didn't have much time. Gish was getting antsy, and he'd remove him from the case if something didn't break soon. He was following a mother with two crabby tired young kids, feeling weary himself, when he saw her.

For a moment he didn't believe his eyes. He stopped short in the doorway to the terminal, and someone bumped into him from behind, said "Excuse me" and squeezed past.

She was there, standing in a crowd of people, tall and beautiful and so familiar—Gab. Something inside him melted like hot wax, and all the years fell away in one magical, glorious moment, and he was buoyed by a joy he hadn't felt for a decade. A big smile spread across his face, a foolish grin that he couldn't help, and he started toward her, his tiredness forgotten, everything forgotten but the fact of her presence. He strode quickly, impatiently, his heart light and young again, and when he stood before her, for one split second he was going to take her in his arms, crush her to him, hold her. . . .

Then he saw the expression on her face, and everything inside him congealed into a lump of disappointment. "Well, well," he said, fighting for control, "this is a surprise."

"I know."

"Does Brian know you're here?" he asked.

"Brian is in Las Vegas with George Lemming," she said flatly.

"I see."

"I have to talk to you," she said, and he saw her worry her lower lip with her teeth.

He looked away. "It couldn't have waited?"

"No. I have to get this off my chest, Jed. I just can't stand it anymore. This all has to end."

It was so natural to start down the concourse, his duffel bag in one hand, her arm in the other. She didn't pull away, either, and she didn't say anything more about what was bothering her.

It was Jed's idea to stop at the Brown Derby out on Scottsdale Road for their talk. It was a well-known spot, and if Gabriela lost sight of his car as she followed him in her Blazer, then she'd know where it was. He drove through the rain ahead of her—a heavy rain that was beginning to form puddles in the streets—and wondered what on earth she had to tell him that couldn't have waited till morning.

At a traffic light, with the Cherokee's wipers swishing the rain away, Jed couldn't help but recall trips to Phoenix he and Gab had made before, Gab excited about the opening of a new shopping center, he planning to stop by to see his dad at police headquarters. They'd shopped and visited and eaten fast food and taken in the latest movies, necking in the back row until they were dying to get home to Tucson, where there was privacy.

They'd been really good together that way, like two halves of a whole. He had been Gabriela's first, and God, how he'd loved teaching her, listening to her gasps of surprise and raw pleasure, feeling her entire body encase him, moving with his body, rising on that tide. . . .

What in hell was he thinking! Hadn't Gish just chewed his butt out? Gabriela was practically a suspect in this murder investigation, for godsake. At the very least she was probably aiding and abetting Brian Zimmerman. Of course, Brian was her husband; Gabriela could never be prosecuted for her silence, but still . . .

Jed's mind twisted and turned as he slowed down for the washed-out stretches on Scottsdale Road. He glanced in his rearview mirror often, unable to stop himself from worrying about Gab in that old car. But Gab knew how bad the driving could get during a downpour in the desert; she'd be okay, he told himself with little conviction.

He waited in the parking lot at the Brown Derby restaurant for her to pull in, and then they both made a dash for the entrance of the adjacent hotel lobby, getting soaked to the bone in the process. Under other circumstances Jed would have laughed at the two of them panting and soaked, but as it was...

"Wow, is it coming down hard," Gabriela gasped, and he couldn't fail to notice the way her blue blouse clung to every curve, the hardness of her nipples under the clinging cloth.

"I don't know about that road up into the mountains," he said, staring at her. "It could be impassable."

"Oh, no," she said, and looked up sharply. "I have to get back tonight. You don't really think...?"

"Maybe it will be okay," he said in a reassuring voice.

"God, I hope so," she whispered.

They took a table in the restaurant, which was nearly closed for the night. Nearby, loud music blared from a bar, and thunder still boomed occasionally. The rain just kept pouring down, and even the parking lot was filling up with water. Traffic crawled by on the road, lights piercing the watery darkness.

They had coffee—decaf for Gabriela, the real stuff for Jed. The truth was, he was so damn weary from a very long day, nothing could have kept him awake.

And he had been planning on staying in Phoenix for the night, anyway, but now, with Gab here...

He stirred sugar into his coffee and then glanced up at her. She was staring out the window, a little forlorn-looking, decidedly nervous. Whatever it was that had brought her here tonight was eating away at her.

"Okay," he said, putting on a professional face, "maybe you better tell me what the problem is."

She met his eyes but then looked away. What if she was harming Brian rather than helping him? What if... Her lower lip began to tremble.

"Gab? Come on, what is it?" He kept his tone hard, but inside his gut was churning.

And then her eyes filled with tears. Angrily, she wiped at them as she came to a decision.

"You didn't make this drive in that old beater to sit here and say nothing. What is it?" he tried again.

Her glance lifted slowly to his. "I . . . I made a mistake coming here," she began. "If it was anyone but you..."

"And what the hell... What, exactly, does that mean?"

"Nothing," she whispered. "I don't know what it means, Jed, I..."

"Listen," he said, determined not to weaken now, "you drove down here to tell me something. I want to know what it is."

"I...can't. I really thought I could. I thought I was going to help somehow...." She took the paper napkin and blew her nose. "I'm sorry," she said. "I made a terrible mistake. I don't know what I was thinking. Brian has to...Brian's still my husband no matter what."

"Yeah," he said in a hard voice, "I know that. And I know you're protecting him."

"I'm not."

"The hell you aren't!"

"Jed," she said, an anguished, "don't do this. Please."

"You're the one who made this trip, Gab. You're the one who sought me out. I think it was to come clean about the Whittakers." He paused. "Look, I didn't mean to shout at you just now. I realize you made a decision but for some reason you've changed your mind. I have to assume it's a loyalty thing. That's okay," he said quietly. "You're entitled. But you've got to come to grips with something, Gab."

She sniffed and stared at him, uncomprehending.

"I'm going to nail Brian. Maybe you don't know what happened on that ledge, and maybe you do. Either way, your husband's going to take a fall."

"You son of a bitch," she whispered. "You'd like that, wouldn't you. We used to be honest with each other," she said. "But you've changed. God, how you've changed!" And then she rose to her feet. "I'm leaving," she said. "I'm sorry, I thought I could trust you."

"Gab," he began, but she was dashing out of the restaurant.

In the end, of course, neither of them could go anywhere. Jed had followed Gabriela to the parking lot, where she was sitting in her Blazer listening to the radio. To the north, Scottsdale Road was impassable, according to the highway patrol. The alternative route into the mountains was in even worse shape; the gullies and washes were full, spilling out onto the roads. No one was going anywhere.

Standing next to her car in the pouring rain, he told her, "I'll get us both rooms for the night."

"I want to go home," she said from where she sat, stuck, stalled near the exit.

"Don't be foolish. You're not going anywhere till the water recedes. You know how it can get down here."

She gripped the steering wheel tightly.

"Come on," he said. "We'll get help to push the car into a parking space."

It took a while, but eventually Gabriela had to give in and go into the hotel. Jed did get two rooms. He even got them on separate floors, not wanting her to think this was anything but business. He dialed her room, though, just to check on her. After all, she was pretty upset. It was his fault, too, for pushing so hard.

The phone in her room rang several times. He sat on the side of his bed, knees splayed, and began to worry. She wouldn't...she couldn't possibly be dumb enough to try to drive into those mountains....

After five more rings, Jed hung up. Gabriela was smart, upset but smart. She'd never pull a stunt like that. Nonetheless, he dialed her number again.

GABRIELA STEPPED OUT of the shower and wrapped a towel around her, then hung up the underwear she'd just washed. She heard the phone ringing, and she opened the door and rushed to pick it up, but it stopped. Most likely it had been Jed. Well, he'd try again.

Then, towel still on, she called the hotel in Apache Springs and got Lorna. "I'm sorry to call so late," she said. "I'm stuck in Scottsdale. The roads are washed out."

"Uh-huh," Lorna said.

"Really, they are."

"I believe you."

"Well . . . I just wanted to check in, you know, so you didn't worry."

"Oh, I'm not."

"Lorna."

"No, really. Just be careful driving back in the morning," her sister-in-law said.

"I will."

"Is, ah, Jed there?" Lorna couldn't help asking.

Gabriela hesitated slightly. "No."

"Oh, okay. Well, good night, Gabriela. See you around noon."

"Good night," Gabriela was saying when the knock came at the door. It was Jed. She didn't have to open the door to know that. She sat on the side of the bed and felt her nerves leap. Insane, she'd been utterly insane to have made this trip! How could she have thought she was going to explain everything to Jed, that she could have told him about the ax without betraying Brian—the fact that he'd lied? What had she been thinking?

He knocked again, louder. Oh, God! Gabriela cried inwardly, and she knew with a flash of certainty that she'd been kidding herself all along, that she'd made this trip for one reason and one reason only—to see *him*.

Suddenly she wanted to cry.

"Gabriela? Gab? I know you're in there. Open the door."

"Go away," she moaned. "Go away, Jed."

"Open the damn door, Gab."

She sniffed. "My clothes are all drying. Go away, Jed," she repeated, but inwardly she longed to let him in; every fiber of her being was crying out to be held in his arms again.

In the end, she wrapped a sheet around herself and opened the door. Without asking, he stepped past her and closed it firmly, standing there tall and lean and so handsome her stomach knotted.

She swallowed hard and moved backward. "This is wrong," Gabriela whispered. "I was wrong to have come here."

"No," he said in a low voice, "you weren't."

"Don't, for God's sake. Don't do this."

"I'm not going to stay quiet any longer, Gab," he said, his blue eyes bored into hers. "I was a fool to let you go ten years ago. I thought it was history. But now..."

"Don't," she pleaded.

"Even my own wife knew. I didn't believe her at the time, but she hit the nail on the head—I never got over you, Gab."

"Oh, Jed," she whispered, and she felt like a trapped animal.

But he put up a hand. "I'm going to finish and then I'll leave, but I can't pretend anymore. I was serious. I'm going to put your husband behind bars, Gab, and I can't let my feelings for you interfere. I wish you'd come clean. But if you don't, I'll have to push. It's going to hurt. Both of us."

But she was crying now and couldn't really hear him as she sobbed, "Brian is innocent! He didn't do anything! Please, Jed, you have to believe me."

"You know I can't just take your word for it. Be reasonable, Gab."

"Reasonable!" she breathed. "You show up without warning after ten years and you say you're investigating an accident that I witnessed. You want me...us...to think it's a coincidence, a coincidence...." She could hardly breathe, and her chest rose and fell too fast as she gulped lungfuls of air, and she could feel the tears on her cheeks. "You act as if we're suspects and then you tell me my husband's a...a criminal and you're going to put him in jail! Reasonable! Jed, don't you...can't you see what you're doing to me?"

He stood there looking at her, his eyes hooded. The moment stretched out, too long, much too long, and still he said nothing. All Gabriela could hear was her own breath, and the pounding of her pulse.

He finally moved, a slumping of his shoulders. He put a hand up and rubbed his face tiredly. "Yeah," he said gently, "I see."

"Then...you have to—" she swallowed "—you have to stop this. You have to...leave us alone."

"I can't," he said. "It's too late."

Gabriela put a hand up to her mouth as if to stifle a moan.

"Gab," he said raggedly.

She shook her head in hopeless denial.

He took a step toward her. "Gab, please..."

And then he was there, reaching out for her. She tried to back away, afraid, but the wall stopped her. He was relentless, standing so close, his hands on her bare arms now as she clutched the sheet to her. "No," she said, "we can't," but her protests sounded weak even to her own ears.

Jed swore softly and bent his head to hers. She shut her eyes and groped for the strength to resist him, but that, too, failed her. And then his mouth was on her neck, a whisper against her skin, and little shock waves ran up her limbs.

"Don't," she managed to moan, but it came out more like an acquiescence, and she was lost.

Their lips met so tenderly, so gently, at first, a brush, a touch. Heat seared Gabriela's insides, a melting, tremulous heat that made her weak with longing. His hands were on her back, on her bare skin, urgent, and he smelled so good, just as she remembered, the knowledge stored in the very fiber of her being. She could feel the roughness of his whiskers, and she breathed in his scent, his very breath.

He pulled her closer, and her arms went around his neck. "Jed," she whispered, and his answer was a throaty groan, and his lips and his hands were hard on her, as if he meant to possess her, to wipe away the years. She opened to him, the sweet nectar of their mouths mingling, their tongues entwining. Her breath came hot and quick, her fingers kneading his flesh, turning in his hair, her breasts flattened against his chest.

He moved his head, and his tongue traced the outline of her lips, and he drew her bottom lip gently into his mouth, then moved lower, his tongue tracing the ridge of her collarbone, sending delicious darts of pleasure through her. Lower still, along the swell of her breast above the sheet, his tongue trailing incandescent bursts of sensation that made her belly curl.

A split second of sanity invaded Gabriela's brain, a moment of fright at the strength of her own passion. She had to fight the desire that swept her; she couldn't give in, not here, not now. It was wrong. Oh, God, it was wrong.

"Jed," she said, breathless, and somehow she got her hands between them and forced herself to go stiff in his arms as she clutched the sheet tightly. It took every ounce of strength she possessed, because she had never wanted a man this way, not even Jed—she'd been too young, too innocent then. But now she knew...

Jed seemed to be coming back into his senses, as well, and he drew in a deep, quavering breath as he moved away a few inches, his hands still on her arms. "Gab," he breathed, "Gab, I'm so sorry."

But she shook her head. "It was my fault. I...Brian and I..."

"What?" he said, and he tilted her chin up gently until their eyes met. "What about you and Brian?"

"I... It's no good between us. It hasn't been for so long. Oh, Jed, oh, damn it! It's not you. We..."

But he said "Shh," and she couldn't go on; it would sound too much like an excuse for what they'd just done.

Instead, she said, "What are we going to do? How can you go on investigating us? Oh, Jed..."

"Because it's my...duty," he said.

Of course it was. He was Max Mallory's son. And yet Gabriela knew he'd also become his own man now. And she knew that for years she hadn't wanted to admit the glimmering of a truth—Jed was suited to this work; it fit him like a glove. So wrong, she'd been so very wrong. She'd denied her love, pushed him away from her ten years ago, and it had been a terrible, terrible mistake.

The weight of the knowledge pressed on her, a burden she would carry to the grave. And yet Jed was there, close to her, and she could talk to him, touch him for a few fragile, precious moments until it became too hard for both of them. She could no more resist the chance than she could stop breathing.

"Will you be okay?" he was asking, holding her hand, playing with her fingers. He used to do that, and she remembered; her body remembered.

She nodded.

"I won't ask if I can stay," he said, his eyes dark in the dim light.

"No," she whispered, then she averted her glance from his. "Jed . . ."

"Uh-huh?"

"I told Brian, uh, when he left for Vegas, that I wouldn't be there when he got back."

"You did?"

"The gambling . . . I told him if he went this time, I wouldn't be there. I moved my things to the hotel." She felt heat creep up her neck. She was mortified, but it had to come out.

Jed looked at her as if he was going to say something, but he didn't. She was grateful.

"I don't know what's going to happen," she said.

"I'm glad, for lots of reasons."

"That's not why I did it," she said. "It's been coming . . . for a long time. It wasn't you, Jed. All I know is that I can't, I won't, divorce Brian until this is over."

His lip quirked in that way she knew so well. "Is that the good news or the bad news?"

"It's all bad right now."

"No, it's not, Gab. This is good. You and me."

But she bit her lip and shook her head.

He drew her into his arms again and held her, just held her. It felt so good, the comfort, the sweet closeness, the hardness of his body against her. She fit against him as if they had been cut from the same piece of flesh. She nuzzled her face into his neck and sighed.

But it had to end, and Jed was the strong one this time. "I'd better go," he murmured into her ear, "while I can." He drew away from her and smiled. "It'll work out, Gab, you'll see."

"That's what Otto said," she mused aloud. "But some things never do."

He left then, and when he was gone, Gabriela sat on the side of the bed and hugged herself, feeling so terribly empty and cold and alone.

They had breakfast together the next morning, but she was very silent. Jed didn't press her, either, about why she'd driven to Phoenix in the first place, and she was grateful.

It was a cloudless, perfect August day as they drove back to Apache Springs, Gabriela in the lead. It was hot, too, until she reached the tall timber country. But she barely noticed. All she could think about was last night, how very close she'd come to adultery. She glanced in her rearview mirror. Yes, he was still back there, his sunglasses reflecting the light, one arm resting on the open window frame, a hand draped over the top of the steering wheel.

How many times in college had she admired the way Jed seemed so sure of himself, always knowing exactly where he was going, what he had to do, how to do it? It had been irritating sometimes, too, that absolute confidence, his lack of an Achilles' heel. But now she could see that Jed was human, and he'd made mistakes. He'd had an unsuccessful marriage. He was vulnerable and not as sure as he'd once appeared, and somehow that only made her feelings for him stronger and more hopeless.

It was just before noon when Gabriela pulled up in front of the hotel. She hadn't even parked when she saw Brian coming through the front doors. Of course, he was back from his trip—she'd known he would be. And Jed had followed her up the drive, right behind her, pulling up in front of the hotel as Brian came down the stone steps, his face tight and pale with anger.

"So this is why you left me," Brian ground out. "This is your reason, huh? It didn't have a damn thing to do with my gambling, did it?"

"Brian, please, I'll talk to you later," she said, getting out of her car.

Then Jed was there, and Brian swung his gaze toward him. "Did you two have a nice time?" he asked, looking from Gabriela to Jed and back.

"Brian," Gab began.

"Let me tell you," Brian said coldly, "you're not getting away with this. Goddamn U.S. marshal! Well, I fixed your wagon. Think you can take my wife, do you?"

"Brian, I can explain," Gabriela began, but he was in no mood to listen. Instead he grabbed her arm, shot Jed a vicious look and began to steer her toward the hotel.

But Jed stepped up and barred their way. Slowly, he removed his sunglasses and fixed Brian with a hard look. "Lay one finger on her and you'll answer to me," he said in a stone-dead voice.

Brian swore viciously. "Get this through your head, Mallory," he spat, still grasping her arm, "she's *my* wife!"

"I mean it," Jed was saying. "If you so much as…"

But Gabriela had had enough. "Stop this!" she cried, and she pulled free of Brian. "Just stop it!" And with that she lifted her chin and walked up the stone steps past Lorna, who only shook her head.

CHAPTER TWELVE

TWO BEARS SET OUT for the big city at the foot of the snowy mountain, a place he'd been to a few times.

He had his amulet and the deerskin bag of feathers and fur and bones. Out on the highway he put out his thumb in the time-honored tradition and waited until a fellow Apache in a new pickup stopped to give him a ride.

"Where to, Grandfather?" the younger man asked respectfully.

"Flagstaff," Two Bears said, and after he and the young man exchanged information about their clans and found they had a common relative in the Standing Rock clan on Two Bears' mother's side, he settled back for the ride, his withered face impassive. But deep inside, well hidden from this man, he was very much troubled. Forces that had lain dormant for so long had now awakened and were moving toward one another on a collision course. Already there had been two killings, and who knew how many more would occur if he waited any longer to act?

Finally, after watching the young Zimmerman man bury that weapon, it had come to Two Bears, the identity of the one who lived with one foot in each world, the one who could be the catalyst to stop this awakened evil.

He thought about these things as his pleasant clansman drove him straight to his destination in Flagstaff and dropped him off.

"You've got a long way to go to get home, Grandfather," the Apache said. "You take care, hear?"

"I always do," Two Bears replied, and he thanked him for the ride and asked him to give greetings to their common relative.

Inside the antiseptic hospital he asked where Jackson Many Goats could be found. He was directed politely with only a few curious stares, and then he was there, finally, across a desk from Lawrence Many Goats' son.

"I am Two Bears," he said. "I've come from the reservation to see you."

The young man was puzzled. Also, he was impatient, wanting to return to his work, Two Bears could see. "This is important," he said sternly in Apache.

Jackson sat straighter, and his face cleared of the white man's expression. "Yes, Grandfather."

Two Bears told him the story of Kokopelli and the Spanish treasure cave, of the cycle of greed and death that had begun again. He related the dreams and visions he'd been having, the warnings. Something had to be done to avert further disaster.

"I don't understand, Grandfather," Jackson said, frowning. "What does this have to do with me? How can I help?"

"You are in the center. You are the One Who Walks Two Paths."

"But, Grandfather, what can I do?"

"You have seen the beginning already. Two people are dead."

"The Whittakers?" Jackson asked, shocked. "Is that who you mean?"

"That is the name I heard, yes. It is for the treasure. You must prevent more from dying."

"But how, what on earth . . . ?"

"You will know at the right time, just as I knew to come to you."

"Old One, please, explain this a little more. Do you have some kind of proof? Do you know something more about the Whittakers' deaths? Did you see them die?"

Two Bears shook his head. "I only know what Kokopelli tells me, and now I have told you. It is for the treasure."

He left Jackson Many Goats' office and walked through the noisy, stinking city where strangers in bright clothes made over the land into their own image. He found his way back to the highway and put out his thumb for the journey home. He was content; he had fulfilled his responsibility for now.

JED WAS STILL STIFF with anger when he drove to the Pines Motel, where he'd kept his room. To see the way Brian treated Gabriela, spoke to her . . . He'd been on the verge of getting real physical there, doing something to stop Brian's filthy accusations. If only Brian knew how good Gab was, how loyal, the torture she was going through. He stared straight ahead through the dusty windshield, and a muscle in his jaw jumped. Brian Zimmerman wasn't worth one hair on Gab's head.

Oh, but you are, Jed told himself mockingly. *You're the good guy, right? And the good guy always gets the girl in the end.*

Not this time.

Gab wouldn't divorce Brian when he was in trouble, and he was going to be in worse trouble soon. The better Jed did his job, the less chance he'd have to win Gab back. A real catch-22. Well, she'd left Brian, so maybe she'd get away from him little by little, move somewhere else eventually, and if Jed couldn't have her, at least he wouldn't have to keep picturing her with Zimmerman.

No, Brian Zimmerman was going to be behind bars.

There were two messages for Jed when he checked at the front desk. One was from a TV reporter also staying at the Pines. It read, "Please give me a call. Interested in any updates you have." Jed crumpled that pink slip in his hand. The other, however, he paid heed to. It was from Arthur Gish. "Call in at once," it read. The time on the message was only five minutes ago.

He dialed the number from his room and got through to his boss right away. Arthur Gish's voice was ominously quiet. "I got a call just now, Mallory."

"Yes, sir?"

"I got a call from Brian Zimmerman, your suspect."

"What?"

"Oh, yes, and the man was pretty ticked off."

Jed's mind whirled. "Brian Zimmerman called you?"

"He sure did. He told me, Mallory, and please say this isn't true, he told me that you're sleeping with his wife. Tell me it's not true, Mallory, or I'll have your goddamn badge!"

Jed closed his eyes and gripped the receiver. Damn.

"Mallory?"

"No, I'm not sleeping with his wife," he replied in a level voice.

"I don't believe you! You're compromising this case because you can't keep your hands off some old flame? Think of how it's gonna look in court—think of it!"

"I've done my job, sir. I have not had any relations with Mrs. Zimmerman that might compromise the case."

"I knew I should have sent Taylor, damn it!"

"You wanted me because I knew the Zimmermans," Jed reminded him tightly.

"Okay, okay, so it's done," Gish snapped. "But I want you out of there, Mallory. I want this case wrapped up immediately. A day, two at the very outside, that's it. If you don't have hard proof by then, you're through, anyway, and I'll send someone else to finish up. You understand?"

"Yes, sir."

"You better not have lost this for us, Mallory. The FBI will be laughing its butt off, you know that? And I won't cover for you on this. It's your ass, Deputy."

"I understand, sir."

"The hell you do." And Gish hung up.

Jed took a deep breath while a sense of guilt swept him. It was as if his father was watching him, disapproving, shaking his head. Jed, boy, can't you see what you've done? Messed up again.

He sat there for a minute riddled with doubt, and then he shook it off. He wasn't a failure and he hadn't compromised the case, damn it! He was a good deputy, and he was doing his job. Forget Gish, forget everyone else. Concentrate on the job, on hard evidence, on the murder weapon and the motive. If Jed found those, the case was made, and it didn't matter about him and Gab.

Okay, he had a day, maybe two. He could stretch that, maybe to three, until Gish pulled him off the case. He'd solve it by then, and...

And what? Return to Arlington, take up where he'd left off? Forget about Gab, forget the way she felt and smelled, and forget the taste of her tears? Leave her alone to somehow get out of a disastrous marriage to a man who might soon be in jail?

God, he'd wanted her last night. Jed ran his hands through his hair and groaned. He'd wanted her so bad that it hurt. And she'd been so frightened, so miserable, so confused. Trying to be fair and loyal. Gab would never betray her husband. There had to be some other way to find out the truth. He couldn't ask her again.

And where was she right now? Was Brian cornering her somewhere in that hotel, swearing at her again, hurting her?

He couldn't do anything to help her. Whatever he did would only make things worse. It was hard not to go back to the hotel or call to see how she was, but Brian's sister was there, and there were guests, and Gab was smart enough not to be alone with her husband. She could take care of herself. He had to believe that or he'd go mad.

Okay, forget it. He had a job to do. *Get a grip,* he told himself.

He stood and went to the wall where he'd tacked all his photographs and lists and put his hands on his hips.

"Okay, Judge, what'd you do to Brian Zimmerman that made the man pull out that ax?" he asked for the hundredth time. He thought a moment. "You were having a good time, a little tired, it was getting late.... Maybe you had something on Zimmerman. But what? He was your host, that was all. Well, then, maybe you had something Zimmerman wanted. Maybe you were working on a court case and Zimmerman wanted a certain verdict.... Oh, hell," Jed said. None of it fit. And that was the whole problem. Motive. What in the hell was it? He couldn't get the truth from Judge Whittaker, and he sure wasn't going to get it from Zimmerman.

Jed went around town that afternoon, covering new ground, asking more questions. He went into the Tippler Bar before the work crowd rolled in, when the barkeep was reading the paper and dust motes danced in the slanted light from the fly-specked windows.

Sure, the guy knew Brian, had known him since high school. A good guy. Yeah, got into debt in Vegas, but he'd manage. Terrible about that accident, wasn't it.

"I'm investigating the accident," Jed said, holding out his badge and ID.

The bartender clammed up then, rattled his paper and refused further comment.

Jed thought of interviewing Brian's parents, but he remembered Ellie Zimmerman, so sick, and Otto wasn't well, either, according to Gab. And what, after all, could they tell him?

He needed to know Zimmerman a whole lot better, needed to know what really made the man tick. He racked his brain. Brian had to have left a clue somewhere; all criminals did, even the smart ones. You had to get into their minds, think like they did, then it became logical. The problem here was that without a motive, Jed couldn't think like Brian.

Gab knew something, though a tiny piece to the puzzle, and maybe if Jed knew what it was, he could use it to figure things out. Maybe he couldn't. Brian hadn't told anyone the whole story, Jed was sure. He couldn't. But somebody knew something.

Brian Zimmerman was a man's man, a good-buddy sort. He'd go to his friends if he needed help. Not his wife, not his parents. His buddies.

George Lemming?

Jed walked back to the motel, hands in his pockets, head bent forward, thinking.

He got into the Cherokee and drove out to Lemming's base camp, hoping he'd catch him there. On the way he framed his questions. Time to put a little pressure on. Gab had told him that he and Brian had just gone to Las Vegas.

Why? All of a sudden, in the middle of everything going on here, Brian had left for Vegas. With George.

Lemming was there, all right, and he scowled when he saw Jed.

"I'm busy," he said rudely.

"So am I, Mr. Lemming, but I'd appreciate your cooperation. If necessary, of course, I can get a subpoena and make you come to Flagstaff, but I'd hate to have to do that."

George swore.

"I understand you just went to Vegas with Brian Zimmerman," Jed said. "What were you doing there, if I may ask?"

"I was gambling. Brian had some business to take care of."

"What business?"

"Ask him."

"All right. Did you win anything?" Jed asked mildly, pushing, annoying Lemming, hoping he'd get angry and slip up.

Lemming gave him a swift look, then shrugged. "Win a little, lose a little."

"You get your room comp, Mr. Lemming?"

"Sure."

"Where?"

Lemming told him.

"That takes more than winning a little."

"Sometimes I win a lot," Lemming said, grinning wolfishly.

"Mind if I call the casino and check on your stay?"

"Suit yourself.

The phone in the trailer rang then, and George answered it. He turned his back on Jed and lowered his voice. Jed didn't really listen, but he heard a few snatches of conversation. A time, a date, something about air time and elevation. Business stuff, broken off abruptly when George said he'd call back later. He hung up and turned to Jed. "Anything else?" he asked belligerently.

"Not this time," Jed said mildly. "Thanks for your help."

Lemming was hiding something. Jed could feel it. It was experience and instinct and some inborn talent that made a good investigator. The man's replies were too easy, too pat, too... prepared. As if he and Brian had rehearsed their stories to get them just right, perfectly coordinated. Something had happened in Las Vegas, if indeed that was where they'd gone. He'd check on it.

Jed drove back to Apache Springs, his mind thrumming with possibilities, scenarios. The motive, the damn missing motive. Why had Brian Zimmerman done it? Revenge, jealousy, power, greed, self-defense? Those were the usual motives, but none seemed to fit in this case.

And he had two days—more like one and a half—to wrap this up. Great.

He planned on returning to his motel, but found himself driving past it, through town and up the Apache Springs Hotel drive. He couldn't stay away another second, worrying, wondering about Gab. He wanted to see her face-to-face, to assure himself that she was all right. If only her husband wasn't there, it'd be all right. If he was . . . Well, Jed would deal with it.

He parked off to the side of the building so that the sheriff's Cherokee was not so obvious and went into the lobby. Lorna Kessler was behind the front desk.

"Well, Deputy Mallory," she said, cocking her head, "I wonder who you've come to see."

"Is she around?" he asked.

"She's in the kitchen, some problem with a delivery." Lorna looked at him. "You'll go easy on her, won't you? I don't know how much more she can take."

"I just want to see if she's okay. Believe me, hurting Gab is the last thing on earth I want to do."

"Well, you have hurt her, maybe unintentionally, but you're making it hard, you and my brother." Then Lorna gestured with her hand. "The kitchen's through there, and don't worry, Brian hardly ever sets foot in it."

It was hot and steamy in the big kitchen, noisy, people chattering, pots clanging. He saw Gab at the back door, her head close to that of a white-hatted chef. She looked up, startled, when she saw Jed, and excused herself.

"What are you doing here?" she asked in an alarmed whisper.

"I wanted to see if you were okay. Look, Gab, I don't want to cause trouble, but I feel responsible, and..."

"I'm okay," she interrupted.

"Brian isn't bothering you?"

"He left. He went somewhere." She shrugged. "I don't know where." She looked around the noisy kitchen and then pulled Jed outside the back door. Sudden quiet encased them.

"I was worried about you," he said. She was so close, looking at him with those clear green, luminous eyes. His fingers itched for the feel of her skin, her hair. He took a jagged breath.

"I'm okay," she repeated, then she searched his face. "Brian said... he said he called your headquarters. He said..."

"Yeah, he did that, all right."

"Are you in big trouble?"

"In a manner of speaking."

"Um" was all she said, then she asked, "What now? Where do you go from here?"

"I keep doing my job, looking for evidence, looking for a motive. It's not over yet."

"Please, stop this," she said, her head coming up. "Just stop it."

"No. It's time you start facing the facts."

"The only fact staring me in the face is you, Jed Mallory," she whispered harshly. "You and that damn stubborn streak!"

But he shook his head, saying, "Just think about it, Gab, just think about what you really saw out there. Was Brian trying to help Clare or was it something else?"

Her eyes flashed. "Go to hell," she said abruptly and then stormed back inside, slamming the kitchen door in his face.

Well done, he told himself as he headed away. *That was really cool, Mallory.* Now he'd lost her for good.

CHAPTER THIRTEEN

THE CLOCK WAS RUNNING OUT for Jed, and as he grabbed a light meal at a local diner he knew he was going to have to push Brian Zimmerman as hard as he'd ever pushed a suspect before. He ate a BLT and picked at a side order of coleslaw, and formed a plan—plan B, because plan A sure as heck hadn't worked.

His plan would have to be implemented tomorrow, because he was darn certain the following day Gish was going to order him back to headquarters.

Jed walked toward the Pines Motel slowly, thinking, absently nodding at people he passed, his hands shoved in his jeans pockets. Plan B had possibilities. He'd have to goad Brian Zimmerman into it. No, Jed thought, and a smile played on his lips, he'd bluff the man. After all, Zimmerman was a gambler. It wasn't going to be easy, but if he handled the plan tactfully, maybe Jed could pull it off.

Back in his room he telephoned an old friend of his dad's in Phoenix, a chief of detectives who was very influential in the metro police department.

"I'm fine, Martin," Jed said. "Yes, still with the Marshals Service. Uh-huh."

"So to what do I owe this call, Jed? If you're anything like Max, I'm betting it's not social."

Jed laughed and relaxed against the pillows of the bed, one arm behind his head. "I was wondering," he said, "if you happen to have someone real good at handling polygraphs." He briefly related the story about the judge and the Zimmermans.

"Lie-detector tests? Sure. You bet. Sammy Kahn's good, been with the force about eight years now. Real reliable."

"I see," Jed said, and he laid his plan on the table. "What do you think, Martin, can I line this Sammy Kahn up for tomorrow?"

"I can get that done for you. The question is, kid, can you get this Zimmerman character to cooperate?"

"I'm going to give it my best shot, Martin."

"Well, good luck. Give me a call if it's a go and I'll get you all fixed up."

"Thanks," Jed said.

"Oh, we always do our best to cooperate with you feds, no problem."

Jed did not miss the undertone of sarcasm. "Sure," he said, and laughed again. He spent the rest of the evening putting in order the questions he wanted Sammy Kahn to ask Zimmerman while he was hooked up to the polygraph. The only thing left to do now was to talk—bluff—good old Brian into going along with it. If Jed couldn't pull this off, Zimmerman might literally get away with murder.

He found Brian the next morning out in the pool pump house, working with a maintenance man on a faulty valve.

Brian looked up from where he sat cross-legged on the concrete floor. "Not you again, Mallory," he growled.

Jed was aware of Gab standing over by the outdoor bar, staring in his direction. He couldn't help but notice the crisp red-and-white-striped shirt she was wearing or the white miniskirt. She was all legs and arms and a mass of wild midnight hair....

He shook himself mentally and turned his full attention to Brian. "Could I talk to you a minute in private?" he asked Brian, very amiably. Mr. Nice Guy.

Brian shrugged, stood, wiped his hands on a rag and motioned for Jed to go outside. "Okay," he said, clearly impatient, "what now? I'm getting damn sick and tired of this, Mallory."

Jed laid it out for him, his tone matter-of-fact. "It's like this, Brian. My boss is getting calls from the president himself demanding that we wrap this case up one way or the other. Now, I'm probably going to be called back to Washington tomorrow...."

"What a pity."

"Anyway, that won't be the end of it. Arthur Gish will just send someone else, and someone else after that. It's not going to end as long as there are any questions. So here's the deal. You submit to a lie-detector test and..."

"Are you joking?"

"Not at all. It would get us off your back for good."

"Or get me arrested! Those things aren't reliable. I mean, they're so unreliable that you can't even use the results in court! Why the hell would I..."

But Jed put up a hand. "That's exactly my point. They aren't totally reliable. No results could be used for or against you. But if the tests are in your favor, Gish will call off the hounds. If the results are iffy, well, Gish is already prepared to hassle you for as long as he's getting it from higher up."

"Hell," Brian muttered, hands on his hips. "I don't know." Then he looked up sharply. "I think I better call my lawyer, Mallory."

"Hey," Jed said, "call him. I'm sure he'll advise you to take the polygraph. Like I said, it can't be used against you in court, but it could get us out of your hair for good. What have you got to lose?"

"I'll call him," Brian said, his brow furrowed, his temper just barely in check. "But this really ticks me off. You read every day about innocent people getting charged with crimes.... I never thought it could happen to me. This is the pits, Mallory."

"Yeah," Jed said, "I'm sure."

Brian did head into the hotel to call his lawyer and Jed sweated it out. It could go either way. Of course, the first thing Brian's lawyer was going to assume was that Zimmerman was innocent. That would make him think the polygraph was a sound idea, a way to clear his client once and for all. And it was true, no matter what the results, a lie detector test was inadmissible in a court of law. Maybe this would just work. All Jed hoped to accomplish was to perhaps get a hint as to what pushed Brian's buttons. Even the smallest clue could lead Jed to uncovering the motive. Heck, he didn't even care if the needle leapt off the graph when Brian was asked the most pertinent questions about the ax and about the accident—Jed already knew the man was as guilty as sin. But without a motive... Well, no arrest was ever going to stick.

While he waited for Brian, he was aware of Gab moving around the pool area, giving directions to waiters who would be serving lunch out here, straightening chairs and lounges, checking inventory at the bar. There were a few guests in the pools, their skin rosy pink. Others sat around glass-topped tables having coffee and croissants. Jed wondered how they could eat with the stench of sulfur in their nostrils—it made him kind of nauseous after a time.

He leaned against the red-stone wall of the hotel, folded his arms and let his gaze drift back to Gab. She was talking to two guests now, fluffing the blond mop of hair on the daughter's head as she spoke. The little girl of maybe five or six laughed and ducked and tugged at Gab's white skirt, teasing her in return, and Jed couldn't help but think that some man should have given Gabriela children. He could have been that man....

"Okay" came a voice at his ear, shaking him from his reverie. "Okay, Mallory, my lawyer says it's all right. He thinks it's bull, though, and said your boss is going to hear from him if you guys harass me one more time. I should have called him days ago, I guess." Brian shrugged. "So when do you want to do this?"

"We can drive down to Phoenix right now and be back by late afternoon," Jed said.

Zimmerman sighed. "Guess I'll go change clothes. Give me ten minutes."

"Sure," Jed said, fighting a triumphant grin, "I'll just call Phoenix and make sure they're ready."

"This stinks," Brian mumbled as he strode off toward his cabin.

Jed called Martin to make sure Sammy Kahn was available. No problem, Martin assured him. And then he went back out to the pool area to find Gab, not knowing if he'd ever have the opportunity to see her alone again. That notion was more unsettling than he'd dreamed.

When he approached her she looked caught somewhere between anger and confusion. "I don't want to talk to you," she began, and started to walk away.

Carefully, hoping no one noticed, he caught her arm. "Just give me one minute, Gab, one lousy minute. Tomorrow I'll probably be out of here for good. Gab...?"

Finally she stopped. He dropped his hand. "What did you want with Brian just now?" she asked. "Where's he going?"

"We're driving to Phoenix. He agreed to take a polygraph."

"A...lie-detector test?"

He repeated his explanation.

"I don't believe you," she said. "You wouldn't make him do it if he had nothing to lose."

"Every word I said is true. I told Brian the same thing."

She bit her lip and frowned. "And he said he'd do it."

"Yes."

"You're trying to trick him."

"Oh?" Jed said. "But how can he be tricked? He's an innocent man."

"You know what I mean," she said and she looked at her feet.

But Jed let that subject drop. "He'll be back here in a couple of minutes," he said. "I only wanted to tell you that...well, I wish we could be straight with each other, Gab."

She stared at him with those luminous green eyes. "I *have* been straight with you. I've told you too much about my life already. I feel like a traitor. Don't push me, Jed."

"I've been straight, too, I guess. It's just that, well, seeing you again made me realize how I feel. I know you're in the middle of a mess here, but I also know it's not going to last forever, and you're leaving your husband...."

"Yes," she said, "I am going to file for divorce. But I told you I'd never begin proceedings until Brian's in the clear and this thing is all over."

"Okay. Look, I just want you to know I'm here if you need help or someone to talk to, Gab. Anything, anytime."

"Stop," she whispered.

"I mean it. Anything..."

"Stop it," she breathed, and he could see the rise and fall of her breasts. "I'm so messed up right now I... I just can't let myself think about anything like that, Jed. Please, don't ask me to. I just can't."

He nodded solemnly. "I'll respect that."

"You're tearing me apart, Jed," she said. And then finally she looked up and met his gaze. "What's going to happen if Brian... incriminates himself today? I mean..."

"Let's just wait and see," he said softly.

She bit her lower lip and he could see moisture collecting in her eyes. God, how he wanted to hold her, just to touch her, comfort her. "Jed," she whispered, "you've got to tell me. I'm just so confused about everything. I know what you said before, but do you honestly, in your heart and in your professional judgment, think Brian... hurt those people?"

He watched as a tear slid down her cheek, and when she unconsciously reached up to wipe it away, he did it instead, tenderly.

"Tell me," she said.

"Yes," he replied quietly, "yes, I do think Brian is guilty."

"Oh, dear God," she whispered. Her hand went up to her chest and she backed away from him, her eyes wide, then she turned and walked quickly across the patio. She walked faster and faster, until she was running, disappearing inside in a flash of red and white and long legs and flying black hair, and he wished to hell he'd had it in him to lie.

THEY REACHED PHOENIX by early afternoon, the two men in the Coconino County sheriff's vehicle. Jed pulled into the downtown police headquarters parking lot and turned the engine off, the air conditioner making a soft hissing noise as it died. Neither had spoken more than two words since they left Apache Springs, but Jed had something he wanted to get off his chest. It was a truth that had to be aired. Another man would never have verbalized it, but Jed was not just any man. Max Mallory had raised him to be a little too honest, he guessed. And then, too, maybe Max had raised him to be very clever, even a little devious when it came to catching criminals. Jed might subconsciously want to rattle Brian just before he went in to take the test. Either way, Jed was going to say his piece.

"Before we go inside," he said, turning to Brian Zimmerman, "I've got to tell you that if there was one chance in hell I thought I could get Gabriela back, I'd do it."

Brian swung his head around in disbelief. "You've got a lot of nerve, buddy, telling me that. Are you nuts?"

Jed gave a humorless laugh. "Maybe I am, but I just know that I want this out in the open. I wouldn't want you to think I'm pulling any underhanded crap with Gab."

"You're talking about my wife, man," Brian said tightly.

"She's moved out."

"It's temporary. We had a fight. We'll get back together. And it's none of your goddamn business, anyway."

"She told me, so I figure it's my business."

Brian swore under his breath. "You're out of here, Mallory, you know it and I know it. You can't prove I did anything and you're in trouble with your boss. You're history. Leave Gabriela alone!"

Jed ignored the speech. "One more thing, Zimmerman," he said slowly, "I swear to God, if you ever lay a finger on her again, you'll have me to answer to."

Brian clenched his jaw. "Just go to hell," he said, swinging open the car door, and it was then that Jed noticed he seemed to sway a little, holding on to the door with one hand, his other going to his head.

"Hey, you all right?" Jed asked.

For a minute Brian said nothing, just braced himself against the door, his eyes squeezed shut. Then finally he straightened and collected himself. "Let's get this over with," he muttered, closing the door, appearing to be perfectly normal.

Sammy Kahn was waiting for them. Earlier that morning, Jed had faxed down to Phoenix the list of questions but of course Kahn was the expert; he'd know exactly how to put them.

Jed waited with his father's friend Martin when Brian, looking abrasively cool and collected, went into a private room with Kahn.

Before the door was closed, Jed heard Brian say, "God, I'm really nervous about this. I don't know what to expect...."

"They all say that," Martin told Jed as they went for coffee. "I guess they figure if the test comes out badly they can fall back on the old I-was-real-nervous excuse."

"Probably some of that's true," Jed said, thinking that maybe he'd outmaneuvered himself, trying to shake Zimmerman like that. Maybe he wasn't so damn smart after all, trying to play God.

"Damn tootin'," Martin replied. "I wouldn't want to be in Zimmerman's shoes. I can't believe you talked him into this."

But Jed shrugged. "He thinks that no matter how it comes out I'll get off his back. And the truth is, without some sort of concrete lead, I am up the creek."

"I've been there myself," Martin said as they entered a cafeteria in the police headquarters.

In the end the test results were inconclusive. Sammy Kahn showed Jed the graph sheets, which he'd marked with red pencil. Each question he'd asked Zimmerman had a pencil mark next to the corresponding needle position on the graph.

"Here's where I began with the simple stuff, his name, age, place of birth, you know. You can see where the needle leapt when he gave his address. He was pretty rattled."

"Is that unusual?" Jed asked, leaning over Kahn's desk.

"Not in the least. Some people are so stressed out that little spurts of adrenaline occur quite randomly. Others try to force it. You know, so that when I ask a pertinent question and the needle goes off the paper, they can say they were a wreck and compare it to the nonquestions."

"Uh-huh," Jed muttered. He'd heard of this before. It was the main reason polygraph results were inadmissible in court.

"Okay," Kahn went on, "here's another big leap on the graph. I asked him if he was married, then I asked if they lived together. The needle flew off the paper when he replied that they were sort of separated. He didn't calm down for several minutes."

"Uh-huh," Jed mumbled, one hand absently rubbing his jaw.

"Now, here—" Kahn pointed to the graph "—I began the questions about the hike he took with his wife and the Whittakers. Right here, the needle took a jump when I asked what the purpose of the hike was. He told me it was a tour offered by the hotel. I asked him the specifics, and he said they went on a treasure hunt. At that point the needle jumped pretty good." Kahn showed Jed, who found that interesting. He made a mental note of it.

"Okay," Sammy Kahn continued, "here we see the details of the hike. Not much response except for the day being very hot. I couldn't guess what that means. Anyway, the next big leap is right here, when I asked if they were hiking near the Apache reservation, like you told me. I wouldn't have expected so sharp a reaction."

"Interesting," Jed said, making a note of that, too.

"So here's where we get to the crux of the interview. Right here's where I ask about the condition of the trail where the Whittakers fell to their deaths. I asked specifically if the trail was dangerous. The needle flew. I asked if the ledge began to crumble, and again the needle flew. Same thing happened when I popped in the question about his ax. But then he settled down right here." Kahn pointed.

"What does that tell you?" Jed asked, shifting his weight.

"That the trail was truly in bad shape and that he had an ax."

"Uh-huh," Jed said.

"Then we go on to the most pointed question—did he strike Judge Whittaker with a weapon. Look at this." Kahn showed Jed where at first the needle just went along on an even line, then took a few small jumps.

"What does that mean?"

Kahn smiled. "He's a real cool customer. He was able to prepare himself for the question but couldn't quite make it all the way through."

"Could it mean he's innocent?"

"Well, now, if I was asked that in a courtroom under oath, I'd have to say his reaction was inconclusive."

"Um," Jed said, disappointed.

Then Kahn showed him what he considered to be a very interesting reaction to one of the last questions. "Right here I asked if his wife saw the victims fall to their deaths. See this? The needle went haywire."

"So?"

"So, I'd say your Mr. Zimmerman is in a panic over what his wife actually witnessed. I put in a question of my own...hope you don't mind...but I asked if his wife remembered more than she'd told the police.''

"And?"

"He showed some reaction. I'd say he's worried about it, but not unduly so."

"Inconclusive," Jed muttered, wishing things were clearer, wishing for some kind of magic here. "Damn."

Kahn shrugged. "Hey, we're dealing with human emotions. They're not an exact science."

"Yeah, I know." Jed sighed. "You've done a great job, really. I'm just over a barrel on this case."

"My overall view of this session is this," Kahn said. "The results are basically inconclusive. The response I got at the mention of this treasure hunt thing and the Apache reservation were just as strong as the questions about the cause of the deaths. Your Mr. Zimmerman is on the edge."

"How's that?"

"Either he's been pushed too far by you, Mr. Mallory, or he's one guilty sucker."

"Great," Jed said, straightening.

"Well," Sammy Kahn said, "my advice is this. Look into the treasure hunt aspect and find out what connections there are to Zimmerman and the reservation." Then he cocked his head. "What the hell is this treasure hunt, anyway?"

Jed had to think. "Oh, it's some gimmick the resort hotel uses to attract guests. You know, old Spanish treasure hidden in the mountains." Jed shrugged.

"I've heard that baloney before," Kahn said, and laughed.

"Yeah," Jed agreed.

The test had taken more time than Jed had antici-
pated, and as they left Phoenix the shadows were long,
the sky splashed with blood red and orange and pur-
ple, a wildly beautiful desert sunset.

Brian finally said, "Well? I hope this gets you off
my back, Mallory. I told you I was innocent. Your so-
called expert medical examiners should be fired."

"What makes you think the test indicated your innocence?" Jed asked.

"What else would it show?" Brian replied, and Jed
felt a muscle tighten in his jaw. Zimmerman was a
cold-blooded murderer, Jed thought, but the SOB just
might get away with it.

IT WAS A LONG, LONG DAY for Gabriela. She felt as if
a terrible storm was brewing overhead, the clouds
massive and black, ready to burst open. And there was
nothing she could do to stop it.

She even told Lorna her fears. "It's awful. I feel as
if something terrible is about to happen, but I can't
put my finger on it."

"It's Jed Mallory, is what it is. He's got you all
botched up."

But Gabriela shook her head. "No, it's not really
him. I've felt this way ever since the accident."

"You're tired."

"Of course I'm tired. I don't think I've had a
night's sleep since that day."

"Everyone feels all shaky and confused when they
get overtired. It's all going to work out, Gabriela.
You'll see. And this mess with my brother... leaving
him, you know, well, that can't be helping. What are
you going to do about that, anyway?" Lorna asked
carefully.

Gabriela sighed heavily. "I'm divorcing him." They were sitting outside at a table, taking an afternoon break, and she looked up and met her sister-in-law's eyes. "You knew he went to Las Vegas again with George? Lorna, I begged him, he promised, then he just turned right around and went."

"He needs help. Real bad."

"It's more. It's... We haven't been together, Lorna, for a long time. I... Oh, God, this is so embarrassing."

But Lorna patted her clasped hands. "Do you love him at all?"

Gabriela tried to search her soul. There was no easy answer. "Not in a married way, not anymore."

The women were silent for a minute, and then Lorna said, "What about Jed? I'm not prying, but do you think that maybe you never got over him? Maybe he was always the right one, Gabriela."

But there was no real answer to that, either. "How can I think about that right now?" she said. "Jed's trying to put Brian in jail, for God's sake!"

Lorna nodded. "But you have feelings for him. You can't deny it, I've seen you two. When you come within twenty feet of each other you look as if you're both going to fall apart."

Gabriela drew in a quavering breath. Everything Lorna was saying was true. But how could she feel that way, be so disloyal to Brian?

"No wonder you feel as if something awful's going to happen," Lorna said. "It probably is."

"Thanks, thanks a lot," Gabriela said. "You're a real help."

And yet it was true. As evening approached and Brian and Jed were still not back, the sense of impending doom persisted. Soon that big thunderhead over her was going to burst and all hell was going to break loose.

She took the elevator up to Otto and Ellie's, then stood in the cluttered corridor for a long time. She was going to tell Brian's parents she was definitely filing for divorce, tell them now before the men returned with news about the polygraph. No matter how that turned out, she never wanted anyone to think her decision was based on anything but the fact that her marriage had been over for a long time.

She finally raised her hand to knock on their door, but something stayed it, a sudden flashing image of Jed that morning seizing her. He'd looked at her with his blue eyes—compassionate, shrewd, assessing, knowing—absolutely, brutally truthful eyes, and told her he thought her husband was guilty of murder.

Even now she shrank from the memory, and she realized that must be the cause of her sense of impending doom. How could she face Brian's parents? What would they do if, God forbid, Jed was right?

She stood there in front of their door paralyzed with indecision. Maybe she should put off telling them about the divorce. They were already so upset. She stood there and searched her conscience, seeking the truth, and it came to her, without a doubt, that she would have left Brian, guilty or innocent, Jed or no Jed, and she felt better, a little better, anyway.

And then, swept with guilt and a terrible knot of anxiety in her chest, she knocked on the door. She took a deep breath and went in.

CHAPTER FOURTEEN

TWO BEARS AWAKENED at dawn with the dream-vision so clear in his head that his lips were still moving in conversation with Kokopelli. The weapon, the thing for which the friend of Jackson Many Goats had been searching, which the strange baying dogs and noisy men had been trying to find, was in a clump of scrub oak. He had watched from afar and seen the blond man bury it. Now, however, he finally knew what to do with the knowledge.

He rose, groaning with the stiffness of great age, but as he walked and the sun rose to warm him, the stiffness subsided, and he was there, already digging with his turquoise-handled knife when the canyon below was still cast in black shadows.

It was not far to the road, and although he had to wait for some time for a car to stop and give him a lift, he had great patience. He got out at the Apache Springs Hotel entrance, and, carrying the weapon wrapped in a cloth he'd brought for that very purpose, he made his way up the drive and around the hotel to the hot sulfur pools.

She was there, of course, the pretty Mrs. Zimmerman, and she was very surprised to see him when he caught her gaze through the rising steam.

He walked around a pool and stood in front of her, giving her a courteous greeting.

"Two Bears," she said, "it's good to see you, but what..."

He laid the cloth-wrapped object down in front of her, knowing it was the right thing to do but not sure why it had to be so. Puzzled, she looked down at the bundle, then up to his face again, but wisely she did not press him for useless talk.

He nodded to her, turned and left that place.

IT OCCURRED TO GABRIELA for a split second that confronting Brian might be dangerous, but her desperate need to know the truth outweighed any other concerns, her disbelief and horror propelling her. She finally found him at the cabin fixing himself lunch. She burst in, flinging the door open, all thought, all feeling, suspended, her body quivering with her need to know, just to know. She said nothing, merely dropped the ax in its wrapping on the table next to his half-made tuna fish sandwich. Her chest was so tight she couldn't talk, but her gaze never left his face.

"What's this?" Brian asked.

Her eyes flashed emerald sparks.

"Oh, for Pete's sake, Gabriela, I'm not in the mood...."

"Open it," she said.

Sighing in exasperation, Brian unwrapped the cloth.

It lay there, some dirt stuck to the leather-wrapped handle, the stainless steel winking dully, the rust-colored stains on the sharp edge faint and innocuous-looking.

Brian stared at it for a long time. He said nothing. Then slowly, as if his head weighed far too much, he raised his eyes to hers. They were frighteningly empty, blue pools without bottom, and she drew in a sharp breath.

"Yeah?" he said finally. "So?"

She swallowed, all her nerves thrumming, the black horror closing in, taking all the oxygen out of the air. "It's your ax," she managed to say, and it was remarkable how normal she sounded.

"Is it?"

"Brian..."

He pushed himself up from the table suddenly, frowning, and she took an inadvertent step back. His voice was too quiet when he spoke. Even and quiet. "Where'd you get this?"

She shook her head. "It doesn't matter."

"You've been spying on me, you and your boyfriend," he said in a dangerously soft voice, "haven't you?"

She gasped. "No, I haven't, no, Brian."

"Then where in hell did you get it?" His tone was angry now, louder.

"It doesn't matter," she repeated.

"Not Mallory, not that jerk Mallory?"

She shook her head, knowing instantly how foolhardy she had been. She should have told Jed, called him right away. She never should have...

Brian was regarding her with a mixture of bemusement and anger. It was almost better than his previous deadly quiet. She had to ask, though. She had to. "You killed Evan with this, didn't you?" she breathed.

Nothing. No reaction. She wanted to scream, hysteria near the surface. Sweat dampened her all over; the cabin abruptly became claustrophobic. "Why?" she cried. "Why, Brian, why?"

For a moment he merely stared at her, and then he did an odd thing. He swayed a little, squeezed his eyes shut, and mumbled as if talking to someone else. Something about his loss of control terrified her, but she couldn't think about it now that his eyes had focused on her once more.

"Why?" she asked again.

He told her flatly. "We found the treasure, Evan and I. And he was going to tell the authorities because it was on the reservation. It was mine, that treasure. I'd been looking for years, and there was no way I was going to turn it over to the Apaches."

"The treasure."

"Yes, the Spanish treasure. In a cave. On the damned reservation, of all places."

"It can't be," she muttered.

"It is, it sure is. It's there, gold and weapons and collectors' stuff. Worth millions. Oh, it's there, all right, Gabriela."

She shuddered, then felt an overwhelming urge to laugh, felt it bubble up inside her like vomit. She fought it down. Jed ... She had to get to a phone.

"I'm rich now, Gabriela, you know that? It's up there waiting, and..." He paused. "I was sorry about Clare, you know. She saw it, though, the whole thing, and she went after me. So I had to push her."

"But you're not sorry about Evan," she whispered.

"Look," Brian said, "you don't get it. I offered to split it with him, fifty-fifty, but he knew the law about artifacts found on reservations belonging to the Indians. He refused to go for it. What was I supposed to do? Use your head, Gabriela."

"It's over, Brian," she said in a low voice, trying to keep her tone logical and matter-of-fact. He was crazy, and she had to get him to see that. "It's all over. You know that, don't you."

He laughed, scoffing. "It's just started. By this time tomorrow I'll be rich."

Her mind whirled. The motive, the missing motive—and the murder weapon. Right here in front of her. She had to get to a phone! She tried to put a sympathetic expression on her face, but she knew the attempt must be grotesque. "Brian, you have to turn yourself in. I'll help you. I'll stand by you, I swear. You'll be all right. We'll get a lawyer, a good one."

"I don't need a lawyer," he said harshly. "I need that goddamn treasure."

"But you'll be arrested, Brian. Be reasonable."

"Who'll arrest me? No one knows where this is—" he brandished the ax "—and no one knows why I did it. Not your boyfriend, not anybody, and they never will." He looked at her, a tic pulling at one side of his mouth. "Except you."

Gabriela backed up another step. Her knees felt like water. "Oh, Brian," she whispered.

"Don't worry, I'll share the money with you. Me and George are splitting it, but there's plenty," he said mildly.

Another step backward, her breath coming fast and quick. He was crazy, absolutely crazy, and danger-

ous. Terror tore at her with sharp talons. Get out! her
mind screamed. Just get out of here. She stepped
backward again, her body tensing as she readied herself to whirl and flee through the open door. A blackness was trying to invade her brain, but she knew she
couldn't give in to it.

"Gabriela," he said then, his voice very quiet, "you
aren't thinking of leaving, are you?"

She spun around and flung herself toward the door,
but he was there so fast, so unbelievably fast, his hand
grasping her arm like an iron band. She struggled,
trying to pull free, gasping and whimpering, trying to
kick at his legs, but he clasped her against his side,
facing out, so she couldn't reach him. Her flailing legs
knocked over a chair, but he was so strong, so terribly strong. She drew in her breath to scream, and his
hand came down over her mouth, hard, cutting the
inside of her lips, and she could taste blood, and the
blackness again began to creep in around the edges of
her brain.

He half dragged her to the table, where he snatched
up the ax, sticking it in his belt, then headed toward
the open door. She tried to grab at things, dug her
heels in, but Brian was in great physical condition, and
she was no match for his strength. She grabbed at a
bookcase, felt her fingers catch, then give away, the
case going over with a crash. But no one would hear,
no one, not out here in this private spot, this quiet,
serene site for the cute little cabin. No one was there,
no one would come. No one ever came to the cabin.

"Stop it, Gabriela," Brian said into her ear. "Stop
it or I'll have to hurt you. We're just going for a ride,

that's all. I was going to do it tomorrow, but I'll go today instead.''

She made noises in her throat, her eyes rolling up, unable to get her breath with his hand over her mouth. He was dragging her, her feet sliding, slipping, her hands clawing at his arm, until finally they were outside and she heard him close the cabin door and lock it with his free hand.

He swung her on his hip to face him. "Will you shut up and walk?" he asked.

She nodded, her chest heaving.

"Okay," he said, "but you'd better not try anything cute."

She fell to her knees when he let go of her and kneeled on the pine-needle-strewn ground, gagging and trying to get air into her lungs. But before she could, Brian closed his hand around her upper arm, lifted her to her feet as if she weighed nothing, and pulled her the few yards to where his truck was parked.

He opened the passenger door, leaned past her to get at the glove compartment and took out a small pistol. "Now," he said, with that awful uninflected tone, "I have a gun and I'll keep it real handy, Gabriela, because no one, not you and not your boyfriend, is going to stop me from getting my treasure. You understand?"

Then he thrust her up onto the passenger seat, locking her door, and ran around to the driver's side and was in before she could get away.

"Okay, now we take a little drive." He pushed her head down so that she was half lying on the seat. "Stay there. Don't move."

She was still panting, and her heart was thudding so hard she was afraid it would burst. *No way to jump out, no time,* she thought. *He has a gun. He'll use it. He's already killed. Oh, God, he'll do it again. Jed was right. Oh, Jed, you were right!* Her head was on the seat; she knew no one would see her; she couldn't get out; and her husband was a murderer, an insane murderer. He was taking her somewhere, and then... Her pulse burst inside her head and she stopped thinking, just stopped, because she was so afraid, so deathly sick afraid, that she couldn't stand it.

Brian started the truck and pulled away from the cabin, driving down the familiar driveway, past the hotel, down the drive, onto the road. She knew every pothole, every bump. The one in front of the sign, the one leading onto the main road. Brian was driving slowly, keeping to the speed limit through Apache Springs. Once she even saw him raise an arm and wave casually to someone, and she wondered at his impenetrable calm. He was crazy, an absolute stranger, not her husband, not her charming, smiling, good-ol'-boy husband.

The truck picked up speed once they were past the town, and she could see his foot pressing harder on the gas pedal, faster and faster as they drove into the wilderness, turning off the main road. Hurtling along now, over bumps, Brian crouched forward over the steering wheel, his hands grasping it like the hooked claws of some big animal. She could see him if she turned her head just a little; she could see his foot and his muscular jeans-clad leg and his wrinkled blue shirt and the intent look on his face, and she crouched there on the floor of the cab, afraid to move, afraid to call attention to herself while this deadly stranger drove her farther and farther away from safety.

"TELL ME AGAIN WHAT this Two Bears said," Jed asked Jackson as he dipped tortilla chips into salsa.

"That stuff is awful hot. Be careful," Jackson said.

"It's great. I've been dying for hot salsa," Jed said, "and the rest of this dinner better be just as good. Now, what did this old guy tell you?"

Jackson chewed pensively on a chip. "Okay, he mentioned something about the legend, the old Apache legend, which is sort of a local joke, that there's a cave full of Spanish treasure that no one's found for four hundred years."

"Uh-huh, I know that part," Jed said. He was impatient. It had been a bad day, another day gone with nothing to show for it. He had in his pocket a message from the motel desk that Gish had called. He hadn't called back, but had driven to Flagstaff instead, avoiding the inevitable. He'd tried to call Gab last night to apologize, but he hadn't been able to reach her, and he was worried about her. God, he'd been such an ass.... A little white lie would have saved her such torment.

"So he starts warning me about danger and deaths and telling me about Kokopelli appearing to him and telling him all this stuff and that I should do something about it. No, that I was chosen to do something about it because I'm . . ." and Jackson said something in Apache.

"What's that?"

"Closest translation is 'The Man Who Walks Two Paths.'"

"He's got that right."

"Come on, Jed. He's a crazy old coot. Supposed to be a hundred years old."

"So? Maybe he is."

Jackson snorted. "He's a spiritual leader. He's respected on the reservation. Here, well, here he's just an eccentric old guy." Jackson paused. "Although, when I was a kid and we visited relatives on the reservation, I saw him do some weird things. Healing and trances and stuff. But I was pretty impressionable back then."

"So he searches you out and warns you about deaths?" Jed asked.

The waitress came then, sliding piping hot plates of Mexican food in front of each of them. Jed drew in the aroma—it smelled heavenly: garlic and onions and cumin and chilies. "There's not a decent Mexican restaurant in the entire Washington area," he said.

"Sad," Jackson replied, shaking his head in sympathy.

"Yeah. So, he warned you...?"

"More deaths, he said. There would be more deaths over the treasure."

Jed took a bite of his bean enchilada and raised his eyebrows questioningly.

"I asked him if he meant the Whittakers, but his answer was sort of indirect, you know, so I wasn't sure."

"There haven't been any more deaths," Jed mused, "but there could be, although who or why in God's name..."

Jackson shrugged, eating, his mouth full.

"More deaths," Jed muttered, then something crossed his mind and he looked up at Jackson, and the medical examiner had stopped chewing and was looking intently back at him.

"More deaths over the treasure," Jed said slowly.

"The Whittakers," Jackson said. "Did he mean they died because of the treasure?"

"You tell me—is that what he meant?" Jed asked.

"Maybe so."

"They found the treasure," Jed said, trying out the theory. "It had to be the judge and Brian Zimmerman, because the ladies stayed behind. They somehow stumbled across the goddamn treasure!"

"Why didn't they tell the ladies, then? Or is Gabriela lying about not knowing anything? Maybe she wants the treasure as much as Brian does, and . . ."

Jed shook his head. "No, I'll swear she doesn't know. Gab wouldn't cover up for a murderer for money. For love or loyalty, maybe, but not money. So the men didn't tell them."

"But why murder the judge? All he had to do was split it with him," Jackson said.

"I don't know. There's a reason. They found it, but it had to be kept secret for some reason," Jed said.

"Why? It doesn't make sense."

Jed pondered. Something was tickling at his brain, something . . . "Holy cow," he said suddenly. "The polygraph results. Zimmerman's reaction to the questions about the treasure hunt—okay, now I get that. But the Apache reservation, that question got his blood pressure up!"

"The reservation," Jackson repeated.

Jed's eyes widened. "He even told me that!"

"Who?"

"Zimmerman. He told me the other side of the canyon was on the reservation!" His voice was low and harsh.

"There you go," Jackson said. "They would both have known you can't take anything off a reservation. It belongs to the tribe."

"My God, that must be it!" Jed hit the table with a fist. "Brian knew he couldn't touch that treasure if anyone found out where it was."

"But the judge said they had to go straight to the authorities," Jackson suggested.

"And Zimmerman is in debt up to his ears, and they argue about it. Or, hey, maybe they don't argue. Maybe Brian keeps his mouth shut," Jed said, thinking.

Jackson took the story up. "So they're on that narrow trail on the way back, and Zimmerman sees a ray of hope."

"Gabriela is ahead of them and can't see, so he nails the judge with the ax, and then the wife screams and attacks him or whatever, scratches him, and he pushes her over, too."

"Then he either hides the ax or heaves it away," Jackson said, "before Gabriela sees it."

"Bingo," Jed said, leaning forward, eyes gleaming. "Motive."

"You really think," Jackson said, "that old Indian was right?"

"Oh, yeah, he was right. It makes perfect sense now." Jed nodded, deep in thought, then he looked at Jackson. "You know, I think I saw this Two Bears. Had to be him. It was the first day I was up at the canyon with Brian Zimmerman. An old Indian was there, just sort of appeared like magic.''

"Yup, that was Two Bears," Jackson said. "I told you I saw him do weird things when I was a kid."

"Hunchbacked old fellow?"

"That's him."

Jed thought a minute. "And then Gab saw him when we were up there. It's like he was some kind of guardian for the canyon."

"Don't get carried away with this Indian lore," Jackson said.

"Maybe Two Bears saw more than he's saying. Maybe he knows something else," Jed said. "I've got to find him."

"Good luck. He can only be found when he wants to be."

The combination plates were forgotten, the melted cheese congealing into grease, the beans and rice getting cold, the tortillas soggy.

"I've got to go, Jackson," Jed said, standing, looking distracted. He reached into his pocket and put a bill on the table. "Pay the check for me, will you? Thanks. I've got to get back to Apache Springs."

"Sure, go on, I'll take care of it. Let me know what develops," Jackson said.

"Sure, sure. Man, you might've broken this case for me. You and old Two Bears."

He left, striding away, feeling like those bloodhounds on the scent, eager and strong and excited. Sure, the treasure was the motive. It seemed impossible, but Jed knew in his gut it was true. The Spanish treasure... And pretty soon Brian was going to make a move. He couldn't wait forever.

Gab... Did she know anything about this? She'd never stay with Brian, though, if she even had a clue. Not her. Hell, she still believed he was an innocent victim and that Jed was the villain!

He got into the Cherokee, started it, pulled on the headlight switch and thought about that. Sooner or later Gab was going to find out about her husband. She'd certainly know something was up if Brian suddenly became a wealthy man.

Jed did a U-turn and headed toward the stretch of interstate that would lead him to Apache Springs. The one thing he hoped was that Gab hadn't already found anything out. If she had, if she had confronted Brian, she was in deep trouble.

CHAPTER FIFTEEN

THE MIST CRAWLED SLOWLY along the ground and clung to the trunks of trees, barely moving, heavy in the predawn coolness. It swirled around Brian's truck, obscuring land and sky.

Gabriela stretched and realized she was still on her back in the truck, knees bent, the steering wheel next to her head. Her hands were tied; Brian had done that late last night with the heavy orange nylon rope he kept in the truck. He'd tied her up because she'd panicked again and started to kick and scratch and scream. For a time he'd even gagged her, but she'd worked his soiled bandanna down to her chin.

Now she was silent, her senses dull. She was bone-tired and cramped and her head was pounding. She wriggled slowly to a sitting position and cursed him out loud, not even caring where he was or if he could hear her. And then she tried, for the hundredth time, to untie the nylon knot at her wrists with her teeth. It was utterly useless; Brian, if nothing else, had been an excellent Boy Scout and could tie a knot that would hold a bear.

After a few minutes she gave up and leaned back against the seat, staring through the fogged-up window. Dawn was upon the meadow now, and with her fists she rubbed a clear spot on the driver's-side window. Yes. They were still in the meadow he'd driven to last night, where she'd tried to fight him but lost the battle. Again.

Gabriela stared as the mist moved in undulating waves across the open space. She couldn't see Brian anywhere—maybe he was resting outside against the truck, asleep. She could try opening the door, try making it into the forest, losing him in the fog. She could sure try that. But she wouldn't. In her heart she believed he'd kill her if he caught her.

A familiar fear crawled along her spine, and she tried furiously to think. Had anyone at all seen her go marching off to the cabin yesterday? Maybe someone had seen her carrying the odd-shaped bundle that was the ax. Or maybe no one had noticed her at all.

She thought about Jed. But he'd told her he was leaving, hadn't he? He was probably already gone.

Someone had to realize sooner or later that both she and Brian were missing. By midmorning Lorna would grow suspicious. She'd ask around. By noon she'd surely be worried. But who in God's name was going to find her out here? And by tonight, well, Brian hadn't come to this spot for a picnic. He was crazy, he'd gone certifiably mad, but he had a plan. He'd driven here directly. He had a plan, all right. The question was, what was he going to do with her?

She was thinking about that when his face abruptly peered in at her through the closed window, and she nearly leapt out of her skin. In the half-light he looked exhausted, crazed, his hair sticking out this way and that, dark circles beneath his eyes, eyes that seemed like windows to his demented soul.

Gabriela cringed.

"Someone's meeting me here in a few minutes," Brian was telling her. "You just stay right here in the truck. If I even hear the door click... Well, you get it."

She looked away and licked dry lips. "Brian," she said, "I have to go to the bathroom. Can I at least...?"

He let her relieve herself behind a stand of pines. She thought a dozen times that now was her chance to run—he'd never, ever find her in this fog. And she had managed to wiggle back into her dirty white slacks, her hands still tied, and was telling herself desperately "Run, go, do it!" when suddenly he was there.

"Don't even think about it," he said harshly, grabbing her wrists, tugging her back to the truck.

"Brian, I wasn't..." she gasped.

"The hell you weren't!" he snapped, and he shoved her back into the front seat and slammed the door. "You're a fool," he said. "We're about to be stinking rich and all you give me is a bunch of grief. So just shut up and sit here and don't try anything." To make his point, he pulled the pistol out of the waistband of his jeans and put the barrel against the window, aimed directly at her head. "You're my wife, Gabriela," he said through the glass. "You're either with me or against me. You better make up your mind." And with that he was gone, heading out into the meadow, the fog swallowing him.

It wasn't long before Gabriela heard a low grinding noise off in the distance. One moment it was audible, the next it was gone, and then she heard it again, an engine sound, like a four-wheel-drive vehicle.

The sound grew louder. She strained to hear, trying to figure out which direction it was coming from. In the fog it was difficult, though, everything was so muffled; either that, or surprisingly crisp sounding. It was eerie, that engine noise, and Gabriela fought a shiver.

After a time, she could hear the vehicle from just across the meadow. And then the engine stopped. She heard a door open and close, and that noise seemed as if it was right on top of her.

Then there were two voices, both men's. Brian and George probably. They were in this together. Fifty-fifty.

She strained to hear, though God only knew what she'd do with the information. Jed, she could tell Jed, but he was gone. She felt a terrible sinking sensation. She'd never know now how it could have been, growing old with the man she had always loved. Children, grandchildren . . . Jed.

"Chopper'll still be here as soon as the fog . . ."

She could hear a man's voice, but then it faded into the mist.

A minute later, ". . . part of murder. If I'd known, buddy, I'd have told you to get lost." That was George, all right, and it was obvious he was telling Brian off.

Then Brian's voice, raised, angry. "Then just get the hell out of here! I'll . . . the helicopter." Brian swore then.

It struck Gabriela suddenly: if she cried out, if George heard her . . . Would he help? But Brian had that gun.

Then there was a long exchange between the men. A lot of cursing. She only caught snatches of it, despite the lifting of the fog as the first rays of sun groped across the grassy meadow.

Gabriela could make out Brian and George now. Even George's truck. They were standing near the edge of the trees across the meadow. They were both still yelling, and then abruptly George gave Brian a shove and turned on his heel, heading back to his truck.

She was thinking frantically that she had to get George's attention somehow when she saw Brian doing something. He was reaching around to his back, his waistband, and he had the gun. George was just about to open his own truck door. Brian lifted the gun....

She screamed. It seemed for an instant that George froze; he began to turn toward the noise when suddenly his body jerked. There was a popping sound and he keeled over toward the truck, clung for an agonizing moment to the door handle, and then went down to his knees. Finally, horrifyingly, his whole body spasmed and he dropped facedown onto the pine-covered earth.

ONCE BEFORE IN HIS LIFE Jed had been gut-heaving afraid. He and three other U.S. marshals had been sent to defuse a hostage situation in Harrisburg, Pennsylvania. The man, who held two small children hostage in their home, had escaped from another marshal en route to prison. He was not a murderer, merely a securities counterfeiter, but apparently he'd gone nuts at the idea of being locked up, taken his escort's gun, fled across the railroad tracks and was holed up with the young hostages.

No one wanted anyone to get harmed. Still, the street in front of the tiny brick rowhouse was swarming with local cops, state police, FBI agents and the U.S. marshals. Ten hours into the hostage crisis the fugitive, Thad, decided to deal. He yelled to police that if someone came in to talk and assured him no harm was going to come to him, he'd let the kids go and give up. To show his good faith, Thad tossed the stolen gun onto the snow-packed front lawn.

Somehow—probably because Jed was the rookie—he was elected to go in and talk. After all, Thad was unarmed now. And so, fearlessly, cocksure, Jed entered the house.

Thad, however, was far from unarmed. Pointed directly in Jed's face was a sawed-off shotgun. Later, they would learn it belonged to the father who'd abandoned these kids and their mother. At the time, where the gun came from was of little importance to Jed Mallory. He knew only one thing: he was scared.

Thad had plans. He used silver tape to secure the barrels of the gun to Jed's head, let the kids go, then, finger on the trigger, pushed Jed ahead of him out onto the street, saying that if anyone took a shot at him he'd still be able to pull the trigger before he died.

In the end it was a junior FBI officer who talked Thad down, calmly promising that no one was going to lock him up. That, of course, was a lie. Everyone knew it—including Jed—but Thad so desperately wanted to believe it that he finally let the shotgun go, dropping it so that it literally hung by the tape from Jed's head.

Jed, bile rising, tore the tape and a lot of hair away in a frenzy of terror and claustrophobia. He fell to his knees and vomited several times, news cameras rolling. To this day Jed couldn't even look at a roll of silver tape without being swept by nausea. Around headquarters, it was a private joke: don't let Mallory near the tape.

Jed was experiencing true fear again, but this time it was not for himself. He'd spent most of last night questioning everyone at the hotel, trying to get a hint about Brian Zimmerman's whereabouts. And Gabriela was missing, too. That was what made Jed sick with that same shuddering fear he'd felt in Harrisburg.

Lorna Kessler was the most helpful so far. Just past eight in the morning she snapped her fingers and said, "You know, I think I did see Brian's pickup going down the drive yesterday. It must have been yesterday, because the day before he was in Phoenix with you, and you didn't get back till late."

They were standing in the lobby, Jed shifting from one foot to the other, vibrating with impatience and a sense of urgency. "Do you have any idea if Gabriela was in that truck?"

Lorna shook her head.

"Think hard. Do you know where Brian might have been going? Maybe he said something. Anything."

Again she shook her head.

By nine, Jed had talked to most of the hotel's employees for the second time in less than twenty-four hours. No one, not a soul, could remember seeing either Gabriela or Brian since yesterday at lunchtime.

At one point Jed roared at a waitress, "Is everyone blind around here!" But then he scrubbed a hand through his sandy hair and apologized.

At nine-thirty, as he was walking across the patio by the pools, he spotted an unfamiliar face—a painter, presumably, since he had on paint-splattered coveralls. Jed approached him.

"Hey, man," the guy said, gaps where teeth should have been, "I just do odd jobs here. I don't need to talk to no police."

Jed persisted. "Were you working here yester-day?"

"Ah, maybe, yes, painting the outside wall of the bathhouse, y' know."

"Sure," Jed said. "Did you happen to see Mrs. Zimmerman?"

The man grinned slowly. More missing teeth. "Now, how could I miss that woman?" He winked. "Y'know, she's got the damnedest pair of legs I ever did see. Ten miles long."

"Uh-huh," Jed muttered. "So did you see Mrs. Zimmerman yesterday, say in the late morning?"

"Maybe."

"Go on."

"Well, it's like this. She was wearing these white slacks.... Well, y'know. I like it a lot better when she's got on a skirt-thing, y'know. Like she's got this real short black one that..."

"I get it," Jed snapped. "So what, exactly, was Mrs. Zimmerman doing when you last saw her yes-terday...in her white slacks?" he added sarcasti-cally.

"Um," the painter said. "She was like maybe talk-ing to that old guy, y'know."

"What old guy?"

"The gardener. Used to work here back a ways. In-dian."

Jed's pulse quickened. Hadn't Gabriela told him on the trail that day that Two Bears once gardened here? "And then what did Mrs. Zimmerman do?" he asked.

"Well, she took that thing the old dude gave her and went running off."

"Whoa," Jed said with forced patience. "What did the old man give her?"

"A package of somethin'. Like wrapped up in cloth, y'know."

What was it? "Okay," he said. "So she ran off. Where?"

The painter nodded. "That way. I'd say she went home."

"Uh-huh." Had she gone off to confront Brian about something? Aloud, Jed said, "Did she come back?"

The man shook his head. "Nah. I even hung around, y'know, to see if she'd changed into one of those short things." He shrugged.

"Well," Jed said, "thanks, buddy."

"No problem."

And then, before turning away, Jed had to add, "Oh, by the way, if I ever catch you staring at Mrs. Zimmerman again, I'll knock the rest of your teeth out, pal." He smiled mildly and headed toward the path that led to the cabin—the one she'd moved out of so recently.

Outwardly Jed appeared calm as he walked along the foot trail. Inside he was seething. It wasn't that idiot painter, either, although guys like him sickened Jed. They ought to get a life. He was deeply troubled, though, about what exactly Two Bears had given Gab. And then she'd gone immediately to the cabin.

Had Brian been there? Had they had a confrontation? And where the hell had Zimmerman been going when his sister saw him driving off?

Jed had already knocked loudly on the cabin door twice last night. He was convinced no one was there. But that package Gabriela had been carrying... Was it inside? Was she inside, injured? His stomach tightened.

He tried knocking again but only briefly. And he only considered for an instant the virtues of obtaining a search warrant before he put his shoulder to the wood and forced the door open. Half falling inside, Jed righted himself and immediately saw the clutter—the overturned chair, the books from the bookshelf scattered on the floor.

He searched the whole place. Nobody. Nothing. No Gab, no package, and sure as hell no Brian. After a time, his frustration eating away at his sanity, he righted the chair, sat, knees splayed, and hung his head.

"Think," he muttered. Two Bears brought her a package; he kept wanting to think it was the ax. She confronted Brian with it, and Brian was seen shortly thereafter driving away. Gabriela hadn't been seen since yesterday morning, either, so it was a safe assumption she was with her husband.

But where had Brian gone with her? To get the treasure? Where else would he have gone, especially when he was feeling the net close in around him?

"Okay," Jed said, lifting his head, staring into the middle distance. Presumably the Spanish treasure was on the reservation, and near that canyon, too. Rough, rough country. He'd had to walk in—three times. But what if the higher terrain was flatter? What if the treasure could be conveyed to a plane? No, a helicopter...

It came to Jed more like a streak of lightning over his head than the proverbial light bulb switching on. George Lemming. That day out at the logging site when Jed had been interviewing him, good old George had been making some sort of flight arrangements on the phone. For a helicopter? Brian and George, a chopper. It fit. And somewhere within walking distance of that canyon lay the treasure.

He rose abruptly and snatched up the phone, dialing Arlington. He waited five minutes before Arthur Gish picked up on the other end. They were five of the longest minutes of Jed's life.

"Where the hell have you been, Mallory?" Gish demanded.

But Jed didn't have time for that. Instead, he launched into the story. He told his boss everything: about the peculiar results of the polygraph, how at the time Zimmerman's reaction to the treasure hunt and the reservation had made no sense. He went on to relate to Gish Two Bears' visit to Jackson Many Goats and how the old man had shadowed Jed near the canyon twice now. He told his boss his theory on the motive and how Mrs. Zimmerman had been seen with a cloth-covered object.

"I'm betting it was the murder weapon, sir," Jed said. "And now Mrs. Zimmerman may be in real danger. I figure they have to be using a helicopter. And it just so happens that I overheard this George Lemming on the phone making—"

"Let's just hold on right here for a minute," Gish interrupted.

"Sir?"

"I want you to listen to me, Mallory, really get this through your head. All this business about Spanish treasure, polygraphs, old Indian spiritual leaders. I mean, if you were in my shoes, do you realize how it would sound?"

"Sir, I see what you're getting at, but—"

"But nothing. Hasn't it once occurred to you that Mr. and Mrs. Zimmerman made up and took off for the weekend?"

"Sir, I can safely assure you that isn't—"

"Now look," Gish said, his tone growing impatient. "I'm afraid you've gone soft over this woman, Mallory."

"Not so, sir," Jed said, emphasizing the sir. "I'm telling you, Zimmerman is out there right now on the reservation collecting his treasure. He's got his wife with him, and she's no willing participant."

"Look," Gish said, "believe what you will, Mallory. You've got no hard evidence, just hearsay and speculation. I don't buy it. Not one bit. I want you back at headquarters."

"Sir," Jed said, his frustration mounting, "I need help out here. I need your authority to order an air search from Phoenix, and I need all the ground help I can get. That terrain is..."

"No, damn it, Mallory, no way! Now get your butt on a plane and get back here. That, Deputy, is an order."

"That's your final word, sir?" Jed asked, suddenly knowing what had to be done.

"Tonight," Gish said, "I want you back here tonight."

"Then," Jed said very evenly, "I quit, sir."

"You...what?"

"I'll have to hand in my badge, sir. If you want, I'll send it by courier."

"Are you joking?" Gish sputtered.

"Not in the least. Goodbye, sir," Jed said. "I'll miss the Service, but I can't say I'll miss that damned climate."

"Mallory?"

But Jed had already put down the phone.

He'd quit. After all these years he'd quit.

Jed stood up and glanced around the room again, saw the books lying helter-skelter on the floor. And suddenly his resignation seemed very small in the face of what was going down here. *Gab,* he thought, *just hold on, I'll find you somehow.*

CHAPTER SIXTEEN

NO TIME. THAT WAS ALL JED could think. He had no time. And he was a civilian now, with no more authority to call up a search than that toothless painter. Okay, but Sheriff Ulrich didn't know that, did he? Gish wouldn't have phoned everyone on this case to tell them Jed Mallory had quit, not yet. He'd do the paperwork, leave it in his out basket for someone else to do. He was an administrator, after all.

All right, there was this window of opportunity, then, and Jed knew exactly what he had to do.

From his motel room at the Pines he phoned Sheriff Ulrich in Flagstaff. "Sheriff, this case has turned ugly. Brian Zimmerman took off with his wife. They're both missing. Nope, no idea where, but he's found the Spanish treasure up beyond that canyon. Yeah, I know it's crazy, but I'm betting he's going in there with a helicopter, and the thing is, Marshal Gish, my boss, is requesting your full cooperation for an air and ground search. We've got to find that treasure cave.

"Now, yes, right now. Start at the canyon. I'm going up there now. I'll have a radio to keep in touch, but you know those mountains. And planes if you can get them, choppers, whatever's fastest.

"One more thing. Get in touch with the Apache reservation. This is a federal case, so it's legit. I think the cave's on the reservation, and they stand to collect on anything up there. One of them may even know where the cave is.

"Yeah, okay, but fast. This is a real volatile situation, and we can assume Zimmerman is armed and dangerous. All right, thanks. The Marshals Service appreciates your help, Sheriff."

It worked. There was nothing a local law-enforcement officer liked better than to be asked to help the feds. He hung up, relieved for about ten seconds, then his skin started crawling and his heart gave a sickening lurch and he was back to worrying about Gab and what Brian was doing with her or going to do to her or had already done with her.

He couldn't wait one more second, not one moment. He sure as hell wasn't going to wait for Ulrich and his men to get here from Flagstaff, he knew that. He took his .38 revolver out of his suitcase, where it had been all this time, checked it, stuffed it in his waistband. No time for water, food, anything like that. Gab could be hurt, scared.... His mind stopped right there and refused to consider an alternative.

He ran outside and started up the Cherokee. Ulrich would see it parked on the road. He drove up toward the canyon, too fast, far too fast, swerving once to avoid a huge motorhome that rounded a corner in his lane. He swore, pounding his open hand on the steering wheel, speeding on.

He braked at the trailhead, skidding on gravel, snatched the two-way radio from the car and started up the trail running. A hundred yards later he had a side ache and had slowed to a trot. He had so far to go, so damn far to the murder site, and then how far after that? And where? Where was that cave, and how on God's earth was he going to find it?

He was half crazed with worry, panting, sweating, walking now, jogging when the trail wasn't too steep. He had nothing to go on but gut instinct: he knew the treasure cave was up beyond the murder site, because Brian and the judge had found it that day, and he was ninety-nine percent positive Brian was headed there.

Of course, the man could be real smart and be holed up somewhere else entirely, keeping Gab hostage, waiting, figuring no one would ever find the cave. He could be, but he wasn't, Jed knew. He wasn't that patient.

Gab. He hoped she wasn't trying any heroics. *Just sit tight, Gab, I'm coming.*

He walked. His side had a dagger in it now, hurting when he breathed. The gun dug into his ribs with every step; the radio in his pocket did, too. He kept going, counting the minutes, trying to figure when Ulrich would get there, listening for planes. Nothing. Too soon.

Panting, trotting along the trail on a flat section, his breath rasping, sweat running into his eyes. Hurry, hurry. What if Brian had already been there and gone? Yesterday, maybe. Jed cursed. And he'd been in Flagstaff, eating Mexican food with Jackson. God, he was dumb. It was so obvious now. Why in hell hadn't he put it all together before?

Treasure hunt. He'd read the brochure that first day he'd walked into the lobby of the Apache Springs

Hotel. He'd had the key, the motive, in his hand then and hadn't seen it.

He got to the murder site, the narrow part of the trail. Here, this was where Zimmerman had decided to take things into his own hands, right here. But how far beyond this had he and the judge walked? And up there—he looked, squinting—up there somewhere they'd found the treasure.

Where, damn it, where?

Jed turned around slowly, desperately searching the canyon walls, the rocks and stunted brush, the canyon floor below, the blue sky. Goddamn it, where? Where did he go now? he thought, as near despair, as lost, as he'd ever felt in his life.

Jed was standing there on the precariously narrow trail, hands on his hips, jaw locked, when he had the damnedest sensation, as if he were being watched. He turned and looked back along the trail toward the curve behind him. Nothing. No one. He shrugged, trying to put his mind back on track, but the sensation persisted, and finally the hairs on his neck lifted. There was someone. . . .

Again, slowly, he looked over his shoulder, and abruptly his heart gave a leap. As if by magic, out of thin air, a bent old man stood in the path. The old Indian, Two Bears. Jed had no time to think, to consider, to wonder, to ask how or why.

"Come with me," Two Bears said, and Jed followed.

THE HELICOPTER APPEARED over the meadow, blowing the grass flat, raising dust, making the very ground shudder. From where she sat in the truck, Gabriela looked up, squinting, into the sun and watched the chopper descend like a very large and angry hornet. The rotors slowed, the whine of its engine wound down, and Brian ran, ducking under the still turning blades, and leaned into the Plexiglas bubble where the pilot sat. She watched as Brian and the pilot talked, as they bent over a map, fingers pointing, tracing routes.

Maybe the pilot would help her.

Maybe, if Brian left her with him alone for a minute, she could explain what was going on and he could radio for help and... But Brian wouldn't let her out of his sight. She knew that. He wasn't stupid, and for all she knew the pilot was in on the deal, knew all about it. She couldn't take the chance, because if she guessed wrong, Brian would kill her, or the pilot would, or Brian would kill both of them.

She shuddered, feeling sick. She'd been fighting down panic for hours, waiting and watching while Brian dragged George's body into the trees at the edge of the meadow and drove his truck into the trees, too, so that no one could see it, coming out with his arms full of heavy canvas bags.

NOBODY KNEW WHERE she was. Jed was probably back in Arlington by now; he'd even said he'd never see her again, and he'd also told her that, yes, he thought her husband was a murderer, and she'd run from him as if he were the devil.

Brian was coming back toward the truck now. He'd lost the crazed look and seemed calm, very much in control. But she knew that could change at any moment. He'd already slapped her once, savagely, when she couldn't stop screaming after he'd shot George, and then he'd been nice and solicitous afterward, asking her if she was okay, apologizing, explaining that they were going to be rich. And then he'd turned ugly again.

He was matter-of-fact this time. "Look, I'm going to untie you for the helicopter ride. I'll be right there every second, though, and the gun's in my pocket." He put his hand on it. "So you behave now. We're going to get the treasure, then we'll come back here and go away together. Okay?"

Woodenly she nodded.

"Good girl." He untied her hands, even rubbed her wrists. "We're going to be awful rich, Gabriela, you know that?"

"Yes, Brian."

"No more talk of divorce, okay?"

"Okay."

"I know I haven't been much of a husband lately. It was all the pressure, babes. But that's over now. I love you, Gabriela. Honestly."

"Yes, Brian."

He glanced toward the chopper. "And don't worry, the pilot thinks we're from the museum in Phoenix, so he won't ask questions." And he smiled smugly. "George thought of that." Then he bent down and shouldered the pile of canvas bags effortlessly and led her to the helicopter, tossing the bags in the area behind the pilot, helping Gabriela in and securing her seat belt and his own. The pilot flipped switches up front, and the chopper came back to full life, whining, howling toward a crescendo. Above their heads the rotors turned faster, then spun, thudding, making the machine twitch and jump. Then they went up, straight up, defying the laws of gravity, and the meadow diminished, then disappeared as the pilot steered them toward this place where Brian had supposedly found the Spanish treasure.

During the flight Gabriela thought about how to get away once they landed. She could run and hope Brian wouldn't shoot her in front of the pilot. But Brian had gone crazy. He still thought he could take the treasure, drive away with it and go somewhere. But what about George Lemming? Someone would notice he was missing, too. Even if they didn't find his body right away, they'd look for Brian to question. Jed knew about George and Brian's friendship, how they went to Las Vegas together. Oh, there'd be plenty of questions....

But Jed was gone. He didn't even know Gabriela was missing. Lorna, Lorna would know by now. And Otto and Ellie. And the deliveryman from Nobel who was going to talk to her today about those missing cases of peeled tomatoes.

She had to hang on. Make Brian think she'd cooperate. No matter what he did or where they went, she'd make him think she wanted the money and would go with him willingly. Sooner or later he'd let his guard down.

It was a short flight, no more than twenty minutes. She knew the treasure was up above the spot where she and Clare had waited that day. Clare Whittaker, with her arms full of wildflowers, saying, "Those guys, just had to prove how macho they were, hiking up so far." Gabriela's eyes filled with tears at the memory. How they'd waited there, gossiping, resting, and she'd asked Clare if her headache was better, because if it wasn't maybe they should walk down. Altitude sickness was something you didn't fool around with, and Clare had laughed and said, "Honey, I'm not going to die of a little old headache, for goodness' sake."

And then Evan and Brian had come back, acting odd and secretive. Now Gabriela knew what the big secret was. Too late, though. Why hadn't Evan told them? Then none of this would have happened. He and Clare would still be alive and Brian wouldn't be a murderer.

Or maybe Brian would still be a murderer, and he'd have rushed back to call the sheriff and report that three people had been killed in an awful, tragic accident.

The helicopter was racing over the rough terrain, its shadow chasing them, dipping into gorges, whipping across valleys and forests. It slowed and hovered finally, and Brian leaned forward for a consultation with the pilot, pointing.

There was a broad, slanted mountainside, scree-covered and rocky, and just below it the mountain split into jagged crevices leading down. It didn't look the least bit familiar to Gabriela, but then why should it? They were coming at the place from above, not below, and she'd never been up the trail this far in any case.

The helicopter settled onto the ground just above where the canyon started down into shadow. A surprisingly gentle bump and they were there. Brian jumped out, dragged the pile of bags with him and yelled to the pilot over the fading engine noise to wait while they collected the stuff, and for a heartbeat Gabriela thought that he was leaving her there with the pilot. But no, her sudden hope burst into shards, because Brian was leaning in the door toward her and saying, "Okay, babes, this is it. You're coming with me."

She got out and hugged herself. It was cool up here, a breeze blowing, afternoon clouds starting to pile up in the west.

"Come on, hurry up," Brian said, pulling at her arm, shouldering the canvas bags.

It wasn't far to the cave, a couple hundred feet, just down below the scree field. Suddenly they were within the walls of a ravine that dropped off below them, and there was a darker shadow in the rock wall. Brian led her, scrambling over boulders, right up to it. He pulled a flashlight out of his pocket, dropped the bags, and turned to her. There was an intensity to him, a smile on his lips, the kind of triumph radiating from him that a general must feel after a victorious battle. "This is it, Gabriela," he said.

He motioned her ahead of him into the dark cleft, and she stepped inside. The sunlight was cut off sharply, the cave pitch-black but for the thin beam from the flashlight that Brian had now switched on. Cold and dry, the cave smelled of dust and rock, its air dead still, its silence total. Her footsteps echoed dully, raising puffs of powdery dust.

Brian was close behind her, and she could hear his too-quick breathing and smell his sweat. Sweeping the flashlight, he nudged her forward with his other hand. "See?" came his gloating voice. "I told you."

She saw it then, the gleam of light on the blade of a sword. Gasping, she stepped closer, and the light touched a crested helmet, and something glaring and white—she drew in her breath—bones. A skeleton. A sense of unreality, of horror, shook her.

Then quickly, in turn, the beam grazed a long-barreled flintlock musket, a piece of body armor, a knife, and everywhere, bones, rib cages, backbones, skulls....

"See?" Brian was saying into the black hush. "See?"

Leather, scraps of half-rotted cloth, boot soles, a lance, more swords. Then, a brighter glint, a chain of dull yellow gold and a crucifix entangled in the small bones of...a hand. Gabriela's hand went to her mouth, and she couldn't fit her mind around the reality of what she was seeing.

"Okay," Brian said, "we've got to hurry. I'll get the bags. You're going to help me, babes. Stuff everything in the bags. No bones, though. Wait there." And his footsteps were gone, blackness enshrouded her, and she fought down a terrible claustrophobic panic.

But he was back in moments, his breath quick in her ear, the light spearing the darkness. He set the flashlight on a rock so he'd have both hands free, handed her a bag and said, "Let's get to work."

Desecrating the dead, she thought, standing there with the bag in her hands. Stealing. But they're dead, all these men. And all the stories were true, that was the amazing thing, the myth, the Apache legend. These bones had once been living, breathing men. Men from Spain searching for treasure. My God, how very far they'd come, so far from home, to die up here in this cave.

"Hurry up!" Brian growled. "We don't have all day."

Gabriela closed her eyes and took a deep breath then bent over and picked up a knife, shoving it in her bag. Then a dented cup, a sword—surprisingly heavy—a helmet, a studded leather belt.

Brian left for only a moment to drag his full bag outside the cave entrance, and she had no time to escape, but she knew sooner or later there would be an opportunity, and she'd grab it.

Suddenly Brian was cursing, scrabbling through the bones and belongings and ancient weapons, kicking at the rubble. "Goddamn it!" he yelled. "Where's the bag of coins? That Lemming came back up here and stole it! He stole it! That dirty..."

His rage frightened Gabriela, and she drew back into the shadows. But Brian finally stopped yelling, took a few deep breaths and ran a hand through his hair. "Okay, no time for that. The gold's gone. No time." He suddenly noticed her absence, and his head snapped up. "Gabriela, where are you? Come on, I can't do this all myself."

Slowly she stepped from the shadows at the back of the cave. In her hand was the gold crucifix.

"Come on," Brian said impatiently. Then he stopped and cocked his head, looking at the relic she held. "Pretty, isn't it?"

Pretty, she thought, but she only nodded.

"I'll buy you even prettier stuff, anything you want, babes."

But she bent over, hiding her face, picked up a helmet and stuffed it into her bag.

When her bag was full, Brian slung it over his shoulder with his and they both walked back toward the helicopter, his eye on her every second. No chance to run, not a sliver of a second. She wondered why the pilot didn't notice her face or her dirty white pants or her blue T-shirt that was ripped on one shoulder; couldn't he see that something was wrong? But he was sitting in the shade of a stunted juniper, reading a newspaper, drinking coffee from a thermos.

"Not much longer," Brian called to him.

"Better hurry," the pilot called back, pointing to the west. "There's some weather coming in."

"Right," Brian replied, hustling Gabriela with him.

Back inside the cave it was cool, the only sounds the ones she and Brian made: the clank of four-hundred-year-old metal, the dry shuffle of their feet, the rattle of bones that had to be pushed aside to get at the weapons and ornaments, the stiff rustle of the canvas bags. It was as if there was no world outside, no bright sun or breeze or birds singing or deer standing startled for a split second. There was only this grisly chore Gabriela was doing and the breath rasping in her throat and the smell of death and fear in the still air.

She thought she was imagining it at first. Then she was sure she heard something, a muffled sound. She saw Brian straighten, a sword clutched in his hand. She heard it again, and so did Brian. He threw the sword down and swore, then ran to the cave entrance. Gabriela shrank into the shadows again, against one hard, cool wall, waiting, her heart pounding in trepidation. What was going on? What new and awful thing was happening now?

But Brian yelled something. Standing there silhouetted against the light from outside, he yelled a name, his voice breaking with fury: "Mallory!"

Gabriela felt as if someone had punched her. Jed, Jed here? She had no time to think, because Brian ran back and grabbed her, holding her in front of him, her feet half off the ground as he pushed her, stumbling, breathless, her mind screaming *Jed, Jed,* and then she was blinking in the light, held fast by Brian, shielding him, and the cold steel of his gun was at her temple.

"Mallory!" Brian shouted, and one arm tightened around her neck. "I'll kill her! I swear I will! I want clear passage to the chopper, Mallory!"

She saw Jed then, about fifty yards down from the cave, his form swimming in her vision like a mirage and suddenly snapping into clear focus. Yes, Jed, and someone else, she realized. Two Bears. Little old hunchbacked Two Bears!

Brian's chest was heaving against her back, and the gun he held pressed to her temple shook with his wrath. She closed her eyes and felt her insides turn over with fear. Jed was here. He'd found her. His name was a litany that kept her from going stark raving mad, but the fear ate at her with ravenous teeth.

"Zimmerman," she heard faintly. "Brian, okay, let's be reasonable about this." It was Jed, his voice so calm, so very cool and in control.

"I want to get on that chopper," Brian screamed in her ear, making her jerk spasmodically. "No one can follow, you hear? No one."

"Okay, that's fine. You can go, you have my word. There's no one here to follow you, see? Just let Gab go. She has nothing to do with this."

"No, she stays with me! You think I'm stupid?" Brian was edging away from the mouth of the cave toward the helicopter, which squatted on the slope above them like a giant silver bug.

Gabriela tried to breathe deeply and evenly, her eyes darting around, looking for a way to escape from Brian, readying herself in case he let her go or loosened his steely grip. His body thrummed with unholy, ferocious power against her back.

"Okay, take her. I just don't want anyone getting hurt, Zimmerman." Jed was holding up his hands to show they were empty. "See, I'm unarmed. It's only me and Two Bears here." He stepped forward slowly.

"Get back!" Brian screamed, waving the gun at Jed, then quickly putting it back against Gabriela's head. "I'll shoot her! You can have her, all right! Dead!"

"Okay, Brian, okay. Just don't hurt anyone. Look, you don't have to hurt anyone. Just calm down, man."

"I'm going!" Brian yelled. "Don't try to stop me." He moved closer to the helicopter, dragging her along in front of him.

"Sure, whatever you say. Just stay cool," Jed called out.

He was lying, Gabriela thought. Of course he was lying. He was trying to defuse a hostage situation, standard operating procedure. He'd been trained for it, hadn't he? He had a plan, an idea. He knew what to do. It occurred to her in a glimmer of thought, a foolish ironic aside her mind could not stop, that she'd been so afraid Jed would get hurt or killed in law enforcement, but it was Gabriela herself who was likely to get hurt.

"Don't move!" Brian yelled, pulling her along. "Stay away!"

"Sure, sure. I'm no hero, Zimmerman," Jed said, but Gabriela could see his eyes, quick and vigilant, locked on her husband's face. He had some plan, he must. Oh, God, he had to have some trick up his sleeve!

GAB WAS WRONG. Jed knew exactly what she must be thinking—if she could think at all in this situation—but he had no plan; there were none, short of trying to talk the perp down.

And with Zimmerman, Jed already knew that was a very long shot.

"Back away from me slowly," Jed told Two Bears. "No sudden moves."

But the old man seemed reluctant.

"Do it," Jed whispered harshly. "I'm not going to get you killed along with me." He turned. "Stay there!" he yelled at the pilot, who had suddenly switched on the engine. "I'm a U.S. marshal. Don't move!"

Then, while Two Bears moved with infinite patience behind Jed and off to the right, Jed tried reasoning one more time with Zimmerman. "Look," he called out, trying to forget that it was Gab the man held in front of him like a shield, "let her go, Brian. You don't want to hurt anyone. You've got the gun, no one's going to jump you. Let her go."

But Brian only swore at him and kept backing up the scree field toward the chopper.

Jed felt frustration overwhelming him. The first thing an officer of the law learns about a hostage situation is that someone—most often the hostage—is going to get hurt. And hurt bad. The rule of thumb for the hostage was, in fact, to never, ever go with an abductor, to take a stand immediately—kick, scream, fight, because if the abductor gets even an ounce of control, he's going to go for the whole pound.

But Gabriela couldn't have known that, and now it was too late. The only thing that might save her was an effort to escape when they reached the chopper. If Jed could just get off a single shot at Zimmerman . . .

He heard Brian yelling at the pilot to get in. Still Gab was being dragged up the slope, Brian's gun to her head. It was killing Jed to see her suffer like this— he knew only too well what it was like to have a loaded gun pressed to your head. If he got his hands on Zimmerman, just one single moment . . .

While Brian kept backing up toward the helicopter, Jed almost imperceptibly inched his way toward them in slow, agonizing steps, one after another. He was unaware of Two Bears, assuming the old man had found cover, but Gabriela . . . Her desperate gaze was on Jed, and even though she was too far away, he could feel her eyes locked to his, pleading, begging, so very afraid.

Jed was able to get a little closer when Zimmerman had to threaten the pilot to make him climb back in the chopper. "Get the hell in there," Brian called over his shoulder, "or I'll pull this trigger. Then you're next, pal!"

Jed took a few steps while Brian shot a glance at the pilot, who was doing as he'd been told. Another mistake, Jed thought. Damn. If all three of them could have defied Zimmerman, there would have been a ray of hope. As it was, Brian was in full control. What he didn't know, hadn't even considered, apparently, was that Jed had his revolver tucked in his waistband at his back. Whether or not he'd have the opportunity to use it was another matter altogether.

They were close to the chopper now, and the pilot had it up and running, the rotors slowly whacking the air, gaining speed. Jed felt a surge of desperation. If Gab's life was going to be saved, it had to be in the next few seconds. Every muscle and sinew in Jed's body tightened.

"PLEASE," GABRIELA SOBBED over the increasing noise, "please let me go! You've got the treasure...."

"Shut up!" Brian commanded, squeezing her so hard her breath wouldn't come. "Shut up and get in there, slow, real slow. I swear, if you pull anything I'll kill you, I swear it!"

He was absolutely mad. He'd kill them all, she realized in a moment of blinding clarity; he didn't even care anymore. It must have been that sudden revelation that made her act.

It was when she was climbing up into the chopper, Brian's gun aimed at her back, that she kicked out. There was no thought involved at the time, only a primitive instinct to survive, to fight and to live. Somehow, miraculously, she caught him hard in the groin and the gun went off, the bullet zinging harmlessly into the air, and at the same instant, as Brian was stumbling, hunched over, holding himself, the helicopter tilted a little.

Gabriela was perilously off-balance, half in and half out, clutching at the doorframe. She was aware of Brian, bent over, the gun in his other hand. He was trying to raise it. The chopper lifted another foot and began to turn clockwise, and she lost her hold, tumbling out, and that was when, from the corner of her vision, she saw Jed closing in on Brian.

She hit the rock field hard, her shoulder screaming with a flash of pain, but she barely noticed. Brian had the gun fully raised now and was bringing it around toward Jed. But Jed kicked at his hand, and the gun went flying, dropping below them all and well out of reach.

Winded, she tried to rise and got to her knees, watching in terror as the two men grappled with each other. She saw it then, Jed's gun in his waistband, but he couldn't reach it. If only she could...

Sudden dust stung Gabriela's eyes. The helicopter was lifting higher, kicking up a storm. And when the air cleared she saw it again, Jed's gun between the two men as they each struggled for possession of it.

Then Brian had it. Jed was holding his rib cage and Brian was scrambling to his feet, his teeth bared, chest heaving. Jed lunged, trying to grab Brian's arm, but he missed. Gabriela bit her fist.

The mistake Brian made was to talk, or rather hiss, at his adversary before cocking Jed's revolver.

"This is it, you son of a bitch! Man, you are history," he got out between clenched teeth. Gabriela righted herself and made a wild, desperate attempt to clutch his arm, but when he pulled the trigger there was only a click.

His eyes wide, Brian suddenly realized that the safety was on. It all happened very quickly then. Jed, grimacing in pain, leapt at Brian when Gabriela missed striking her husband's arm. Brian was scurrying backward, feet sliding on the rocky down slope, but he had the safety off now and...

There was a sudden *thunk*. From out of nowhere it seemed, a small, heavy sack struck Brian's outstretched arm and knocked the gun clean into the air, where it hung for an instant and then dropped into a crevice.

Gabriela couldn't believe it. Two Bears. He'd thrown a leather sack.... She stared in disbelief at the gold coins, struck by a shaft of sunlight, as they tumbled and spilled among the rocks.

"The gold," Brian sobbed. "You took it!" But he was sinking to his knees, trying desperately to snatch up the pieces of eight that were disappearing down the scree field. "No, no," he wept, scrabbling insanely.

Jed retrieved the gun, favoring his side, and Gabriela could only stand there staring at Brian clutching at the coins, weeping, rocking, his eyes tightly closed, his face contorted, as if he were in excruciating pain. She heard Two Bears saying, "I knew that bag of gold would come in handy, I just did not know exactly how."

And then the sun disappeared behind a gathering storm cloud and it was over. After four hundred years it was over at last. She bit her lower lip and found Jed's eyes as the sound of Brian's sobs mingled with distant thunder.

CHAPTER SEVENTEEN

FOR SEVENTY-TWO HOURS the media had a heyday. They used their own helicopters to land on the scree field above the cave, filming everything, the now-empty, echoing cavern, the scenery, the canyon, even the fat brown marmots who lived in the rocks. They quickly researched the Spanish expedition of 1589, some even going to Mexico for ancient archives, and anchormen spoke knowingly of Henrique Estancio and Fray Benedicto as they stood, backlit and spooky, in the cave, their own well-known faces alternating with pictures of the treasure.

Gabriela saw Jed for the first time in three days when she happened to catch him on television trying to duck an interview. Evidently Jed was still in Flagstaff, because she recognized the county building behind him. She listened to his interview, stared at his face—he looked tired—but all she could remember was their last minute together, Jed holding her close until the paramedics arrived by helicopter and checked out Jed's bruised ribs and her contused shoulder. The sheriff and his men had handcuffed Brian, read him his rights and flown him out. It had been . . . awful.

And since that moment there'd been nothing but an endless flood of questions and more questions and the media frenzy.

Jed's television interview ended, but the cameras weren't through; they turned to another facet of the case. One of the Apache tribal elders was being interviewed, and he was speaking of the legends surrounding the Spanish treasure and Kokopelli. The camera showed a millennium-old petroglyph of Kokopelli. Gabriela was instantly reminded of Two Bears.

It wasn't until the next day that the hoopla began to fade and the Zimmermans were finally able to draw free breaths. Gabriela sat in the office where it was quiet and tapped a pen against her teeth, staring into the middle distance. Finally she had time to reflect and put her mind in order instead of merely reacting like a turtle being poked with a sharp object.

Brian—he was in Phoenix in a hospital, a psychiatric ward, being evaluated. She could relinquish responsibility, emotional responsibility, for him; there was nothing more she could do.

Jed. Oh, Jed ... Her mind and her heart were full of him, her memories sharp and clear, but her emotions were still raw and confused. A dozen times that morning she reached for the phone to try to call him in Flagstaff, to try to tell him ... What? That no matter how confused she was, her mind just kept conjuring him up? That she was obsessed with him? No. She couldn't tell him that. Not yet. It was all too soon, too soon.

He came to the hotel one last time that day, and she knew he wanted to hear something from her that she wasn't ready to tell him.

"Look, Gab," he said, "I'd like you to know that I'll wait until everything's taken care of here. I won't push you, but I'll be there. Just call, just let me know."

She looked into his eyes and felt him take her hand and play with her fingers, and her heart swelled with love and a great sadness, too.

"Jed, I... I don't know..."

He drew her close and kissed her, softly, gently, then pressed her cheek against his and just stayed that way. She could feel his heart beating and smell his own special scent. His whiskers scratched, just a little, more than they had when he'd been in college, but his hands were gentler.

"Oh, Jed, I don't know what to tell you. Please, I need some time now. There's so much going on. I just can't..."

He held her at arm's length and grinned, the crooked grin she knew so well. "I've waited ten years. I guess a little more time won't hurt."

"Jed, I'm sorry."

"Don't be. It's going to work out just fine."

"What will you do now?" she asked, leaning back in his arms.

"I'm not sure. But I'll figure it out."

"Please don't give up your whole career, not for me. I couldn't bear it. I was wrong the first time, and I know better now. You can't live your life being afraid, and you can't impose your fears on someone else. Do what you have to do, Jed."

"Uh-huh," he said, and he kissed her again, long and lingeringly and so very, very sweetly.

He didn't make it hard for her and he didn't press her. In fact, he went back to Arlington.

He phoned the hotel once or twice over the next week, usually getting Lorna, who screened calls like an overzealous press secretary. So Gabriela knew he'd been asked by his boss to reconsider his resignation. He'd stuck to his guns, though, despite inquisitive rooting by the press, and packed up to leave the East Coast, only saying to the media that it was time for a change.

She wondered if he was in Tucson with his family or if he was still on his way west. She wondered end- lessly where Jed was. Every minute of every day she thought about him. Yes, she'd asked him for time, and maybe that had been the second biggest mistake of her life.

Oh, Jed, she thought, *why am I so afraid to be happy?*

It was on one of those days when Jed filled her mind that the heat wave finally broke and the first hints of autumn touched the mountains of northern Arizona. A sweater around her shoulders, Gabriela sat on the patio with Brian's family and saw the blush of orange and red on the scrub oak that dotted the rock cliff be- hind the hotel. Autumn, she thought, an end and yet a beginning for her, and for the Zimmermans.

She dragged her glance from the hills and looked back at the lawyer—Brian's lawyer—who was brief- ing the family on the latest aspects of the case against him.

"The results of Brian's initial psychiatric examina- tion are hopeful from the point of view of the de- fense," Morton Selman was telling them.

"Explain that, please," Otto said, and Gabriela saw him squeeze Ellie's hand.

"Your son shows signs of paranoid schizophrenia. I'm filing a motion with the court requesting an insanity hearing next month."

"And just what will that mean?" John Kessler, Lorna's husband, asked.

Morton Selman leaned back into the lawn chair. "If Brian is found incompetent to stand trial, then he'll be remanded to the state psychiatric hospital for an indefinite period."

"Then he could be set free in a few years?" Lorna asked.

"It's a possibility," Selman told them, looking from one family member to another. "For now, though, why don't we just take things one step at a time."

Gabriela listened, saying nothing, but thinking to herself that under the circumstances Brian would be lucky if he was found insane. In her opinion, he *was* insane—the pressures of insurmountable debt and his compulsive gambling had driven him over the edge, though the signs had been there all along. She should have seen it coming—they all should have—but now it was water under the bridge. She felt an immense sadness—for Brian, for his parents and Lorna, for herself. Somehow you got through, though. Somehow you managed.

Ellie Zimmerman leaned forward. "Whatever my son needs, whatever it takes, you'll see to it that he's well taken care of, Mr. Selman?"

"Of course," he replied, and he smiled warmly at her. "He's quite comfortable in the Phoenix hospital. And although it's a lockup situation, it's a marvelous, caring facility."

"Good, good," Otto muttered, and he patted his wife's hand.

"Can we visit?" Ellie asked.

"Anytime you want," Selman replied.

The meeting broke up after lunch on that crisp, early September day. Ellie and Otto retired to their fourth-floor apartment, and John and Lorna went on with their move into Gabriela and Brian's cabin. The plan was to remodel the entire structure so that the family of four would fit in comfortably. They were, after all, relocating back to the hotel. The Kessler daughters had already begun the school year in Apache Springs. There'd been some squawking at first on the part of the girls, but they were settling in.

Gabriela had been living in the hotel for the past ten days. Her time was taken up showing Lorna and John the ropes, and, of course, she was still running Ellie into Flagstaff twice a week. The good news was that Ellie's doctor was hopeful they'd arrested the cancer. To Gabriela it was more than good news, it was a blessing.

The day after the lawyer's visit, Gabriela drove to Phoenix to see Brian. It was something she had to do, something she wanted to do. On the drive she was able to reflect without distraction. She considered the barrage of emotions that had consumed her since Brian's arrest that awful day. She'd been so angry and afraid at first. Then had come guilt—hadn't this all been somehow her fault? And then, finally, slowly, had come acceptance and a sort of numbness, an exhaustion of her emotions. Now she could start the healing process, and this journey was the first step.

Brian looked good when he was shown into the visiting room at the hospital. He was wearing regular clothes, his hair was neat and shorter than she'd seen it in years, and his eyes were clear and bright.

"Hey, Gabriela," he said, and he seated himself across the table from her in the small, gray-walled room, observed by a burly attendant through a barred window. "I didn't expect you."

Gabriela gave him a weak smile. "I thought I should come and see how you're doing."

"I'm okay. Better, I think, than I was."

"That's good to hear," she said.

"Did my lawyer explain everything?" he asked, his hands folded calmly on the table.

"Yes, most everything, I guess."

"Good," he said. "I'm seeing a bunch of doctors here. It's helping, Gabriela, I really think it is. For a while there, you know, it was like I was living in this haze. Man, I barely remember..."

"Don't," she said, looking away. "You can think about all that later. Don't torture yourself."

"George," he said in a whisper. "I think I..." And then suddenly he looked frightened, and she knew how very ill he still was. It was as if he couldn't really recall the dreadful things he'd done. Maybe he didn't remember a thing about threatening her life. Maybe he never would. When something is too painful, too terrible to acknowledge, the mind shuts down.

"So how are you?" he asked abruptly, the cloud clearing.

"I'm doing okay."

"I guess you came here to ask me for that divorce, huh? Well, I expected it."

"Brian, I..."

"No, don't feel bad. I blew it big time. I can't be married right now. I've gotta...deal with things. I've got to get myself in gear, you know. The doctors said, well, that it's going to be a long road." He looked at her in earnest. "Get the divorce, Gabriela. I can't be worried about you and getting better at the same time."

"Brian," she said softly, "this can wait. We don't have to..."

"Yes, we do," he said. "I've got enough problems, babes. Get on with your life."

"Are you sure?" she asked. "Are you positive, or is this the doctors talking?"

He shook his head. "It's me. I have to do things this way. Like you always knew, babes, we were history a long time ago."

She looked at him for a heartbeat and nodded slowly. "You're right," she finally said. "But you know if you need me..."

"Yeah, I know. You always had a soft heart, too soft."

"I guess so," she said. "I guess I always did."

JED ARRIVED UNANNOUNCED at the hotel two days later. He took Gabriela by surprise, coming up behind her as she was bent over out by the pools picking up a discarded soda pop can.

"Gab?" came his beautifully familiar voice.

Her hand flew to her heart, and she stood up so fast she felt dizzy. "Jed? My God, I didn't expect..."

"I know," he said, standing there tall and handsome, the most wonderful sight she'd seen in so long, so very long now. "Can we take a walk? Someplace a little more private?"

"Well, sure," she said. "Of course we can."

They headed up the trail that led to the rock overhang above the town, to the spot where she'd gone so many weeks ago to try to sort out her thoughts. She was still trying to sort them out as she walked beside Jed, only this time it was very different.

Jed had come back.

"So, how have you been?" he asked, studying her.

"Better," she said.

"That's good."

"And you? Have you . . . I mean, have you made plans?" Oddly, she felt shy with Jed, full of trepidation.

"Oh, yeah, I have lots of plans."

And then she was afraid to ask, so she started up again, walking out onto the red rocks where they overlooked Apache Springs.

"Aren't you curious?" he asked, and when she turned to face him she saw a smile on his lips.

"Of course I'm curious."

"I've got a new job."

"Oh. Where?"

"Flagstaff."

"You mean . . . ?"

He nodded. "Yep. Full circle. Ulrich hired me on as a deputy. I'll be doing detective work. Pay's lousy, but the cost of living out here is nothing compared to back East."

"Right in Flagstaff," she mused, and her heart began a heavier rhythm.

"You know," he said, "I guess I just screwed up the past ten years trying to be someone I'm not. You were always right about that, Gab, that I wanted to go one better than my dad. Be just a little more important. I screwed up, all right. I always belonged out here."

"But you did...do belong in law enforcement, Jed. I was very wrong about that."

"This is true," he said, smiling again, the sunlight dancing on his hair, in his eyes. "I'm a real careful guy, though. I want you to know that."

"I know. But that day up at the cave, you could have been ... Oh, Jed, I was so scared Brian was going to shoot you."

Jed did a strange thing then; he laughed.

"What?" she asked.

"Gab, that was for you and you alone. I learned my lesson about hostage situations in my rookie year. I don't put my butt on the line like that anymore."

"You did that for me," she whispered.

"Only for you, and for you I'd do it again."

Gabriela looked down at her feet. "The Apaches think you're a real hero. You and Two Bears. Did you know that they're setting up a museum on the reservation with all the treasure in it? They figure if they charge admission, they can run the place forever. Guess what it's going to be called?"

"The Jed Mallory Commemorative Exhibit."

Gabriela shook her head and smiled. "No, silly, the Kokopelli Treasure Cave. It's going to be shaped like a cave, you know, lighting and all that."

"Sounds good to me."

"Um," she said, looking at her feet again.

After a moment he said, "Have you seen Brian?"

She nodded. Then she told him everything. Even about the divorce.

"Have you called a lawyer?"

"Yesterday."

"Um."

"It will be final pretty quickly."

"Um. And what about the Zimmermans?"

"Oh, they're all for it. Even Ellie says I should get on with my life."

"Gab..." he began, and she could finally lift her gaze to his. He was looking at her lips, though, and her heart beat just a little faster. "Oh, Gab," he said again. He put his hands on her wrists, then he moved them up her arms to her shoulder blades, drawing her close. She settled into the curve of his shoulder, her hand on his heart, and she looked up as he inclined his head. At first it was a mere brushing of lips, a meeting after their long separation, a greeting, a reuniting. Her head moved indolently, an answer to his query, their lips barely touching, teasing, tickling, remembering.

Their tongues met in passing, and he touched the corners of her mouth, wetting it. Their embrace deepened, and Gab's hand reached for Jed's neck to stroke with her fingertips the well-remembered texture of his skin, the cords of his neck, and she drew in his own singular scent.

Their tongues mingled, melded together, tasting the sweet nectar of each other's mouths, and he held her head with his hands, delving deeper into her mouth, while she entwined her fingers in his thick, curling hair.

Jed drew back first, his eyes a stormy dark blue. "Oh, God, Gab, it's been too long."

"Yes." Her voice was a bare thread of sound.

"I like that," he said very quietly.

"What?" she breathed.

"That 'yes.' You said it once before to me, ten years ago. But we blew it. I blew it."

"Maybe we were too young."

"Maybe I was a fool."

"And me, too."

"Well, will you?"

Gabriela smiled. "Will I what?"

"Will you marry me? And don't give me a hard time, don't tease."

"Yes," she said.

"Yes. You mean it."

"I mean it, Jed."

"I rented a three-bedroom house in Flagstaff. But we'll build."

"For a growing family?"

"You bet. A big family. You up to it?"

"Yes, oh yes, Jed."

He took her hands and squeezed them, and her heart sang with love.

Above them, in the pine and juniper woods and the tumbled red rock, stood an Apache Indian, hunched over and immeasurably old. He smiled to himself and turned away from the white man's place and remembered that Kokopelli had been known as a very powerful god of fertility in addition to his many other talents.

Ah, yes, he'd almost forgotten that aspect of Kokopelli.

HARLEQUIN SUPERROMANCE®

WOMEN WHO DARE
They take chances, make changes
and follow their hearts!

The Father Factor
by Kathryn Shay

Amanda Carson has helped many parents in her job as
guidance counsellor but never has she come across one who
challenges her as much as Nick DiMarco. The single father of
two is determined to prove he can handle everything—even
his difficult teenager. Fiercely proud, he wants no help from
"outsiders." But the DiMarco kids—and their stubborn
father—have found a special place in Amanda's heart. Now
all she has to do is convince Nick to let her into his.

**Watch for *The Father Factor*
by Kathryn Shay**

**Available in September 1995 wherever
Harlequin books are sold.**

MILLION DOLLAR SWEEPSTAKES (III)

No purchase necessary. To enter the sweepstakes and receive the Free Books and Surprise Gift, follow the directions published and complete and mail your "Win A Fortune" Game Card. If not taking advantage of the book and gift offer or if the "Win A Fortune" Game Card is missing, you may enter by hand-printing your name and address on a 3" X 5" card and mailing it (limit: one entry per envelope) via First Class Mail to: Million Dollar Sweepstakes (III) "Win A Fortune" Game, P.O. Box 1867, Buffalo, NY 14269-1867, or Million Dollar Sweepstakes (III) "Win A Fortune" Game, P.O. Box 609, Fort Erie, Ontario L2A 5X3. When your entry is received, you will be assigned sweepstakes numbers. To be eligible entries must be received no later than March 31, 1996. No liability is assumed for printing errors or lost, late or misdirected entries. Odds of winning are determined by the number of eligible entries distributed and received.

Sweepstakes open to residents of the U.S. (except Puerto Rico), Canada, Europe and Taiwan who are 18 years of age or older. All applicable laws and regulations apply. Sweepstakes offer void wherever prohibited by law. Values of all prizes are in U.S. currency. This sweepstakes is presented by Torstar Corp, its subsidiaries and affiliates, in conjunction with book, merchandise and/or product offerings. For a copy of the official rules governing this sweepstakes offer, send a self-addressed, stamped envelope (WA residents need not affix return postage) to: MILLION DOLLAR SWEEPSTAKES (III) Rules, P.O. Box 4573, Blair, NE 68009, USA.

SWP-H895

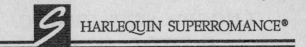

The Dunleavy Legacy
by Janis Flores

For more than a century, the Dunleavy name stood behind the winners of horseracing's most prestigious prizes. The family's wealth and fame was recognized in the most powerful circles.

But times are different now, and the new generation of Dunleavys is about to claim its legacy. Meet the three grandchildren of Octavia Dunleavy, matriarch of the family, as they deal with old feuds and jealousies, with family pride and betrayal, in their struggle to restore the Dunleavy dynasty to its former glory.

Follow the fortunes of Carla, Nan and Seth in three dramatic, involving love stories.

#654 DONE DRIFTIN' (August 1995)
#658 DONE CRYIN' (September 1995)
#662 NEVER DONE DREAMIN' (October 1995)

This eagerly awaited trilogy by critically acclaimed writer Janis Flores—a veteran author of both mainstream and romance novels—is available wherever Harlequin books are sold.

DLL-1

RUGGED. SEXY. HEROIC.

OUTLAWS *and* HEROES

Stony Carlton—A lone wolf determined never to be tied down.

Gabriel Taylor—Accused and found guilty by small-town gossip.

Clay Barker—At Revenge Unlimited, he *is* the law.

JOAN JOHNSTON, DALLAS SCHULZE and MALLORY RUSH, three of romance fiction's biggest names, have created three unforgettable men—modern heroes who have the courage to fight for what is right....

OUTLAWS AND HEROES—available in September wherever Harlequin books are sold.

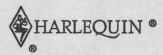 HARLEQUIN ®

As a Privileged Woman,
you'll be entitled to all these Free Benefits.
And Free Gifts, too.

To thank you for buying our books, we've designed an exclusive FREE program called *PAGES & PRIVILEGES™*. You can enroll with just one Proof of Purchase, and get the kind of luxuries that, until now, you could only read about.

Big HOTEL DISCOUNTS

A privileged woman stays in the finest hotels. And so can you—at up to 60% off! Imagine standing in a hotel check-in line and watching as the guest in front of you pays $150 for the same room that's only costing you $60. Your *Pages & Privileges* discounts are good at Sheraton, Marriott, Best Western, Hyatt and thousands of other fine hotels all over the U.S., Canada and Europe.

Free DISCOUNT TRAVEL SERVICE

A privileged woman is always jetting to romantic places. When <u>you</u> fly, just make one phone call for the lowest published airfare at time of booking—<u>or double the difference back</u>! PLUS— you'll get a $25 voucher to use the first time you book a flight AND <u>5% cash back on every ticket you buy thereafter through the travel service</u>!

𝒻REE GIFTS!

A privileged woman is always getting wonderful gifts. Luxuriate in rich fragrances that will stir your senses (and his). This gift-boxed assortment of fine perfumes includes three popular scents, each in a beautiful designer bottle. <u>Truly Lace</u>...This luxurious fragrance unveils your sensuous side. <u>L'Effleur</u>...discover the romance of the Victorian era with this soft floral. <u>Muguet des bois</u>...a single note floral of singular beauty.

YOURS FREE!

$50 VALUE

𝒻REE INSIDER TIPS LETTER

A privileged woman is always informed. And you'll be, too, with our free letter full of fascinating information and sneak previews of upcoming books.

𝓜ORE GREAT GIFTS & BENEFITS TO COME

A privileged woman always has a lot to look forward to. And so will you. You get all these wonderful FREE gifts and benefits now with only one purchase...and there are no additional purchases required. However, each additional retail purchase of Harlequin and Silhouette books brings you a step closer to even more great FREE benefits like half-price movie tickets... and even more FREE gifts.

L'Effleur...This basketful of romance lets you discover L'Effleur from head to toe, heart to home.

Truly Lace... A basket spun with the sensuous luxuries of Truly Lace, including Dusting Powder in a reusable satin and lace covered box.

Complete the Enrollment Form in the front of this book and mail it with this Proof of Purchase.

PROOF OF PURCHASE

Pages & Privileges

Offer expires October 31, 1996

HS-PP4